I0760574

NICHOLE HEYDENBURG

DEADLY BETRAYAL

BOOK 2: THE SHADOW BOUND CHRONICLES

Deadly Betrayal

Deadly Betrayal

Poisoned Ink Press LLC

Contact Information: www.nicholeheydenburg.com

poisonedinkpress@gmail.com

Cover Design: Miblart

Editors: BlackQuill Editing

Three Owls Editing

ISBN 978-1-961608-11-5 (eBook)

ISBN 978-1-961608-12-2 (paperback)

ISBN 978-1-961608-13-9 (hardcover)

Dedicated to Mr. B—not only the best dog in the world, but my best friend, and the inspiration for Brody.

I love you, buddy.

Adult books (crime thriller series):

The Long Shadow Series

The Long Shadow on the Stage- Book 1

The Long Shadow of Memory- Book 2

The Long Shadow of Death- Book 3

Young adult books (standalone thrillers):

The Quiet Girl- Revenge thriller

Don't Look Inside- Psychological thriller

Dead Girls Can't Smile- Psychological thriller

Young adult books (Urban fantasy series):

The Shadow Bound Chronicles

These Deadly Words- Prequel

Deadly Vows- Book 1

Deadly Betrayal- Book 2

Deadly Portals- Book 3

Deadly Legacy- Book 4

Murder, violence, kidnapping, swearing

PROLOGUE

Ammitt paced the long, narrow room, the polished concrete floors cool against his bare feet. "I promise you, brother, this is the demon hunter the prophecy spoke of. It must be her."

"Taylor Windsor is merely a human. You claim she only discovered her powers mere weeks ago. She is not trained. How can she possibly be The Chosen One?" his brother asked.

"If you had been there . . . If you saw what I did . . . No demon hunter has ever been able to banish a demon back to our realm without assistance. How do you explain that if she isn't The Chosen One?" Ammitt questioned, seething at the fact that his brother didn't believe him.

"Are you quite sure her aunt didn't have something to do with it?"

"No, it wasn't her. She's the one I tricked into the deal, after all." Ammitt sneered.

"Ah, yes, your foolish deal that ended when a teenage girl banished you here. All things to be proud of," his brother said mockingly.

Ammitt sighed and stopped his pacing, shoving the aged parchment toward his brother. "Read the prophecy again. It must be the young Windsor girl. Who else would it be? This is our best chance at defeating them once and for all. We have to kill her."

"Correct, but you cannot return to the human realm, leaving me to deal with this."

"If you're the one who kills her, Ray will be pleased," Ammitt said.

His brother took the parchment from him at last, scanning it.

Ammitt peered over his shoulder to read it once again:

There will come a time when demons will cease to exist. When The Chosen One is born and becomes of age, they will be the most powerful demon hunter to ever exist, borne of two ancient demon hunter families, their combined powers elevating The Chosen One to a level not yet reached by demon hunters. The Chosen One will be the one to ensure humanity is safe from the evils of the underworld at last. With the erasure of demons from existence, humans will be free from evil . . .

His brother scoffed and held the parchment aloft, then handed it back to Ammitt. "This does not prove it's Taylor Windsor. She is not of age yet, so how will we know?"

"Go to the human world. Find a way to slither into their lives, like you do so well."

"How am I to get close to them? They will not fall for another deal like the one you made with Melanie," his brother mused.

"You will find a way, brother. You always do," Ammitt replied.

Chapter 1

Taylor

Mel sighed and ran a hand across her face, which appeared infinitely more wrinkled than it had a few months ago—or at least, it did to fifteen-year-old Taylor, whose skin was blissfully smooth. "Taylor, concentrate," she chided.

Taylor huffed and tightened her light brown ponytail, scrunching up her face in annoyance. "I am."

Mel put her hands on her hips and stared her down. "Then why haven't you mastered the spell yet?"

Taylor wanted to tell her aunt that it was impossible. No one could possibly be expected to learn how to practice magic so quickly. But it was pointless. After everything that had happened that summer, she needed to be prepared. She hadn't been able to perform any spells since that night in the woods.

She shivered, wishing she could erase the memory of Ammitt's glowing red eyes and the way he had sucked Camille's soul out of her body, then tossed her aside like a piece of garbage. The image still haunted her nightmares.

"Taylor?" Mel said in a softer tone. "Are you okay?"

She nodded and concentrated on the spellbook, her eyes scanning the incantation once again, although at this point, she had it memorized.

For the past few weeks, Mel had focused on teaching her the basic spells to prepare her for attending Grimwood Magical Academy, the school for teenage demon hunters, in the fall. Taylor would be far behind the other students who had grown up in the world of demons and magic, learning spells from a young age. Demon hunters started their formal training at the academy at age twelve, so Taylor was almost four years behind everyone else.

Mel had scheduled a meeting with the demon hunter's council to make a special request for them to let Taylor enroll for the fall semester. She was a Turner, and the Turners were one of the five original ancient demon hunter families, so they hoped an exception would be made. Taylor was willing to work hard, and she was determined, but she didn't like sticking out or being different. Mel had already warned her not to tell anyone about the banishment spell she had somehow managed by herself. It was safer if no one else knew about Taylor's extraordinary capabilities. Apparently, what she had done wasn't normal for a demon hunter of her age.

By the end of their training session, Taylor was exhausted, and they hadn't even done any physical training. The past few weeks felt more like a year. Mel locked up the spellbook in the ancient steamer trunk and tucked the key into her pants pocket. She gestured for Taylor to leave the room first.

They had turned the formerly forbidden room into a training room. Mel had finally gone through her parents' belongings and gotten rid of some of their stuff. Then they repainted the walls, put down mats, and made the room into a safe place to practice magic. They told anyone else outside of the demon hunter world it was a storage room, and no one suspected a thing.

Trudging down the hallway to the kitchen, Taylor entered the living room, throwing her weary body onto the couch. "Ughhh," she groaned as she sank into the cushions. She relaxed slightly as she lay down.

Brody, a small, white terrier with brown and black patches, trotted over to her. He sat on the floor in front of her, expectantly wagging his tail.

"Come here, Brody." Taylor patted the seat next to her so he could hop up, which he immediately did.

He shoved his head under her hand until she giggled and started petting him.

Mel came into the room and laughed when she spotted her niece forced into petting their new dog.

Brody had belonged to Camille, a servant of the demon Ammitt, but after Camille died, Taylor hadn't wanted to abandon him. She had convinced her aunt to bring him home, and now he was part of the family. At first, he had been sad and refused to eat. Taylor suspected he missed Camille, but he had settled into his new life. The strange part was they hadn't found out his age. Mel had taken him to a vet to make sure he was vaccinated and healthy, and the vet had been shocked, claiming she had never seen such a healthy, well-behaved adult dog.

"I'll get you some water," Mel offered.

Taylor perked up a bit. "And a snack?"

Mel laughed again. "Sure, if you want a banana or a protein bar."

Taylor wrinkled her nose. "Gross."

"You need to keep up your strength." Mel paused. "And besides, I need to go grocery shopping. I'm pretty sure those are the only edible foods left in the house." Mel disappeared into the kitchen and came back a few minutes later with a glass of ice water. "Here."

"Thanks." Taylor took the glass and sipped it gratefully. "So, were the bananas rotten?"

Mel smirked. "How did you know?"

Taylor shrugged a shoulder and chugged the rest of her water, wiping her hand across her mouth with a satisfied sigh. "Lucky guess. I've been living with you long enough. Should we go grocery shopping?"

"We can always order takeout. Mexican food or pizza?"

Taylor hesitated, unable to decide. "Both? I want tacos and pepperoni pizza with jalapeños. And maybe some cheesy bread."

"Can do, kiddo," Mel said, going into the kitchen to place the orders.

Taylor leaned back into the couch cushions, resting her hands behind her head. She closed her eyes. She could almost fall asleep, but the food would arrive soon. *I'll go to bed early*, she promised herself.

Mel returned and flopped onto the couch next to her.

Brody nestled in between them and sighed with contentment, closing his eyes once he was sure neither of them was leaving.

"Pick a movie." Mel handed the remote to Taylor.

Without a word, Taylor took it from her and searched through the various streaming services her aunt paid for every month. She scrolled past several movies she had watched with Kylie earlier in the summer. A pang of guilt stabbed her. Mel had warned her not to spend too much time with Kylie and Sarah until she learned how to control her powers. She didn't want any accidents occurring. It might be overkill, considering she hadn't performed a basic spell in weeks. The most she had managed was a few measly purple sparks, hardly enough to do any damage.

Taylor dropped the remote onto the scuffed, old coffee table without selecting a movie. Burrowing her head into Brody's tiny chest, she inhaled his comforting dog scent. She had just given him a bath, so he smelled fresh and clean.

"What's wrong?" Mel asked.

Taylor didn't respond and kept her face hidden. She didn't want to admit the truth—she was depressed and didn't feel like watching a movie with her aunt. What she really wanted was to text Kylie and go out somewhere, *anywhere*, and be around normal people. She missed Kylie, but she also missed her old life back in Minnesota, before her parents died and she was forced to move to Grimwood, North Carolina, and live with her aunt Mel. Before she learned about the existence of demons and magic. Before she found out she came from a long line of powerful demon hunters. So much had changed that summer. Too much.

Mel gently nudged her shoulder. "Taylor, you can talk to me." She paused before asking, "Is this about your parents? Do you miss them?"

Taylor scoffed. "No. I mean, of course I miss my parents. But this isn't about them."

"What, then? Kylie?"

"Sort of."

Mel briefly closed her eyes. "Can you please tell me? I can't read your mind."

Taylor pulled her face away from Brody's soft fur to peer at her aunt. She kept Brody on her lap, his small, fluffy body reassuring and comforting.

He laid his head down and settled in.

"I want my old life back," she whispered.

"I know, and I'm sorry again for everything. I hope you know that. I never meant to hurt you or your parents. It's my fault you have to cope with so much loss, while learning how to master your newfound powers. It isn't fair, but this is what we have to deal with for now. It will get better eventually, I promise."

The doorbell rang.

Mel jumped up to get their takeout. "Be right back with the food."

But Taylor didn't think her life would get better. She didn't see how it possibly could.

Chapter 2

Mel

Mel strode into the circular room, with her shoulders pulled back and head held high. Months had passed since she had seen any of the council members, so she was apprehensive about the meeting, but she had to do it for Taylor's sake. If she could help her niece, then she would endure seeing them all again. It was the least she could do after the chaos she had caused.

The floors in the council meeting room were swirls of polished gray-and-white concrete—gorgeous but durable and practical. The circular room was encased by stained-glass windows depicting different major events throughout their history: the first demon's appearance, the creation of the five ancient demon hunter families and the council, their war with the demons and the eventual defeat of the demons, and the celebration for the demon hunters afterward. She stood there, taking it all in. It was magnificent, especially since she had only been in the room a handful of times. It never failed to take her breath away.

"Well, well, well, Melanie Turner . . . How long has it been?" one of the council members, a tall, thin woman with pale white skin and long black hair, greeted her.

Clarissa Cromwell was the head of her family. The council had been founded with a matriarchal structure. The only exception to this rule was Alastair Price, whose wife had died tragically seven years ago, leaving him to raise three children on his own. Since his children were still too young to take the family's place on the council, he was acting as the interim council member until his eldest daughter came of age.

"Two years, I think," Mel said with a tight-lipped smile at being called by her full name. Everyone knew she preferred Mel.

Mel knew exactly how long it had been since she last saw Clarissa—since her parents' funerals. Clarissa and Gideon had been kind enough to make an appearance and give their condolences, though Mel knew it was partly for show. They didn't care about her wellbeing; they had simply wanted the gossip about who would take over the Turner family's vacant spot on the council. Mel's older sister, Christa, should have taken the spot, but since she had moved away years ago and forfeited her right as the eldest daughter, Mel was the only one left. But she hadn't wanted to join the council, anyway.

The other council members greeted her in turn. There was Alastair Price, a handsome widower with flowing white locks; Vanessa Ellis, a short blonde with three kids; and lastly, Lavender Thatcher, a brunette with two kids. Mel forced a smile and greeted them, shaking hands with each member.

"Have a seat, Mel," Vanessa said, gesturing to the single chair in front of the raised dais where the council members all stood.

Mel complied, and the council members sat in their respective seats.

"Thank you for seeing us today," Lavender started, shuffling a stack of papers in front of her.

Each council member had an identical stack of papers on the long, raised shelf in front of them.

Mel hid her bewilderment at the statement, considering *she* had requested the meeting, not the council. "Of course," she said politely, not wanting to start off on the wrong foot. She wanted to remain on their good side.

"Melanie, you must realize what a terrible mistake you made," Clarissa began, "making a deal with that demon, putting the entire town of Grimwood in danger, not to mention—"

"How do you know about that?" Mel interrupted sharply.

Clarissa chuckled, and the other council members appeared amused as well.

This time, Alistair spoke up. "Mel, you don't honestly think we just sit back and let all the demon hunters do as they please? We're constantly watching everyone in the community. We have eyes *everywhere*. We know everything you do. What kind of council would we be if we didn't take such measures?"

Mel's face paled, and her heart rate sped up. She hadn't expected this. She needed to ask for a favor, but now she felt sure they wouldn't grant her request. If they knew about her deal with Ammitt, then . . .

"Why didn't you intervene?" Mel demanded, her anger flaring. If they were aware of the situation, they could have stepped in. They could have protected her and Taylor, given them a safe house to hide out, or helped in any way besides ignoring the situation and waiting to see how it played out.

"We know about Christa and Nick too," Clarissa added with a faux sympathetic smile. "It's terrible what happened to them, but with the Turner family spot vacant on the council and your lack of involvement over the years, we had to make a decision."

"What kind of decision?" Mel asked, not liking where this was going.

Alastair rubbed the bridge of his nose. "It gives us no pleasure to do this, Mel, but we voted—three to one—about taking drastic measures to ensure no incidents like this happen again. The Turners had their time."

Mel's heart thundered in her chest. She resisted the urge to clench her fists and show her agitation until she knew the outcome. She could guess who had voted against her. "What is it? What are you planning?" she demanded.

"We're taking away your powers," Clarissa said in a tone that almost sounded gleeful.

Mel stared at the council members, one by one, uncomprehending. She shook her head. "You can't be serious! You can't take away my powers. There are protocols. It can't—"

"Actually, we can. As I said, we already voted. All we need is a majority vote to make such a decision," Alastair responded, sweeping his long white hair from his face.

"Don't you need a consensus? For everyone to vote yes?" Mel asked, trying to find a way out of this. How could she train Taylor, much less protect her, if she didn't have her powers? How could she do *anything* without magic? Sometimes being a demon hunter was a nuisance, and it wasn't the life she would have chosen for herself, but with Taylor in her life now, she needed magic. She needed every advantage she could get.

"In extreme cases, a three-to-one vote is sufficient," Clarissa said. "We didn't want it to come to this, Mel, but you left us no choice. You put the demon hunters' secrecy in danger, and you knowingly put humans in danger too, not to mention your niece. Our powers are a gift from our ancestors; they aren't meant to do with as we please. We must respect—"

"Yes, yes, respect the magic," Mel finished the age-old adage. "So what are you going to do, then? Banish me? Kill me?"

Lavender chimed in, "No, nothing so rash." She ducked below the shelf in front of her. A moment later, she popped back up, holding an amulet—a silver chain with a green stone hanging from it.

Mel gasped and put her hand to her mouth. "Is that what I think it is?"

Lavender nodded. "Indeed. The Emerald Vacuus Amulet. You are to wear it at all times. We'll enchant it so you can't take it off, and it will suppress your powers." She let it dangle from her fingers, the green stone catching the streaks of sunlight shining through the stained-glass windows, creating a beautiful, multicolored prism.

"I thought the amulet was destroyed," Mel replied, inching away from the dais in front of her.

She wasn't powerful enough to fight off all four of them, but perhaps one or two . . . Or she could make a run for it. She and Taylor could go into hiding; they could move somewhere far away and start over. Although that brought up a new series of issues.

Grimwood Magical Academy was one of the best schools for demon hunters in the country. Mel didn't have connections to other schools. Besides, they had tried running away before, and that hadn't exactly ended well.

As Mel backed further away from the council, Alastair gasped. His pupils turned white, and he stared off absentmindedly, as if gazing into the distance. The expression on his face remained blank for several seconds.

Clarissa turned to him and put her hand on his back, rubbing soothingly. "What is it, Alastair? What did you see?" she asked when his eyes returned to their normal green color.

"Lock the doors!" Alastair yelled, his voice booming across the polished concrete flooring.

Clarissa raised her hand as if to lock the doors with magic, but Taylor came bursting into the room.

Chapter 3

Taylor

"Taylor, you have to help Mel!" a voice warned her.

"Wh—what? Who are you?" Taylor asked, inching closer to the figure standing in the hallway of her home.

Black wavy hair flowed past the mysterious man's shoulders. His striking blue eyes stared back at her. She remembered seeing him before . . . But where?

The boy rolled his eyes in annoyance. "Seriously? You don't remember me? How many people do you know who can dreamwalk?"

"If this is a dream, then you aren't real," Taylor said, putting a hand on her hip. Sparks of magic fizzled from her hands.

"My name is Julian Cromwell. I'm a demon hunter too. Your aunt is in trouble. You need to go to her."

"Wait, how do you know Mel is in trouble?" Taylor squinted at him in confusion. "Can you see the future?"

"Something like that. It's usually hazy, but I know she's in trouble. The council is going to take away her powers. You have to stop them. They want to punish her for making a deal with that demon and putting so many lives in danger," Julian explained.

"They can do that? The demon hunter council doesn't sound very ethical . . ." Taylor said, wavering about whether she should trust the mysterious demon hunter who had appeared in her dreams.

"It can be an issue, but we don't have time for a history lesson. If you care about your aunt, you'll stop them from taking away her powers."

"I was enjoying such a nice nap," Taylor lamented, throwing her arms up in the air.

Julian narrowed his eyes. "Really? You don't want to save your aunt?"

Taylor sighed. "No, of course I do."

"Okay, then go to this address," Julian said, rattling off an address in Grimwood. "Good luck, Taylor. Be careful."

"Wait! What do I do when I get to the—" Taylor started.

He snapped his fingers and disappeared.

The book slipped off her lap and fell to the ground with a thud that shocked her out of sleep.

Brody barked at the loud sound.

"Crap," she muttered, realizing what had happened. She sat up from her horizontal position on the couch and stretched her arms above her head. "It's okay, Brody. A book fell."

Taylor picked up the book she had been reading before she dozed off and set it on the coffee table. She glanced at the time on her cell phone—3:00 p.m. *Mel must be meeting with the council now. I still have time to make it, but how will I get there?*

Taylor contemplated asking Kylie to drive her, but Mel would be pissed off if she involved her human friend. Taylor didn't turn sixteen until October, though, and it was only August, so she couldn't legally drive. *What to do, what to do . . .*

She threw her hair into a ponytail and grabbed the house key. She patted Brody on the head before leaving. "Be a good boy. Hold down the fort!"

Brody barked in response and wagged his tail, remaining by the front door as if on guard.

Taylor sprinted next door to the Anderson's house. She hesitated before knocking on the front door. For the past two weeks, Taylor had ignored Kylie's many calls and texts. Mel had made up an excuse about Taylor being busy when she showed up at their house. Eventually, Kylie had given up. So was it smart of Taylor to ask her for a favor now? Probably not, but Kylie and Sarah were the only other people she knew in town. What choice did she have?

She rang the doorbell, waiting with bated breath for someone to answer the door.

A moment later, the door opened. Kylie tilted her head when she saw her. "Taylor?"

"Hi, Kylie. I know I've been hard to reach lately, but there's a lot going on. I don't have time to explain it all right now. Mel's in trouble. I need you to drive me somewhere," Taylor blurted out in a rush.

"What? Are you kidding me?" Kylie asked, blowing her bangs out of her eyes.

"Cute bangs," Taylor said, a weak attempt to dissolve the tension.

"Uh, thanks. I was bored last week." Kylie bit her lip. "Anyway, what kind of trouble is Mel in? Is she going to be okay?"

Taylor shook her head. "It's a secret, and it's too dangerous for you to know the truth. I'm sorry I can't tell you more, but I really need your help." She hesitated before adding, "Otherwise, I'll take Mel's spare car, but I don't want to get in trouble for driving without a license."

"No, don't do that. That would be stupid." Kylie partially shut the door. "Let me get my car keys and tell my mom I'm going out for a bit. Any idea how long this will take?"

"Why? Do you have a hot date tonight?" Taylor smirked.

Kylie rolled her eyes. "Right. You know me so well." She disappeared into the house.

Taylor vaguely heard Kylie talking to someone, presumably her mom, before she returned.

"Ready?" Kylie asked.

"You're really going to help me?"

"Of course. But it's not for you. Mel has always been a great friend to me and my mom. I'm doing this for her. I don't want anything to happen to her if she's in danger," Kylie said.

"Sure. Well, I appreciate it either way," Taylor replied.

Taylor followed Kylie to her car and climbed into the passenger seat.

Kylie sat in the driver's seat and pulled out her phone. "Where are we going?"

"Here. Let me type in the address."

Taylor set up the phone navigation, and Kylie swiftly pulled the car out of her driveway.

Based on what Julian had told her, this situation was urgent. She didn't want Mel to lose her powers. That would be catastrophic for so many reasons.

Kylie pressed her foot down harder on the gas pedal, and the car sped out of their neighborhood. Taylor hoped they made it in time.

Taylor

They pulled up in front of the building Julian had told her about. The outside appeared old and weathered and the stones fragile, like the entire building could crumble at any moment. Grass grew throughout the small parking lot, sprouts of green popping up where it shouldn't. There was even graffiti across the back of the building, where Kylie parked her car.

Kylie stared at the decrepit building with apprehension, raising her eyebrows at Taylor. "Are you sure this is the right place? What kind of trouble is Mel in?"

Taylor gave a slight nod. "Pretty sure." She unclipped her seatbelt and opened the door. "Go home. I have to deal with this on my own."

Kylie pursed her lips. "What? Are you crazy? I can't let you go in there by yourself! This place is—"

"I know, but you have to trust me. I'll be fine," Taylor promised.

Kylie hesitated before reaching across the seat to hug her. "Please be careful. Do you at least want me to wait here for you? I don't have to go inside, but if Mel is in trouble . . ."

Taylor shook her head. "No, I don't want to put you in danger. It isn't safe for you to be here."

Kylie's green eyes widened. "But it's somehow fine for you to go inside? I'm so confused."

"Maybe someday I'll be able to explain, but trust me when I say that it's better for you to leave." Taylor pulled her phone out of her pocket and waved it back and forth. "I have my phone with me so, worst-case scenario, I can call you if I need a quick getaway."

"Or maybe you should call the police."

Taylor shook her head again. "I can't do that. It's a long and complicated story, but the police won't believe me. I have to handle this by myself."

Kylie groaned. "You worry me." She exhaled loudly. "Okay, I'll leave, but I won't go home yet. I'll wait somewhere close by just in case. Call me or text me if you need to. I won't abandon you, despite my instincts screaming at me to go home and get the heck away from here."

Taylor laughed nervously and scratched the back of her neck. "Yeah, same." She grabbed her backpack from underneath the seat and hoisted it over her shoulder.

"Be careful!" Kylie yelled, as Taylor shut the passenger door.

Kylie drove away. Taylor made sure she was gone before she steadied herself and headed to the back entrance of the building. Julian hadn't told her which entrance to use or how to get inside, so she was officially on her own. She guessed that the back door was smarter if she needed to make a sneaky entrance.

She put her hand on the doorknob to see if the back door was unlocked. A zap of electricity shot through her hand, followed by a stab of pain. She jerked her hand away and flipped it over, examining it for injuries. It looked normal.

Great. So the door is enchanted to keep out uninvited people?

Taylor played with her ponytail, twisting it around her fingers and contemplating what to do. She left her house so fast to ask for Kylie's help that she hadn't fully thought through this plan. In fact, she didn't *have* a plan. How could she get inside? Part of her predicament was her inability to tap into her magic. She didn't have lock-picking skills, and she suspected that wouldn't work on an enchanted door, anyway. There had to be a solution.

She wished she had Julian's phone number to ask for his advice. Or that he was there to help her. If he was a demon hunter like he claimed, then he must have some idea of how to get into the building. Then again, if he did know, why hadn't he warned her? He had given her the absolute minimum instructions.

Taylor drummed her fingers against her thigh, debating her next move. She unzipped her backpack and dug around inside to find something useful. An item that would help her unlock the door. Her fingers touched the cool, leather-bound, ancient spellbook that had apparently belonged to her family for generations. She pulled it out and gazed at the cover. There must be a spell that could help her. She just needed to concentrate.

Taylor opened the book to the intermediate spell section. Based on her previous readings, she already knew that whatever she needed wasn't a basic spell. She had memorized the basic spells, even if she hadn't mastered them all yet. She skimmed the intermediate spells until she found one that seemed perfect.

Reserare spell: unlock. This intermediate spell allows demon hunters to unlock enchanted doors and objects. Raise your hand over the object or door in question and recite the spell.

Spell: "Reserare. Please stop the enchantment and grant me access to this place."

Taylor cleared her throat, raising her hand above the doorknob, and recited the spell. The doorknob jiggled, making Taylor gasp. She waited, but nothing else happened.

Focusing her energy on the door, she raised her hand above the knob again. She needed to get inside and stop the council from harming Mel. She needed to protect her aunt. It wasn't the time for her magic to fail her. This was life or death.

She took a deep breath. She could do this. "*Reserare*. Please stop the enchantment and grant me access to this place."

This time, the doorknob jiggled back and forth even harder before turning, as if by an invisible hand. Hesitantly, Taylor reached out and grasped it in her hand, anxious about being zapped again, but all she felt was the cool metal of the doorknob. She pulled open the door. It worked!

Taylor fist-pumped the air before remembering she was supposed to be stealthy. She recalled a spell for that too, so she flipped to the basic spell section, where she found the *Furtim* spell.

Furtim spell: stealth. Another spell that is particularly useful for covert missions, this spell allows demon hunters to sneak around unnoticed. While it doesn't allow for invisibility, it makes the demon hunter less noticeable, and most humans won't see them.

"*Furtim*. Please let me stay hidden from my enemies. Keep me safe from unwanted eyes," Taylor recited.

Warmth spread throughout her body, from the top of her head down to her toes clad in black combat boots. She wasn't sure what it was supposed to do, but the tingly feeling suggested *something*.

Well, it must have worked.

Taylor put the spellbook back in her backpack, zipped it shut, and crept into the building. She glanced around before pulling the door closed as quietly as possible. Peeking down the hallway, she didn't see anyone, so she continued moving forward. She kept close to the wall on one side in case she needed to duck into a room and hide. Although she wasn't sure what any of the rooms were used for, she wasn't sure she wanted to find out. She could only imagine the sorts of secrets the demon hunter council kept hidden here at their headquarters. They clearly didn't want any humans or other beings stumbling across this place and uncovering their secrets.

Soon, Taylor came to a set of grand-looking double doors. *This has to be it.*

"Lock the doors!" an authoritative male voice yelled.

Quickly, she turned one of the doorknobs and opened the right-hand door. She spotted Mel standing in the center of the room in front of a dais where four people were seated—three women and one man.

"Taylor!" Mel screamed.

Taylor rushed into the room toward her aunt before the double doors slammed shut.

Mel

Mel moved closer to her niece. "Taylor, what are you doing here? How did you get here? How did you know where to find me?"

Taylor hugged her aunt before whispering, "I'm here to save you."

"What? But how did you—"

Taylor interrupted her questions, "I'll explain later. Let's get the heck out of here!"

Alastair stood from his chair behind the dais, and the other council members followed suit. "Ah, Taylor, it's a pleasure to meet you."

Taylor narrowed her eyes at him. "Who are you?"

"Alastair Price," he answered, swishing his long white hair behind his shoulders.

The others introduced themselves to Taylor as well, and everyone returned to their seats.

Clarissa cleared her throat. "Now that the introductions are out of the way, can we get back to the matter at hand, please?"

"Are we going to allow the young Turner girl to be here during our meeting?" Lavender asked with her nose upturned.

Taylor crossed her arms over her chest. "It's Taylor Windsor, actually."

Vanessa shrugged a shoulder and smiled kindly. "We might as well. She's going to find out, eventually."

"Find out what?" Taylor asked, relaxing her arms by her sides and taking a step toward the council members.

Clarissa leaned forward over the dais, smiling smugly and dangling the amulet from her hand. "Your Aunt Melanie's powers are going to be taken from her as punishment for making a deal with a powerful demon."

"What? Why? Is that a normal punishment in this world?" Taylor questioned.

Alastair tugged at the collar of his dress shirt. "This is a waste of time. She's a child who knows nothing of our world. We don't have to explain any of this to her." He snatched the amulet from Lavender's hand. He muttered under his breath, and the green stone on the necklace began to glow.

"What are you doing?" Taylor demanded, moving closer to the dais.

A look of immense sadness crossed Vanessa's face like a shadow. "They're doing what they think is best for the demon hunters and for all of humanity. I'm sorry, Mel."

Clarissa and Lavender joined in the chanting with Alastair. Vanessa remained silent, leading Mel to assume Vanessa was the one person who had voted not to take her powers away. But it didn't matter. Three demon hunters from the original five families teaming up against her? That was an immense amount of power. Mel hadn't practiced magic in years . . . until recently. Mel didn't stand a chance.

Mel braced herself. If they couldn't put the amulet around her neck, then she would be safe. She grabbed Taylor's hand, intending to make a run for it and make sure her niece was safe before a catastrophe occurred. But, of course, Taylor thwarted her plans.

When she turned to her niece, Taylor's entire body was glowing. Purple sparks flew from her fingers, and she could hear the electricity vibrating from her niece's body. Taylor's light brown ponytail flew up into the air, fanning out around her head.

"Don't hurt my aunt!" Taylor screamed in a voice so high-pitched that all the stained-glass windows in the room shattered. Glass exploded from the windows, spraying across the room. Taylor raised her right hand, directing the glass to fly toward the dais.

Alastair ducked under the dais to hide. Clarissa screamed in a high-pitched whine. The others threw themselves to the floor too.

Mel stood frozen for a moment before lurching toward Taylor. "We have to leave. Now!"

Taylor's chest was heaving as she stared around at the destruction she had caused. Mel wondered what was going through her mind.

"Taylor, it isn't safe. We have to go," Mel repeated, reaching out for her hand.

Taylor grasped her hand, and they ran out of the room.

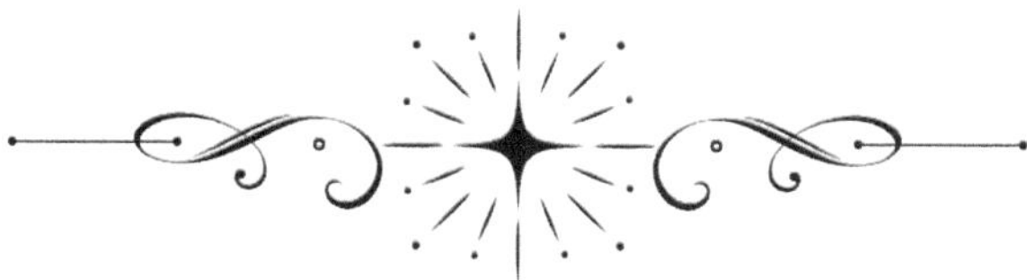

During the drive home, Taylor bombarded Mel with questions. "Is it normal for demon hunters to be punished by having their powers taken away?"

"No, it's extremely rare and a punishment that shouldn't be taken lightly. I didn't agree to it, and they were about to force me to wear the amulet. Once it's on your neck, it can't be taken off unless the person who enchants it grants permission. In that case, it would have been the three council members who would need to undo the enchantment," Mel explained.

Taylor clenched her jaw. "I can't believe they would do that to you. Haven't you known them for years? Aren't you friends with them?"

Mel laughed. "Not exactly. We all went to school together, and we got along fine back then, but that changed over time."

"What changed?" Taylor pried.

"Sorry, kid. I don't want to get into it right now. How did you find me, anyway? And how did you get there?"

Taylor's face flushed. "Oh, crap. I need to text Kylie." She pulled out her cell phone, and her fingers flew over the screen as she sent a text.

"So . . . ?" Mel prompted.

"I asked Kylie to drive me there," Taylor mumbled in a barely audible tone.

"Okay, apparently that's the least of my worries. How did you know where I was? I didn't give you the address."

"Um . . . I had a dream, and there was this demon hunter who told me you needed help. He gave me the address."

"Another demon hunter contacted you in your dream?" Mel questioned, tilting her head to the side.

"Yeah," Taylor said.

Mel thought for a moment before responding, "I suppose it was one of the Cromwell children? Dreamwalking is one of their family's powers."

"He told me his name was Julian."

"Yup, he's Gideon and Clarissa Cromwell's son. Why would he help you, though? Clarissa was *definitely* not on my side today," Mel said.

Taylor shrugged. "I don't know. He was insistent that I go stop them, so I did. It was weird, but for some reason, I believed him."

"He must have overheard his mom's plans and decided to warn you," Mel said, more to herself than to Taylor. Mel hesitated before asking her burning question. "Are you okay? What spell was that? Were you performing a spell you found in our family's spellbook?"

Taylor gulped loudly before answering. "I'm fine. Just tired. And, uh, not exactly. I wasn't reciting any spells. It just sort of . . . happened."

Mel gripped the steering wheel tighter until her knuckles turned white. "That's what I was worried about. Now do you understand why it's dangerous for you to be around people while you're untrained? If you become emotional, then you could lose control again."

"That's different! They were going to hurt you. Or at least take away your powers, and that's bad enough. It wasn't fair," Taylor said.

"I don't want you to hurt anyone, Taylor. Even the council members. Imagine if you accidentally hurt Kylie or Sarah. If you did, the punishment would be worse than losing your powers."

Taylor bit her lip. "What would it be?"

Mel paused for what she knew was too long, but she could barely choke out the word. "Death."

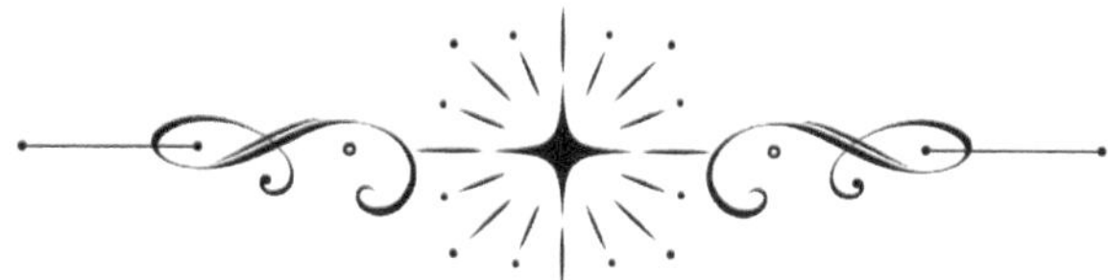

Back at home, Taylor fell asleep on the couch. Mel knew she must be exhausted after exerting such a great amount of energy. She wasn't sure what spell Taylor had used, but whatever it was had been powerful. It also proved that Taylor's powers were out of control, and she needed to keep a closer eye on her. Mel thought her niece would be fine if she left her at home—Taylor had been napping when she left for the meeting earlier—but clearly, that wasn't the case.

Chapter 6

Taylor

Taylor woke up to Brody licking her face. "Brody, stop it," she chided, gently pushing him away.

Glancing around the room, she discovered she had fallen asleep on the couch in the living room. She must have been too tired to go upstairs to her room. Her entire body ached, and she felt as if she had just run several miles. Groaning, she stood from the couch to find her cell phone. She winced. It was the next day, and it was already after 11:00 a.m. She had several missed phone calls and texts from Kylie. After her initial text saying she was going home with Mel, she hadn't replied again because she had passed out.

Kylie must be worried.

Taylor sent her a quick text reassuring her friend that she was fine and headed into the kitchen. She poured cereal and milk into a bowl, then sat at the kitchen table to eat her late breakfast.

As she was scooping another spoonful of cereal into her mouth, her cell phone rang. *Kylie.*

She didn't want to ignore Kylie after they had sort of made amends, so she answered the call. "Hello?"

"Uh, hi. Are you alive?" Kylie asked.

"Yeah . . . that's why I texted you."

"Do you have any idea how worried I was? I didn't hear from you all night!"

Taylor groaned, holding her hand against her aching head. "I know. I'm sorry. I was so tired that I didn't check my phone again after we got home. It was a . . . a crazy night," she responded, purposely remaining vague. She couldn't let Kylie get wrapped up in this mess. She had already gotten her involved when she shouldn't have, and she didn't want to make it worse.

"Yeah, about that . . . What happened? Is Mel okay?" Kylie asked.

"She's fine."

Kylie gave a loud, dramatic sigh. "Is that all you're going to tell me? I drove you to a creepy, abandoned building and waited at the grocery store nearby until you texted me that you were heading home. I was there for hours worrying about you and Mel."

"Sorry, Kylie. I wish I could tell you more, but—"

"Mel isn't, like, in a cult or something, is she? Or is it drugs or alcohol?" Kylie continued hypothesizing.

"No, nothing like that. We're both fine. It had to do with the debt Mel was in and the debt collector wanting her to pay him back . . ." Taylor lied. "Her debt is paid off now, though, so they should leave her alone."

"Oh. Huh. I thought it was more dramatic than that. It seemed really important to you that you got there."

"It *was* important, so thank you for helping. I know Mel appreciates it too," Taylor said.

"Anyway, do you want to go shopping later? My mom wants me to do some chores, but I'm free this afternoon," Kylie said.

Taylor could hear the hope in her voice. She debated what to do until Kylie spoke up again. She could never stay quiet for more than a minute.

"I understand if you're busy. I know you've had a lot going on this summer. Or, I assume you have, since you've been ignoring me," Kylie said.

Well, she certainly couldn't say no to her now. She was only human—or a demon hunter, apparently.

"Sure, we can go shopping later. Come over when you're done with your chores. I have a few chores to take care of before then too," Taylor said.

"Really?" Kylie asked.

"Yup. See you later," Taylor said, hanging up the phone before she decided otherwise.

Mel would be so pissed when she found out. Unless she didn't . . .

In the afternoon, Taylor told Mel she was taking Brody on a walk around the neighborhood and that she would be back later. At first, Mel had protested because it was about a thousand degrees outside—or at least ninety-five degrees—so it was unbearable to be out for too long. But Mel eventually relented. Taylor suspected she felt guilty for keeping her trapped in the house. And it was true. Taylor longed for the days of freedom when she had been able to come and go as she pleased. The days before she knew about the existence of demons and demon hunters. Before all the curses and deadly vows . . . Before her entire world had changed.

Taylor peeked out the curtains in the living room and spotted Kylie coming up the driveway. She needed to intercept her before she rang the doorbell.

She grabbed Brody's leash and clipped it onto his collar. "We're leaving, Mel. We'll be back soon."

"Okay. Have fun. Come home if you start overheating. You'll get dehydrated or sunburned if you're out there too long. Make sure to bring a water bottle with you," Mel warned her. "I'm ordering pizza for dinner, so don't stay out late."

"Don't worry. We'll be fine," Taylor promised, leaving the house to enjoy her freedom.

"Hi," Kylie greeted her as she walked up the front steps.

"Hi, Kylie. Is it okay if we go over to your house?" Taylor asked. "And can Brody come too?"

Kylie beamed, bending down to scratch underneath Brody's furry chin. "Of course. You know my mom always loves having you over. Both of you."

Taylor's face must have paled because Kylie quickly asked, "What's wrong? You look scared."

"Oh, uh . . . I guess I didn't think your mom would be home."

Kylie stood back up after greeting Brody and tilted her head sideways. "Well, she's at work now, but she'll be home in the evening. I asked her if you could stay for dinner."

"I can't. Sorry," Taylor blurted out.

Kylie's gaze went skyward to the fluffy white clouds, the perfect backdrop against the pale blue sky. "What's going on? I know you can't tell me about whatever happened with Mel, but something is wrong. You're acting weird." She paused, then added, "Weirder than usual, I mean."

This was a lot easier when I was able to tell her everything.

"Yeah, it's just that . . ." Taylor scrambled to come up with a decent excuse, one that wouldn't make Kylie never want to talk to her again. She didn't want to lose the one friend she had made since moving to Grimwood. No one could expect her to become a loner and not have any friends. "I really miss my parents, and it's hard being around you and your mom. You're so close, and it reminds me of how me and my mom were." Taylor paused, letting her excuse sink in. "I miss them a lot," she added.

Kylie lurched forward to hug her, wrapping her arms tightly around Taylor. "I'm so sorry, Tay. That thought hadn't crossed my mind. I know you've gone through a lot this summer. I'll try to be more understanding." She tapped her chin. "Wait, is that why you were pulling away and didn't talk to me for weeks?"

"Ye—yes," Taylor agreed, capitalizing on her new excuse.

Part of Taylor felt like a terrible person for using her parents' shocking deaths as an excuse for her rude behavior toward her friend, but it wasn't a lie. Just stretching the truth a bit. Besides, she needed to get out of the house and away from Mel for a while. She needed to spend some quality time with someone her own age—not to mention, take a break from training.

Kylie patted her arm. "I'll be here for you as much as you need me. Shopping should be a good distraction."

Taylor smiled. "I think it will be just what I need. As long as we go somewhere we can bring Brody with us?"

Kylie glanced down at Brody, who expectantly stared back, wagging his tail with excitement about whatever adventure they were about to go on.

"Absolutely," Kylie responded. "I think the market downtown is mostly outside and dog-friendly, so we could head there."

"Perfect," Taylor said, bumping shoulders with Kylie. "Thanks for inviting me, Kylie. You're a good friend."

"Yeah, better than you," Kylie teased.

Taylor laughed, but Kylie had a point. "You're right."

Mel

Waking in a panic, Mel rubbed her bleary eyes to focus on the clock on her bedside table. *4:30 p.m.*

"Four thirty?!" she muttered, stumbling out of bed. She scrambled to find a clean T-shirt and shorts, then threw her hair up into a messy ponytail. "Taylor? Brody?" she called, wandering into the hallway and heading to Taylor's bedroom. She paused, waiting for an answer or the sound of Brody's nails tapping against the hardwood floor, but the house was silent. "Taylor!"

Mel knocked before twisting the doorknob and entering Taylor's bedroom. She peeked into the bathroom too, but there was no trace of her niece or Brody. The events of the past twenty-four hours had been tiring and stressful, but she still couldn't believe she had fallen asleep for several hours during the middle of the day.

She checked her phone, but she didn't have any missed calls or texts from Taylor. Taylor had promised she was taking Brody on a walk, but she left hours ago. If she hadn't lied, then she should be back by now. Unless . . . unless something bad had happened.

Mel took the stairs two at a time, checking the rest of the house before accepting that Taylor was, in fact, still gone. She called Taylor, but her phone went straight to voicemail.

"Damn it!" Mel cursed, tucking her phone into her purse.

She slung her purse across her shoulder, grabbed the first pair of shoes she found, and headed next door. She could ask Kylie if she had seen Taylor today. She didn't think Sarah would be home from work yet. Mel had only taken the day off because of her meeting with the council the day before. The chaos of the meeting had ensured she didn't want to go into the office.

Mel sprinted over to the Andersons' house and banged her fist on the front door, praying Kylie answered. She kept knocking for about thirty seconds before deciding no one was home. Sighing, she called Taylor again before giving up and heading back into her own home.

What if something had happened to Taylor? The council hadn't been pleased with either of them. *What if*—but Mel stopped herself from finishing the thought. They wouldn't harm Taylor, would they? It went against the demon hunter's laws. They couldn't break the law without repercussions. Then again, after they had attempted to forcefully take her powers with the Emerald Vacuus Amulet, she wasn't sure what to think anymore.

Mel took off her shoes, threw them toward the entryway, and headed into the kitchen. She wiped down the countertops and washed all of the dishes piled up in the sink.

She called Taylor again. Still no answer.

She decided to wait until dusk before deciding what to do next. She would call the police or contact another demon hunter for help. The only problem was deciding who would be most likely to help her. Maybe Vanessa.

By the time Mel had finished mopping the floors downstairs and was elbow-deep scrubbing one of the toilets, she nearly jumped out of her skin when she heard the front door open. Mel raced to the front of the house, anxiously expecting to see her niece, but it wasn't Taylor standing there in the entryway with their nose turned up in the air as if they smelled something rotten. It was Alastair.

"Alastair . . . what are you doing here?" Mel questioned, smoothing down her messy hair.

Sweat dripped down her back from all her cleaning and running around, and she tried not to grimace at how unattractive she must look—not that she cared if Alastair saw her in such a state.

They had known each other since their days at the academy. He was handsome in a cool, Lucius Malfoy sort of way, but not her type. Besides, now wasn't the time for her to focus on romance. She had a teenage demon hunter to raise. And considering she had lost her niece, she wasn't doing a very good job.

"Mel." He nodded in acknowledgement and closed the front door with a wave of his hand.

"Wait, how did you get into my home?"

A snide smile curled up on Alastair's face. "Ah, yes, the protection spell." He pointed a long, thin finger at her. "Your spell work isn't bad, but I was able to break through it."

Mel's forehead wrinkled. She hated how stupid he always made her feel. "Protection spell?"

Alastair put a hand to his forehead and sighed deeply, as if her questions were inane and ridiculous. "You don't need to pretend you don't have a protection spell on your house. Most of us do. You don't need to hide it. Although perhaps you should be ashamed that it was so easy for me to break through. I expected more of a challenge." He removed his hand from his forehead and stared at her with the full intensity of his green eyes. "Anyway, back to the reason I'm here . . ."

Mel still felt bewildered—for multiple reasons—but she chose to ignore her questions in favor of finding out why one of the demon hunter council members had shown up unannounced at her house. "Okay." She crossed her arms over her chest, leaning defensively against the wall in the hallway, angling her body away from him. "Why are you here?"

"Mel, please . . . Let's not pretend there hasn't been something between us since our days at the academy. If you hadn't been so stubborn back then, I probably would have married you instead of Priscilla."

Mel cringed and backed further away from him. *Did he just admit he would have chosen me over his wife who died from cancer? What a jerk.*

Alastair took a step closer to her, then another until he was mere feet from her. He slowly extended his right hand until he stroked her chin. Mel froze as shockwaves overcame her. What the heck was he doing?

"Alastair, stop it!" she shouted.

Almost as soon as he made contact with her skin, Mel reacted. Instinctively, purple sparks shot out from her hand, not quite burning his fingers, but heating them enough to make him stop touching her.

"Ow! What the hell was that for?" Alastair protested, rubbing his hand and wincing.

"Alastair, I'm not sure how you got the idea that was okay, but I don't want you to touch me ever again." Mel held her hands by her sides, palms out, prepared to attack again.

Alastair's frown turned into a smirk. "I was simply being nice, Mel. Of course I didn't mean any of it. I was giving you one last chance to get out of this mess. If that's the way you're going to be, then unfortunately, you're out of chances." He moved quickly, pulling an object from his pants pocket.

He darted toward her.

Mel shot purple sparks at him again. This time, he was ready. He raised his hand to deflect the magic bursts. Mel ducked into the hallway leading to the kitchen. All too soon, he caught up to her. A cool, metal object slipped around her neck. He pulled her hair out from underneath the chain. Then Alastair enchanted the amulet so she couldn't remove it.

Mel yanked at the amulet, attempting to pull it off. It was too late.

"*Magicae uptis*! *Ignis*! *Unda*!" she recited the magic burst spell, then the fire spell, water spell, and every spell she could think of off the top of her head. But it was no use. Her magic was gone.

Chapter 8

Taylor

In the evening, Taylor came home to find her aunt in the living room surrounded by junk food. She was weeping and watching one of those terrible Lifetime movies her mom had loved to watch when she was feeling sad. Brody hopped up onto Mel's lap, licking her face to make sure she was okay. Mel patted him on the head.

"Mel, I'm home. What's wrong?" Taylor said, tentatively approaching her aunt.

"Taylor! Oh, thank God you're home! I was so worried when I couldn't reach you, and you weren't next door at the Andersons'."

"Oh, sorry. My phone died. I forgot to charge it last night," Taylor lied.

Mel frowned. "If you're going to leave the house, you need to make sure your phone is fully charged. I was worried about you. I thought something happened."

"Um, well . . . something kind of did happen," Taylor admitted, scratching the back of her neck and avoiding eye contact.

"What?" Mel snapped, pausing the movie and sitting up from her slouched position on the couch.

"Kylie and I went to the outdoor market downtown and—"

Mel interrupted her explanation and stood from the couch. "*You what*? Please tell me you didn't hang out with Kylie and go out in public to be around a large group of people when *I specifically told you not to*."

Taylor groaned, throwing her hands up in the air. "I know, but can you blame me? I'm fifteen years old. I should be out in the world, hanging out with friends, going to fun places, enjoying my summer . . ."

"And avoiding trouble," Mel finished. "You aren't a normal teenager, Taylor. You have to be careful. We've discussed this. Until we understand your powers or you have a better grasp on controlling them, I forbid you from leaving the house again."

"Are you kidding me? You can't do that! This is so unfair!" Taylor protested.

"I don't care if it's unfair. As your guardian, I have to do what I think is best for you. You lied to me about what you were doing, so that proves you aren't responsible. You're still a child, and you clearly don't understand the repercussions of your actions," Mel said.

"Well, I think I'm starting to," Taylor mumbled.

"What was that?" Mel asked.

"Nothing," Taylor snapped. "Come on, Brody, let's go upstairs."

"Where are you going?" Mel demanded, moving toward her.

"To my room. If I have to stay in this house, I don't want to see you."

Mel narrowed her eyes. "Taylor, I'm not doing this to be cruel, but you gave me no choice. What were you thinking dragging Kylie into this? Again?"

"Yeah, yeah," Taylor started, before noticing a necklace around Mel's neck. She pointed at the necklace and stepped closer to see it more clearly. "Is that new? Where did you get it?"

It wasn't like the type of jewelry Mel normally wore. In fact, besides the occasional simple sterling silver earrings or bracelets, she hadn't seen Mel wear anything remotely like that necklace. Her aunt wasn't the type of woman who wore such ostentatious jewelry. The gem in the center was a gigantic emerald. It was . . . ugly.

Mel clasped the necklace, her cheeks pinkening. She cleared her throat. "Oh, this? It was a gift."

Taylor snorted. "What? Do you have a secret boyfriend?"

"No."

"Fine. If you aren't going to tell me, then whatever. I don't care." Taylor called for Brody again, and he raced her up the stairs to her bedroom.

She shut her door and plopped onto her bed. Absentmindedly, she turned on the TV. Brody hopped up onto her bed and curled up next to her, yawning and closing his eyes. He must have been tired from all their shopping and walking around. Taylor scrolled through the movies until she found one mindless enough to distract her from her current reality. She welcomed anything that let her escape.

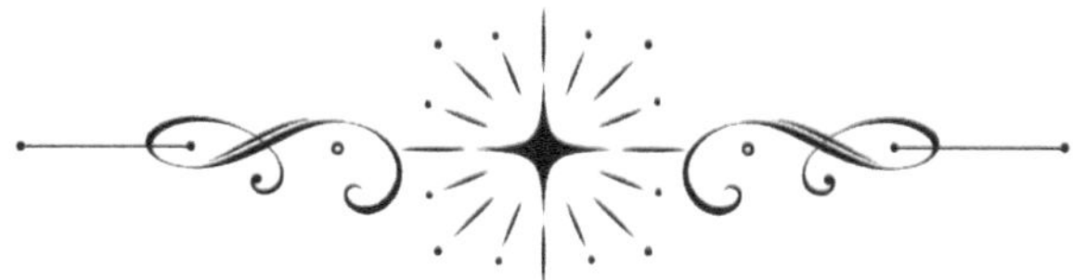

Taylor tossed and turned for most of the night. Unable to sleep, she finally gave up and grabbed her cell phone to look at memes and scroll through social media. Distracting, sure, but was it productive?

She fumbled for the lamp on her nightstand and found the switch, flicking it to the *on* position. She wished she had the spellbook. Then she could read more about the spells she hadn't learned yet and maybe even practice some of them. She was excited to learn more of the advanced spells. Mel had taken the spellbook from her after she saved her from the council, but Taylor knew it was locked away in the steamer trunk again.

Quietly, she crept across her room to the door. As she reached for the doorknob, Brody opened his eyes and stared at her, his dark eyes appearing eerie in the dim light. He tilted his head and let out a low whine.

"Shh, Brody, go back to sleep. It's okay, buddy," Taylor whispered.

He whined again and put his face in between his paws. His eyes widened until they were nearly as big as saucers and irresistible.

"Ugh, fine. You can come with me. But stop whining and be quiet, okay?"

Brody wagged his tail silently, as if agreeing to her terms, and jumped off the bed to follow her out of the room. Taylor snuck down the stairs slowly and stealthily, while Brody practically bounded down. She winced, knowing there was no way Mel hadn't heard him. Maybe she would get lucky and Mel was so tired she didn't hear them sneaking around. Then again, it was Taylor's house too, so she wasn't sure why she still sometimes felt like a guest. Maybe part of it had to do with the fact that she now felt trapped in a prison. Home was supposed to be a safe place, not somewhere you were stuck and never allowed to leave.

Taylor didn't want to turn on any of the hallway lights and risk Mel seeing them, so she recited the *lux* spell. She cupped the white ball of light in her hands and let it float in front of her, guiding her path through the downstairs hallway. She headed toward the spare room that Mel kept locked at all times.

When Taylor first moved in, her curiosity about the locked room had nearly killed her. She wondered what Mel was hiding and had only cared about finding answers to her mysterious aunt's life. Now she wished she hadn't been so curious and that she had never broken into the room with Kylie. Then her life wouldn't have drastically changed over the summer.

Taylor reached up to the top of the doorframe, feeling around for the key that unlocked the room. Nothing was there.

"Where is it?" she whispered to Brody, swiping her fingers across the doorframe again.

Brody wagged his tail and stared at her, waiting for something to happen.

"It should be here."

Just as Taylor was trying to recall the unlocking spell she had used previously, the hallway light flickered on.

Her aunt appeared at the end of the hallway, coming toward her like a ghost in the night. "Looking for the key?" Mel asked, with her hands on her hips and a fierce expression on her face.

Chapter 9

Mel

Mel had caught Taylor red-handed trying to get into the locked room. "What were you planning to do? Use the spellbook?"

Taylor scooped up Brody into her arms and silently headed to the stairs.

"Taylor, answer me. Why are you down here in the middle of the night? You woke me up, and you owe me an explanation. I have to work tomorrow," Mel said.

"Sorry. I tried to be quiet. It's my house too, you know," Taylor said in a defensive tone.

Mel's face softened. "I'm sorry. Of course it is. I want you to feel at home here, but we need to trust each other. Why were you trying to get into the spare room?"

Taylor stared at her, her hazel eyes narrowing. "You don't trust me."

"That isn't true. I—"

"It is true, though, Mel. You're keeping me locked in the house like Rapunzel being locked in her tower. I can't do this. That's why I snuck out earlier and lied to you to hang out with Kylie. And I didn't tell you what happened, but it . . . it wasn't good."

Mel beckoned her toward the living room. "Let's go sit on the couch and chat. I'll get us some ice cream since we're already awake. This sounds like it might be a serious conversation. Ice cream makes everything better."

Taylor scoffed. "Ice cream doesn't fix everything, Mel. I'm not five."

She sat on the couch. Mel went into the kitchen and made the most elaborate ice cream sundaes that she could. She returned to the living room carrying two heaping bowls of ice cream piled high with whipped cream, chocolate syrup, gummy bears, and a maraschino cherry on top.

"Wow." Taylor gawked at the sundaes. "You went all out."

Mel grinned, taking a spoonful from her bowl. "I figured we might as well enjoy it. I don't want the night to be ruined."

Taylor dug into her sundae, swallowing a bite of ice cream before responding, "Well, don't speak too soon."

"Taylor, don't you know by now that you can talk to me about anything? Whatever it is, we'll figure it out together," Mel said.

"But you're going to be angry. You haven't let me leave the house. I don't think what I did was that unreasonable."

"I'm sorry, Taylor. None of this is fair to you. Your entire life was turned upside down this summer. I'm aware that I haven't been the best guardian, but I promise I'm trying. I only want to protect you. Please tell me what happened. We'll deal with it together. I can't help you if I don't know what's going on," Mel said.

"Okay." Taylor exhaled loudly. "When Kylie and I were browsing the outdoor market, we decided to go to the coffeeshop downtown for Frappuccinos. I had Brody with me, so I couldn't go into the store. I asked Kylie to order for both of us and bring the drinks outside. I grabbed one of the outdoor tables and waited for her. It took forever for her to come back outside, and she was empty-handed when she finally returned. Apparently, the barista bullied Kylie at school last year. He was so mean to her, Mel. Like, you wouldn't believe half the things she told me he did to torture her. He spread nasty rumors and made most of the people at school stop talking to her. Anyway, he must have said something mean because she came out crying. I asked her what happened, and she said that Isaac was working there and she couldn't get our drinks. I asked her to watch Brody and handed her the leash, then I went into the coffee shop. At that point, all I had planned on doing was ordering the Frappuccinos and leaving, so Kylie didn't have to face him again, but that . . . uh . . . didn't work out."

Mel held a scoop of ice cream in front of her mouth and stared at her niece with her lips pursed together, refraining herself from judgment until she knew the entire story. "What happened next?"

"I asked to speak to Isaac. When I found out who he was, I asked what he said to Kylie that upset her so much. He smirked and said she deserved it. But she didn't do anything. She was just ordering drinks, and he thought it would be funny to tease her and make her cry." Taylor took another bite of ice cream. "He started laughing, and I could feel the rage coming over me. The next thing I knew—"

Mel gasped, putting her hand over her mouth. "Oh, no. Taylor, please tell me you didn't perform a spell in that coffee shop."

Taylor focused on her ice cream, taking another bite before telling the rest of the story. "I may have burned his hand when he handed me the Frappuccinos. But I swear it wasn't on purpose!"

Mel couldn't help herself from bursting out laughing. "That's it? It sounds like he deserved it."

Taylor snuck a glance at her aunt. "Wait . . . so you aren't mad?"

Mel shrugged. "Do I wish you hadn't performed magic in front of humans? Yes. Do I wish you hadn't risked exposing us? Also, yes. But it already happened, and he sounds like a jerk."

Taylor let out a sigh of relief. "Thank God."

"But, Taylor, you do realize this means I was right. You can't go around unleashing your magic without knowing how to harness it and control it. This situation turned out okay, and I hope you didn't seriously injure the kid, but next time, something much worse could happen. You could have hurt the people in the vicinity, and I know you don't want that."

Taylor ate her ice cream in silence. "Okay," she finally said, setting her empty bowl on the coffee table a moment later.

"Okay? Well, we need to figure out where to go from here. It might be difficult to train you now because—"

Mel's sentence was cut off by the door bell ringing.

"You aren't expecting Kylie, are you?" Mel asked, eyeing her niece curiously. "It's a little late to have a friend over."

Taylor shook her head and headed to the door with Mel on her heels.

"Let me answer it," Mel said, pulling the door open. She wasn't sure who it was, but it couldn't be good.

Brody barked at the new guests in their doorway.

On the front steps stood a teenage boy and Clarissa Cromwell. He must be her son.

"Clarissa," Mel greeted in a cold tone. "It's the middle of the night. What are you doing here?"

Taylor

"Hi, Taylor. Aren't you going to invite us inside?" Julian asked, with a grin on his handsome face.

Taylor opened the door wide and dramatically gestured for them to come in.

Clarissa made the introductions, and Mel told them all to sit in the living room. Clarissa and Julian sat on the couch. Mel let Taylor take the comfy armchair and pulled a kitchen chair into the living room for herself.

"Why are you here, Clarissa?" Mel asked, leaning forward with her hands on her knees.

Taylor gripped the armchair on either side, digging her fingers into the soft, worn fabric. Why were the Cromwells at their house? Besides that anxiety-inducing question, she had only seen Julian in her dreams and felt nervous about finally meeting him in person. He was even more attractive than in her dreams. It was too late to worry about her leggings and T-shirt, and the fact that she hadn't showered since yesterday.

Clarissa gazed at Mel, her eyes dropping to Mel's neck, where the ugly green stone rested. Her mouth opened slightly. Taylor glanced at it again, perplexed. It was only a necklace.

"Melanie, why is the Emerald Vacuus Amulet around your neck?" Clarissa asked. "We didn't complete the enchantment ceremony because you fled."

Mel's gaze dropped to the floor. "Alastair came over earlier. He assaulted me and forced the amulet onto my neck. It must have worked because my magic is gone."

"He did *what*?" Clarissa said, her green eyes narrowing.

Taylor jumped into the conversation. "Why didn't you tell me your magic was gone?"

She couldn't believe it. Mel's magic was gone just like that? The thought was terrifying. Taylor had only learned about her powers recently, but she couldn't imagine losing them, much less having them taken by force.

"I assumed he was acting on the will of the council, but still . . . To come over here unannounced, while I was home alone and attack me . . . " Mel took a deep, shuddering breath. "I'm glad Taylor wasn't home when it happened."

"He most certainly was not acting through the council! We didn't approve of this. We were going to ask you to come back and speak with us again at our headquarters, as we always do. We wanted to reach a compromise, since you were against the use of the amulet. Taylor's intervention made the rest of us rethink the decision to use the enchantment," Clarissa said, rubbing her forehead as if she had a migraine. "I can't believe he did this without speaking with me. Or anyone else, for that matter."

"Well, either way, it's stuck around my neck unless he reverses the enchantment. I've already tried casting every spell I could think of. I can't use my magic. I'm defenseless. I can't even protect Taylor," Mel said quietly in a defeated tone.

"I can protect myself," Taylor insisted. "I don't want you to worry about me. I'll be fine."

"That's part of the reason we're here, although I didn't know about the amulet. The council wants Taylor to start training at the academy in the fall. She'll be safe there and watched after. She can live in the dorms, as most of the students do, and integrate with the other demon hunters. However, because she can't control her powers and hasn't gone through the same training as the other students and will inevitably be years behind them, we agreed it was best to give her a sort of mentor to watch out for her and intervene if a . . . situation arises." Clarissa gestured to her son before making eye contact with Taylor. "Julian stepped forward and offered to act as your mentor."

"*Mentor*?" Taylor said, standing from the armchair, her hands balled into fists at her sides. "But he's the same age as me!"

"I'm sixteen," Julian said with a cocky grin. "And I'm more than qualified to take on this responsibility. It's my duty as a demon hunter to minimize the risk of our exposure. You're dangerous to all of us if you accidentally use magic with humans around, not to mention if you hurt someone."

Julian might have a point, but Taylor knew next to nothing about him and didn't like the idea of being forced into spending so much time with a stranger. She pictured him being glued to her side at all times. Even though he was hot, that sounded both awkward and annoying.

"That isn't a bad idea. Julian has been attending the academy since he was twelve, and I'm assuming you and Gideon have trained him too. I'm sure he will be a worthy guardian," Mel said calmly, shooting Taylor a warning look to be quiet.

Taylor crossed her arms over her chest. "I don't need someone to babysit me. I'm not out of control. I haven't hurt anyone," she said, ignoring the incident earlier with Isaac's burned hand in the coffee shop. That was irrelevant to this conversation. Anyway, he was fine. Probably. "Besides, won't there be adults or professors at the academy? Can't they look out for me?"

"Of course, they'll have your safety in mind too, but they can't spend all their time focused on one student. The professors have their hands full already. There are dozens of students at Grimwood Magical Academy. There isn't enough time for you to get caught up, but you'll be in a better place than you would have been otherwise. Julian is going to start training you as soon as possible, so you'll be better prepared in September when classes start," Clarissa explained.

"Mel is already training me," Taylor interjected, attempting to find any way out of this. Although the more Clarissa told her, the more excited she became about the possibilities. Training with Julian had to be more fun than training sessions with Mel. Her aunt had been practically working her to death. Not to mention the fact that she would get to leave the house.

"Yes, but she hasn't been involved much in our community for years. And now that she doesn't have use of her powers, it will be difficult for her to train you," Clarissa said.

Julian turned to Taylor. "So when do you want our training to start? I'm all yours for the next month." He winked.

Taylor hid her face in her hands for a moment, pretending she was upset about the idea. She didn't want him to get an even bigger head about it, but she was excited to learn more about magic and the other parts of the demon hunter world Mel couldn't teach her. It would mean she wouldn't be as much of a beginner when she went to the academy. She didn't want to stick out when she should be more advanced at her age.

"We'll start tomorrow," Taylor said.

Julian's bright blue eyes widened slightly before he collected himself. He stood and walked to the armchair she was standing in front of before extending his hand to her. "Fine. Is 8:00 a.m. okay? I'm an early riser."

Taylor shook Julian's hand. He clasped her hand in his for a moment too long, prolonging the physical contact while gazing at her with those irresistible blue eyes. Her heart fluttered in her chest, and she broke eye contact while extracting her hand from his.

Taylor hated waking up early, especially in the summer, but she didn't want Julian or his mom to think she was lazy. "Let's make it 7:30 a.m., and you have a deal."

Mel snorted. She knew Taylor's sleep schedule and was probably thinking she wouldn't be able to wake up so early. Taylor was determined to prove herself—to her aunt, Julian, Clarissa, and all the other demon hunters. She could do this. She was going to be the best damn demon hunter their world had ever seen.

"Perfect," Julian said. "We can practice at the demon hunter council's headquarters. They have a practice room with all the materials we should need. Plus, it's soundproofed, and the building is enchanted so humans can't enter it. It's the perfect place to practice."

"I don't have my driver's license," Taylor said, fidgeting with the seam on her leggings as she admitted it. "My birthday isn't until October."

At the same time, Mel and Julian both said, "I can drive you there."

Then Mel said, "Thanks for the offer. In hindsight, I have to be at work tomorrow, so it would interfere with my regular morning schedule if I had to drive Taylor to meet you there. Are you sure you don't mind picking her up?"

"No, it's no trouble. I'll be here bright and early tomorrow," Julian said.

Clarissa stood from the couch and headed toward the front door. "Thank you both for agreeing to this arrangement. I think it's the best outcome for all of us. Julian is a good teacher, and you have a lot to learn, Taylor. We'll see ourselves out. Come on, Julian." She gestured for her son to follow her.

Julian shot one last smile at Taylor and waved as he left the house. He shut the front door behind him.

Mel turned to Taylor. "Please try to look at this in a positive light. You'll get to learn magic in a stable, safe environment, and maybe you and Julian will become friends. At least you'll know someone when you start school there. I know how hard it must be to have to start over again."

Taylor chewed on her bottom lip, mulling it over. "You're right, but I'm still not happy about it."

Mel

The next morning, Mel woke up at 6:00 a.m. like usual, despite their late-night guests. She took a shower and got ready for work, then headed downstairs to the kitchen to brew a half-pot of coffee for her thermos. Her eyes nearly popped out of her head when she saw the coffee pot already full of freshly brewed coffee and a toasted bagel waiting on a ceramic plate. The toaster dinged, signaling the bread was done cooking.

Mid-yawn, she spotted her niece standing in the kitchen.

Taylor whipped around from her position facing the fridge to pull out the cream cheese. Then she grabbed the second bagel from the toaster. "Good morning, Mel."

"Y-you're awake," Mel stuttered.

Taylor giggled. "Why are you so surprised?"

Mel rolled her eyes. "Yeah, okay. As if you being awake before the sun rises is normal. Who are you, and what have you done with my niece?"

Taylor spread cream cheese on both bagels and handed one to Mel. "People can change, you know. I don't want to disappoint you. I know the training is important, and I need to be as prepared as possible when I go to the academy in September."

Mel squeezed Taylor's shoulder. "You could never disappoint me. You've dealt with a lot this summer, and you're doing considerably well despite all that. I'm proud of you. I hope you know that. You're going to accomplish great things."

Taylor smiled, but it looked forced. "Thanks, Mel." She paused, leaning against the counter and taking a bite of her toasted bagel. "Julian should be here soon," she added, her voice wavering.

Mel raised an eyebrow, contemplating her niece's statement. "Are you nervous about training with him?"

Taylor shrugged. "Maybe? I don't know him very well. Are you sure we should trust his family?" Her hazel eyes lingered on the amulet around Mel's neck before flicking back up to make eye contact with her.

"Of course," Mel replied tersely, tucking the amulet into her blouse so it wasn't as visible. *As if she had a choice.*

"Okay. Well, have a good day at work," Taylor replied.

"Thanks, kiddo. I'll see you later, okay? Call me if you need anything," Mel said. "I mean it. Anything at all."

"Okay," Taylor said, then continued eating her bagel.

Mel took that as her cue to leave.

She could have stayed and waited for Julian to pick her up, but she decided it was better to let Taylor deal with this situation by herself. For now, at least. Mel was determined to find a way to take off the amulet.

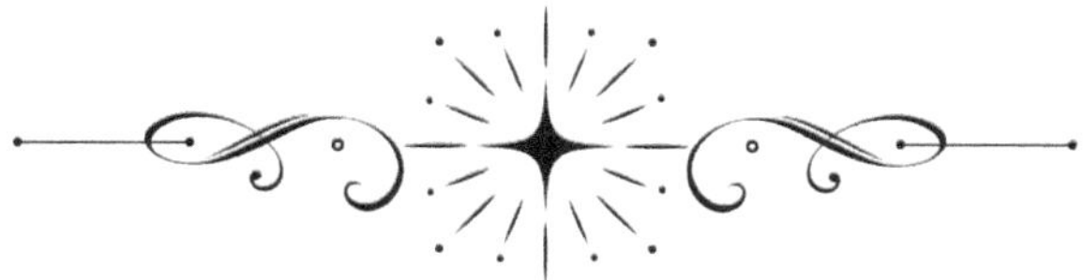

After work, Mel opened the spellbook, skimming through it, already knowing it was useless. As far as she knew, there wasn't a spell in it that could help her. The only way to get the amulet off was for Alastair to reverse the enchantment. But the chances of that happening were slim to none, so she had to try.

She futilely searched the spells. In the intermediate spell section, there was *reserare, praesidium, lux,* and *silentium.* Nothing to disenchant a necklace. This called for a more advanced spell. *Retinentia, exilium, portalis* . . . None of those would do. She scanned the rest of the advanced spells until she found one that seemed promising.

Delustro spell: disenchantment. This is an advanced spell to break an enchantment.

Spell: "Delustro. Please break the enchantment I cast and free the object from its spell."

Mel recited the spell, stretching out her fingers and waiting for the familiar tingling sensation. "*Delustro*!"

The council members had stated the Emerald Vacuus Amulet could only be disenchanted by whoever cast the enchantment spell, but it had been worth a shot. Sighing, she shut the spellbook and placed it back in the steamer trunk.

Mel decided to try a few basic spells to test her powers. If she couldn't get rid of the necklace, perhaps she could still use her magic somehow.

"*Magicae uptis. Ignis. Furtim*!"

Nothing happened. No tingling sensation in her fingers. No purple sparks or bursts of magic. Nothing. She was devoid of magic and what made her special. For so many years, she had longed for this to be her reality. To be a normal human who worked a regular job and lived a normal human life. But absolutely nothing about her life was normal, and almost as soon as it had been taken from her, she missed her magic.

Besides, how was she supposed to keep Taylor safe without her abilities? That was what worried her the most. Above all else, she didn't want any harm to come to her niece. She had already dragged her into enough danger this summer.

Mel supposed she could try talking to Alastair, but after he had assaulted her and gone against the wishes of the rest of the council, she didn't expect him to agree to it. She needed to ask someone else for help. And she knew the perfect person.

Taylor

Pale blue sparks of magic shot toward her. This time, Taylor managed to dodge Julian's attack. She had already been hit enough times, so she felt relieved about not getting hit for once, although she assumed Julian wasn't using his full powers on her. She could only imagine how much sorer she would be if he were.

She yelped with glee and raised her arm to do a fist pump, but more blue sparks flew toward her. She tried to duck in time, but she was too slow. The magic hit her square in the chest, knocking her flat on her butt.

"Ouch," she muttered, sitting on the padded floor that had somewhat cushioned her fall.

Julian rolled his eyes playfully. "Oh, whatever. The floor is padded. It couldn't have hurt that much." He held out his hand to help her up.

She took his hand and let him hoist her to her feet. "Okay, let's go again."

"Are you sure? We've been practicing for hours. Don't you want to take a break and get lunch?"

At the mention of food, Taylor's stomach rumbled loudly. She patted her stomach.

Julian laughed. "I'll take that as a yes. Come on. I know a great spot not too far from here. We should take a break to refuel, then we can practice more later."

"Fine," Taylor agreed.

"You're not picky, are you?" Julian eyed her with suspicion.

"Not at all."

Julian held the door open for her.

"Thanks."

They walked to Julian's car. He held the passenger door open for her, and she climbed in.

"You don't have to do that every time, you know. I can open my own doors," she said.

"I'm being polite."

"Well, stop it. I'm only training with you because I have to," Taylor retorted, buckling her seatbelt.

"Can't we be friends?" Julian prodded. "It will make this more enjoyable."

She glared at him. "I don't need any more friends, and this isn't supposed to be enjoyable. Let's stick to practicing together, and watch out for me or whatever you're supposed to do. Just don't expect me to enjoy this. I was forced into it, and trust me, I wouldn't willingly choose to spend time with you," Taylor shot back.

"Okay," Julian replied, backing his car out of the parking spot and heading toward the main road.

Taylor had no clue where they were going, and she didn't care. She stared out the window as Julian drove, remaining silent until he stopped the car in front of a food truck parked a few blocks away.

"This is it?" she asked, staring at the food truck incredulously.

"You said you weren't picky. Their food is fantastic—not normal stuff you'd find in a food truck. Their specialty is corn arepas with all sorts of fresh toppings. The family who owns the food truck is from Colombia." Julian exited the car and headed toward the food truck before realizing she wasn't following him. "Coming?"

"Uh, yeah. Sure." She stumbled out of the car, finding her legs weak and shaking as she followed Julian. Whether that was because she was hungry or exhausted from practice, she wasn't sure, but she needed to eat.

"You okay?" Julian asked, noticing she was walking slowly.

"I'm fine."

Julian ordered two arepas, then turned to her and asked what she wanted.

"I'll have the same as you," she said.

"Okay." Julian pulled out his wallet and handed his card to the man working inside the food truck.

"Oh, you don't have to pay for mine," Taylor said, blushing as she realized she didn't have her debit card. "I didn't bring my purse with me, though."

Julian laughed. "It's fine. You can pay next time."

"Deal," Taylor said with a small smile. She hated to admit that he was sweet—holding doors for her, buying her lunch, driving her around, even the fact that he was willing to train her. He must have endless patience.

Julian gasped dramatically. "Is that a smile I see? Did I *actually* make you smile?"

"Shut up." She stopped smiling and scowled at him.

"You don't have to try so hard to pretend you don't like me. It's okay if you do," Julian said in a lilting tone.

Taylor's mouth gaped wide open, and she stared at him, unable to think of a good enough response.

"Order number thirty-two!" the man working the food truck announced.

"That's ours," Julian said, grabbing the tray from the pick-up counter. "Thank you," he told the employee.

"You're welcome. Enjoy!" the man said.

"There's a picnic table over there if you don't mind eating outside," Julian said, gesturing toward a few picnic tables on the other side of the parking lot, in a semi-shaded area.

"That's fine. The heat doesn't faze me," Taylor lied. She didn't know why she was lying. Apparently, cute guys brought out her weird side.

"Aren't you from Minnesota?" Julian inquired over his shoulder, leading the way to one of the picnic tables.

"What does that have to do with anything?" Taylor asked.

"Isn't there, like, snow there for most of the year? Perpetual winter and all that?"

Taylor snort-laughed. "No, just for a few months. And sometimes in the spring. It gets hot there too, but not like this."

Julian smiled as he set the tray on the picnic table and sat down. "Do you miss it?"

Taylor sat across from him. She bit her lip. "Yeah. Grimwood is very different."

Julian pushed one of the plates with arepas toward her. "What do you miss the most?" he asked before taking a giant bite of his own food.

"My parents," she blurted out without thinking. She blinked rapidly, attempting to stop the tears before they started falling. She hadn't meant to bring up her parents. She had no desire to talk about them with Julian.

He reached across the picnic table and squeezed her hand, sending tiny electric shocks throughout where their skin touched. Taylor jerked her hand back, surprised. Could he feel it too? He didn't mention it, so she chose to ignore it.

Not wanting to dwell on whatever had just happened, Taylor picked up an arepa and dug in to her lunch. The arepas were fantastic. Julian had been right about the food truck. Not that she would admit that to him.

After they finished eating, she turned to Julian. "Back to practice, then?"

"Nah. I think we've both had enough for today."

Her eyes dropped to her empty plate. "Oh. Okay then."

Julian smirked, his usual playful attitude returning. "What? You want to spend more time with me today? Aren't you sick of me yet?"

Taylor glared at him, not wanting to give him the satisfaction of thinking she wanted to be with him longer than necessary. "Of course I don't want to spend more time with you, but since you're my trainer, I don't have a choice, do I?"

Julian rolled his eyes. "Fine, but can you at least be civil? I'm trying to be nice, but you're not making it easy."

"Oh, really? Maybe I pegged you wrong, then."

"What do you mean?" Julian asked, his eyes narrowing.

"I thought you were the type of person who liked a challenge." Taylor stood from the picnic table, picked up their trash, and threw it into the nearest trash can. "I guess I was wrong."

Julian's blue eyes smoldered as he stood and stepped closer to her. "No, you were right. I do like challenges. I didn't say I was giving up on you yet."

"I hope not. It would be sad if you couldn't make it through our first day of training," Taylor said, inching closer to him, despite herself. Everything inside her body was screaming for her to reach out and touch his skin again. To feel that thrilling little shock between them once more.

"You have no idea what I can endure, Taylor Windsor," Julian said.

Taylor smirked. "Is that a promise?"

Julian gulped before nodding. Then he shook his head, as if clearing his thoughts. "Come on. I'll drive you home."

Taylor

After Julian dropped her off at home, Taylor was greeted by Brody waiting in the front entryway.

"Hey there, buddy. Did you miss me?" she asked, bending down to pet his head.

Brody jumped up, putting his paws on her legs and licking her face.

"I'll take that as a yes. Wanna go on a walk?"

Brody ran toward the row of hooks where his harness and leash hung and stared up at them, patiently waiting for Taylor to put them on.

Once they were outside, Taylor took time during the silent walk to reflect on the past twenty-four-hours' events. How had everything gotten so messed up? Mel didn't have her magic anymore. Taylor was being trained by a demon hunter who was annoying and cocky and—admittedly, very cute, but that was beside the point. Taylor didn't want to fall for someone whose mom had voted for Mel to wear the amulet and lose her powers. If Clarissa was okay with such a terrible decision, Julian must be too. She couldn't be friends with someone who was comfortable with her aunt being weak and powerless. None of this was okay.

Taylor walked around the massive neighborhood of historic homes, trekking up several particularly steep hills, with Brody leading the way. Soon, she was sweating from the heat and Brody's tongue was hanging out of his mouth, so she turned around and headed toward home. On the way back, Brody walked slower than before, probably feeling as hot and exhausted as Taylor did. They made it back inside, and Taylor made sure to refill Brody's food and water dishes.

She glanced at the time on her cell phone: 5:35 p.m. Mel should be home soon. Usually, she was home by now.

Taylor couldn't recall her aunt mentioning a plan for dinner, so she decided to cook spaghetti and meatballs. Her aunt was stressed, so if she could do something to help, even a task as small as cooking dinner, then she would do it.

By the time the meatballs finished baking in the oven, Taylor heard the garage door open. Shortly after, Mel entered the kitchen.

"Hi, Taylor." Mel greeted her with a weary smile.

"Hey, Mel. How was your day?"

"Fine," Mel said tersely, glancing at the stove. She froze while setting her coffee thermos on the counter. "You made dinner?"

"Yup. Spaghetti and meatballs. I figured you would be tired after a long day of work," Taylor said.

"Thanks. That was nice of you. How was your day? How was practicing with Julian?"

"Uh . . ." Taylor hesitated, thinking of a suitable response.

"That bad, huh?" Mel joked. "I think we have garlic bread too. I'll throw it in the oven really quick."

"It wasn't . . . It wasn't terrible. He's just so conceited!" Taylor said, unable to contain her frustration any longer. At least Mel would understand if she complained to her. Besides, whom else did she have to talk to?

"We can eat dinner together, and you can tell me all about it. I could use a distraction," Mel said.

Taylor grabbed two plates from the cupboard and handed them to Mel, who dished up servings of spaghetti and meatballs for both of them.

"Should we wait for the garlic bread to finish cooking?" Mel asked.

"I ate a late lunch. Julian and I went out to eat, so I can wait a little longer for dinner if that's okay with you," Taylor replied.

"Sure. Where did you go for lunch?" Mel prompted.

"Julian took me to this amazing food truck that serves arepas. We'll have to go there together sometime."

"And then what? How was training?" Mel asked. She opened the fridge and pulled out a pitcher of sweet tea.

"He's a pretty good teacher, but after one day, he's already driving me crazy. He acts like he knows everything about me, but we just met. How can he possibly think he knows me? He asked me to take it easy on him, but—"

"Whoa, hold on." Mel raised her hand in a stop gesture. "Why did he ask you to take it easy on him? What were you doing?"

"Oh. Um . . ." Taylor scratched her arm and avoided eye contact. "I may have given him a hard time. But it wasn't my fault! He knocked me on my butt, like, five times during practice. I was sick of falling."

"Are the practice rooms cushioned? Or do they have mats for you to fall on, so you don't get hurt?" Mel asked, peering closer at her as if checking for injuries. "Are you okay?"

"Ye-yes, I'm fine. There are mats, but it still hurt. He looked so smug when he did it too," Taylor said.

"Oh, Taylor . . . Sorry, but I think you'll have to learn to work with him. You don't have to be best friends."

"I already have a best friend. Why can't I hang out with Kylie? What if I bring Julian with me to supervise?" Taylor begged.

"Hmm, that's not a bad idea. I can run it by Clarissa and see if she's okay with it. In the meantime, you could talk to Julian about it too. You would need to come up with a backstory for how you met Julian, and obviously don't mention magic or demons around her," Mel said.

"Yeah, but Kylie already knows about all that, remember?"

"True, but if the council finds out, they'll erase her memories and make it so that she forgets meeting you," Mel explained. "Be careful."

"Great. Another thing to worry about." Taylor stared glumly down at the kitchen table. "Any luck reversing the enchantment on the amulet?" Taylor changed the subject, not wanting to dwell on her sad social life any longer.

Mel shook her head. "Not yet. The spellbook doesn't mention a way to reverse it, besides having the person who cast the spell undo it. I skimmed through the entire spellbook and tried every spell I thought would help. I'm not sure if there's another way to get it off."

"So you're without magic for the foreseeable future?" Taylor asked.

"It looks like it. I'll have to learn how to deal with it. When I drop you off at the academy, I can speak with one of the professors or the headmistress. Someone with influence may be able to get Alastair to see reason. If he won't listen to the rest of the council, though, I don't know if he'll listen to anyone," Mel said.

"Shouldn't Alastair be punished for what he did? I thought people couldn't go around doing spells without permission. Especially on another demon hunter."

Mel pursed her lips. "Alastair is a very powerful demon hunter. If anyone can get away with this, it's him."

"So that's it? You're giving up?" Taylor asked, throwing up her hands in frustration.

"Of course not. I just need to find another way to get this amulet off."

The oven timer dinged, signaling that the garlic bread was done cooking and effectively ending their serious conversation.

The scent of freshly baked cheesy garlic bread wafted out into the kitchen as Mel opened the oven. She slid an oven mitt onto her hand and pulled out the tray, setting it on the counter.

"Mm, that smells so good," Taylor said, her mouth watering.

Mel set a piece of garlic bread on each of their plates. "Dig in. Thanks again for cooking."

"You're welcome."

Silence ensued as they both enjoyed their dinner. Taylor chewed on the garlic bread as she pondered how she could help Mel get her magic back.

"Are you training with Julian again tomorrow?" Mel asked as they were wrapping up dinner.

"I think so. He didn't officially say he would pick me up tomorrow, but I feel like it was assumed."

"Like I said, you don't have to be best friends. But be polite to him, please. His mother is a council member, and the way you—"

"Yes, yes, I know. I can't be mean to him because his mom is powerful. Got it," Taylor retorted in a sarcastic tone.

Mel picked up her plate and gestured to Taylor. "Are you done eating?"

"Yup."

Mel took the plate from her and set both plates in the sink. "I'll do the dishes tonight, since you cooked dinner," she offered.

"Sounds good. Thanks." Taylor stood from her chair and called to Brody, who was curled up underneath the table. "Brody! Let's go. Come on."

He jumped up, alert and ready to go wherever Taylor wanted. He trotted after her out of the kitchen.

"What are you up to for the rest of the night?" Mel called from the kitchen.

Taylor paused in the hallway. "I'm feeling pretty tired. Do you want to watch a movie together? I'll probably go to sleep early tonight."

"Sure, as soon as I finish cleaning up in here," Mel yelled back.

Taylor settled onto the couch, patting the cushion next to her so Brody could hop up and cuddle with her. "Good boy," she told him, hugging him against her chest.

Even if she didn't have any friends, at least she had Brody and Mel.

Chapter 14

Taylor

During their second training session, Taylor managed to dodge several of Julian's attacks.

"Are you going easy on me today?" she asked, only half-joking. She hoped not, because she wanted to be able to beat him at his best.

"Nope. You're already improving. With time, I think you'll be a great demon hunter, just like your parents were," he said encouragingly.

Taylor had been prepping her stance for the offensive, hands raised and right foot slightly forward, but she froze at the mention of her parents. "What do you know about my parents?"

Julian tilted his head and peered at her with curiosity shining from his blue eyes. "Are you messing with me? Or do you really not know?"

"*Know what*?"

"Come on, let's take a short break for a little field trip." Julian headed toward the door and pushed it open, holding it for her.

"Where are we going?" Taylor asked, annoyed about stopping their practice. She put her hands on her hips and stared at him defiantly.

"Trust me, it will be worth it," Julian promised.

Taylor sighed and followed him to another room further down the hallway at the headquarters. She opened the door and stepped inside, surprised at what she saw. Books filled the room, stacked in shelves against every wall. A rolling ladder was propped against one bookshelf. A chandelier sparkled from the ceiling in the center of the room, over a pair of red velvet chaises. In between the chaises was an oval-shaped, white, marble-topped table with gold accents.

She turned to Julian. "A library? Why are we in here? We should be practicing."

He climbed the ladder, searching for a specific book, which he pulled from the shelf when he found it. After disembarking from the ladder, he handed the book to Taylor. "You might want to read this."

"Is it like a regular library? Do I have to check it out?" Taylor asked, her forehead wrinkling in confusion as she took the book from him.

"No, the books are enchanted, so the librarian can find them. If you don't return it within two weeks, they'll come after you," Julian said with a straight face.

Taylor froze for a moment, imagining a demon hunter librarian hunting her down for a book. "And do what?"

"I'm kidding," Julian said, laughing. "Write your name on the check-out sheet." He gestured toward a desk at the far end of the room.

"You mentioned a librarian. Where are they?"

Julian shrugged. "Not sure. Taking a break, I guess."

Taylor inspected the book. It was navy blue with tiny gold stars on the front. The title shone under the glimmering light of the chandelier. *Tales of the Turner Family.*

Taylor gasped, flipping the book over to read the back, but it was blank. "This is about my parents? But why?"

Julian eyed her curiously, crossing his arms over his chest. "This is so weird—having to explain it to you. I just—everyone in our world knows the history of the Turners, so it's strange that you don't know your own family's history." He exhaled loudly before continuing, "Your parents were two of the best demon hunters to ever exist until they were captured by a demon and tortured for months.

"No one knew where they were being held. One day, they disappeared, and everyone assumed the worst. No one knows how they escaped because they never told the full story, but somehow, they did. And they killed the demon who held them captive.

"I think parts of the book may have been embellished over time, but whatever happened, they were worshiped as heroes. Everyone assumed your mom would be the one to take over the Turners' spot on the council. She was the eldest daughter, so it was her rightful position, and she was perfect for it. But months went by, and she and your dad backed off from their duties. Eventually, they announced that they were moving away, and they didn't want to be involved with the demon hunter world anymore. No one heard from them after that. I don't think your mom spoke to her parents much after they left."

"But why? What made them leave?" Taylor asked, clutching the book to her chest. She held on to the hope of feeling close to her parents again, fighting off the stinging betrayal of learning yet another secret they had hidden from her.

"I don't know. Obviously, I wasn't born yet when all this happened. I've only heard the stories, and I read that book because I was curious." Julian gestured to the book he had given her. "I don't have all the answers, but your Aunt Mel might know more than me. That book is a good place to start."

The more she thought about her parents and what had happened to them—the fact that they hid their lives from her—was becoming too much to bear. Silently, tears dripped from Taylor's eyes and onto the leather-bound, navy-blue book. She sniffled and turned to leave the room, not wanting Julian to see her cry.

Gently, he grabbed her arm and stopped her from leaving. "Hey. I'm sorry. I'm sure it's tough to deal with this. You must miss them a lot. I didn't mean to make you cry." His face turned bright red, as if he was embarrassed.

Taylor began sobbing, unable to hold back her emotions. She set the book on the marble table. "Why are you being so nice to me?"

Julian caressed her arm as he gazed into her eyes. "Because you deserve kindness."

Taylor cleared her throat, attempting to stop her sobs. "Sorry."

Julian's forehead creased. He dropped his hand from her arm. "For what? You didn't do anything wrong."

"For crying. I know how weirded out most guys get by women being emotional." Taylor rolled her eyes, brushing it off.

"Don't apologize for crying. It's healthy to cry, and you lost your parents. It's normal to mourn them. Besides, I think you're—" Julian stopped, not finishing the sentence.

"You think I'm what?" Taylor asked, desperately wanting to hear the rest of the sentence.

"Strong."

"Is that it?" she asked, her gaze dropping to the floor. Until this point, she had done her best to fight off the feelings at war within herself. Taylor was beginning to think Julian might be more than just a hot demon hunter. He couldn't help who his parents were, and he seemed nothing like them.

Julian chuckled. "No. You're also intelligent, funny, creative, a fast learner, and . . ." Julian hesitated. "You're beautiful."

Taylor looked back up at him, and without saying a word, embraced him and leaned her head against his chest.

"Where's my compliment?" Julian asked in a breathy voice, stroking her hair.

She playfully whacked his arm, disentangling herself from his embrace. "Don't ruin the moment, Julian."

"You can't hide from me anymore, Taylor Windsor." Julian smirked at her. "Now that I know you like me too."

Chapter 15

Mel

Mel stared up at the towering, two-story, red-brick house before knocking on the Ellises' front door, bracing herself for the difficult conversation she was about to have. As she raised her fist to knock again, the door swung open, revealing Vanessa wearing a short-sleeved, silk, peach-colored sleeveless shirt and white capris. Her blonde bob streaked with gray was slightly messy, and she was barefoot, her toes painted the colors of the rainbow.

"Mel, it's good to see you," Vanessa said, smiling brightly. "Please come in."

"Hi, Vanessa." Mel followed her into the magnificent but cozy home. She wasn't sure how such a large house could feel so welcoming and comfortable, but Vanessa and Randall had somehow managed it. The aesthetic was cozy chic with a touch of hippy flair. The scent of freshly baked pastries wafted throughout the house.

"Would you like some tea or coffee? I baked some cookies earlier too," Vanessa offered.

"Coffee would be great. Thank you."

"I think I'll have some too. I'll brew a new pot. I'll be right back." Vanessa gestured toward the sitting area, where three walls lined with bookshelves were bursting with books. A few comfy-looking chairs were scattered throughout the room. "Have a seat wherever you'd like."

Mel nodded and wandered to the bookcase, staring at the framed pictures of the Ellis family. Randall was tall and imposing with a hook nose, but a sweetheart. Then there were their three kids—Grace, who was sixteen; Oliver, who had graduated from the academy last year; and Molly, who was twelve and about to start her first year at the academy. Their family's special abilities were healing and cleansing, and it showed in their calming, kind personalities.

As Mel was browsing the book selection, Vanessa returned with a tray containing a plateful of cookies, a coffee carafe, two mugs, and saucers full of creamer and sugar.

"Here we go!" Vanessa said cheerfully, setting the tray on the large coffee table off to the side. "The cookies are chocolate chip. Help yourself."

"Oh, this is lovely. Thank you so much," Mel said, pouring coffee and creamer into a mug and selecting several cookies. She took a bite of a cookie and nearly moaned out loud. "Oh my gosh, these cookies are amazing. Are they homemade?"

Vanessa beamed, looking proud and sitting up tall in her chair. "Yes, it's my grandmother's recipe. She was a wonderful baker. Baking became one of my passions after she taught me. She passed on all her recipes to me. She wanted someone in the family to continue her tradition, and I'm happy to honor her legacy."

"That's sweet," Mel said, finishing off the first cookie and restraining herself from grabbing ten more.

"So . . ." Vanessa started. "I have an inkling about why you asked to speak with me today. Clarissa told me about what Alastair did." She shook her head, her lips set in a straight line, clearly disappointed. "I'm so sorry he did that to you.

We—the council—didn't approve that decision. Unfortunately, there isn't a way to reverse the enchantment. The only person who can do that is Alastair."

Mel's heart sank. "There must be something you can do. I need to be able to protect Taylor. You know about the demon who tricked me—clearly, Grimwood isn't safe anymore. Who knows if other demons will show up? Taylor and I watched him take the soul of one of his . . . employees, but we never found out if he was working with anyone else. He could still have allies in the area."

Vanessa's face paled. "Oh, my. We hadn't thought of that, but I suppose you're right . . . We'll deal with it when the time comes, but until then, I'll try talking to Alastair. I'm sure he'll see reason and agree to reverse it. He can't expect you to keep that amulet on forever."

Screw it. They're too good to resist, Mel thought, reaching for another cookie.

"Besides protecting my niece, I also don't like being defenseless against other demon hunters who may not agree with my choices." Mel paused, chewing her cookie. "Like what happened with Alastair. And that was when I still had my magic."

"You don't have to worry, Mel. Alastair acted of his own accord. Myself and the other council members don't feel the same way, and we will try to—"

"But you did, or most of you did, at least. That's what I was told when we met at the headquarters. The vote was three to one," Mel countered, taking another cookie. If Mel couldn't get her powers back, the least Vanessa could do was provide a good snack.

"I was the only one who voted no," Vanessa replied in a quiet voice.

"I assumed so, and I appreciate your support. You were always a good friend back at the academy. That's why I thought I could count on you. I never imagined I would be the guardian to a teenage girl, but here I am. Taylor is my responsibility, and I have to keep her safe. You know I would have your back if the situation were reversed. I would do anything for you if one of your kids was in trouble."

Vanessa sipped her still-cooling coffee for a moment. Slowly, she peered at Mel, her dark eyes swimming with tears. "Would you?"

"Would I *what*?" Mel asked, taken aback by the sudden display of emotion.

"Do anything to help my kids?" Vanessa clarified, clearing her throat.

"Yes."

Vanessa set her mug back on the tray and leaned toward Mel. "Okay, then, let's make a deal."

"Whoa, hold on a second. What's going on, Vanessa? What's wrong with your kids? Are they okay?" Mel asked. Surely, it couldn't be Molly. She was only twelve and basically looked like an angel. It had to be Grace or Oliver.

"It's . . . It's Oliver. When he first graduated, he seemed fine. He started going on missions with Randall and me. He was excelling, just like he did at the academy. We were trying to prepare him as best as possible for his future, to set him up with a good career. Obviously, Grace will be the one to take over as the head of our family and represent us on the council, but he still needs to be ready to take charge if necessary. And if anything were to happen to Randall and me, we would want Oliver to look out for his sisters. He's the oldest, after all." Vanessa sipped her coffee and set the mug down on the coffee table. "At the beginning of the summer, he made some new friends. At first, we weren't worried about it. He's always been shy, so I was glad he had some people to hang out with. He didn't get close to anyone at the academy, and we worried about his social life. He started spending more and more time with these new friends. Randall asked to meet them, but Oliver was hesitant to bring them over. They didn't go to the academy. They aren't Shadow Bound. They're demon hunters, but"—Vanessa took a deep breath—"they believe in merging with the demons, not fighting them or banishing them.

"They practice dark magic. I don't know what Oliver got involved in, but he's been sick for weeks now. I don't know what those 'friends' of his did to him, but I don't think he'll make it much longer. I've tried every spell I can think of, but nothing has helped. He's only getting worse. I'm at my wit's end trying to save my son. You don't know how awful it feels to have healing and cleansing powers that won't cure your child . . .

"Mel, I think Oliver is cursed."

Taylor

"So, where are you going again? I don't get it," Kylie said, her forehead wrinkling.

They were sitting side by side on the porch swing in the front of Mel's house, swaying gently as they chatted.

"Um, it's an old boarding school. My parents met there. I want to see where they grew up and feel closer to them. A few of the same professors still teach there. They might have known my parents, and it would be cool to talk to them and hear about what they were like in their younger years," Taylor rambled, hoping she wasn't blowing her cover.

"What's it called? Is it close by? You don't have to move again, do you?" Kylie pried.

"Grimwood Academy," Taylor blurted out, unable to lie quickly enough in response to the unexpected question. "And yeah, it's still in Grimwood . . . hence the name." At least she hadn't said the magical part of the name.

"Huh. Sounds creepy. Well, at least we'll still be living next door to each other. We can hang out after school and on the weekends," Kylie said with a smile.

"I'll be living in a dorm on campus. Like I said, it's a boarding school."

Kylie's smile faltered. "Seriously, Tay? I'm trying to be happy for you because it sounds like this is what you want, but I was excited to have a friend at school for once. And it's not like you know anyone else here." Kylie dug her heels into the porch, halting the motion of the swing. She stood and stared down at Taylor. "I know you were having a rough time this summer, and you probably still are, but I thought we had moved past the issues from earlier. Now it seems like you're trying to push me away again. I feel like there's something you aren't telling me. What is it?"

Taylor debated telling her the truth. But she didn't want to disappoint Mel or risk the exposure of the demon hunter society's inner workings to a human. She couldn't tell Kylie the truth—not yet, at least. Maybe eventually she could.

Kylie lowered her voice. "Is this about the demon? We haven't talked about it much since the night at the cabin. Did something else happen? Are you and Mel in danger again?"

Taylor quickly interrupted before Kylie could say something potentially dangerous that could get her in trouble with Mel. She didn't want Mel to overhear their conversation and ban her from seeing Kylie again. "No, it's not like that. I only want to go to the school because of my parents."

"Promise?" Kylie asked, sitting back down on the swing and holding out her pinky.

Taylor linked her pinky with Kylie's. "Promise."

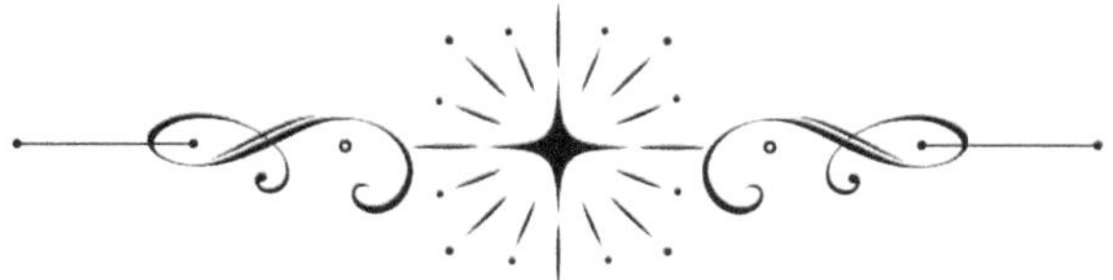

Taylor spent the next week packing. Grimwood Magical Academy had sent a list of required school supplies, textbooks, and the dreaded uniform options. Slacks with a white oxford shirt and a purple tie for the guys, or a dark gray polo and shorts in the warmer months. If anyone preferred a more feminine wardrobe, they could pair the polo with a gray or purple skirt—as long as it wasn't above the knees.

At least the uniform colors were dark purple and varying shades of gray, so they weren't too bad. However, Taylor was used to having freedom with her clothing and being able to express herself however she wanted, not being restrained by a set, limited list of clothes. Not being forced to dress the same as everyone else. She supposed it would make it easier for her to blend in, though, if they were all dressed the same.

She attempted to squeeze another book into her suitcase, but it wouldn't zip shut. She pulled harder on the zipper until it ripped off. She looked at the zipper now lying on the ground.

"Crap."

Brody ran over to investigate and sniffed the zipper before deciding it wasn't something he could eat. He trotted back to his dog bed by the window, where the last few rays of the sun were sneaking through the curtains and warming his little body. He snuggled into the blanket Taylor kept in his bed for him, and he sighed happily.

Mel knocked on the doorframe, since the door was open, band then entered the room. "Hey, Taylor. How's packing going?" Mel asked, her eyes wandering from Taylor, crouched over her stuffed suitcase, to the piles of items left to be packed.

"It's fine," Taylor replied, huffing and finally giving up on the suitcase. "The zipper broke." She bent down to pick it up and showed it to Mel.

Mel laughed while staring at the full suitcase. "You may have overpacked it. Don't worry. There's a spell that can help." She snapped her fingers and started to recite a spell, then stopped herself. "Oh, right. No magic. Do you want me to teach it to you?"

"Have you ever gone this long without using magic?" Taylor asked, pondering the situation. For someone like Mel, who had grown up using magic her entire life and was raised with the demon hunter lifestyle, it must have been awful to suddenly not be in touch with that part of herself. Taylor could only imagine how bad it felt.

"No. There was one time—okay, maybe twice—that my parents banned me from using magic as a punishment after I got into trouble. But it was usually for a few days, and obviously they let me use it again after that."

"Did my mom get into trouble?" Taylor questioned.

Mel snorted. "Oh, yeah. Not as often as I did, but we both snuck out and went to parties when we were younger. And when we were at Grimwood Magical Academy, we were roommates for a few years when our time there overlapped. Christa was two years older than me, so she had a different roommate before I started at the academy."

Taylor smiled fondly at Mel's reminiscing. "I just thought of something. Do demon hunters go to a regular human school before they start at the academy? Or are they home-schooled by their parents? They still have to learn how to read and write and do math and stuff, right?"

"It varies from family to family. Our parents enrolled us in a private school, so that's where we both went until we turned twelve. Then they told the school system they were home-schooling us, so it didn't seem suspicious that we were pulled out of school when we each turned twelve," Mel explained.

"I wonder what Julian's parents did, and if he went to a human school?" Taylor blurted out.

Mel raised an eyebrow. "Yeah? How do you feel about Julian these days?"

Taylor's face flushed as she turned away from her aunt. It wasn't that she was embarrassed or uncomfortable to talk about boys with her, but she wasn't sure how she felt about him.

Sure, she liked him. It was hard not to. He was handsome—that much was obvious. He was also kind and caring—so patient with her when she had been difficult to deal with—and he had helped her practice magic for the past few weeks. It was hard not to like him after all that. But getting close to someone terrified her for reasons she couldn't let herself think about.

"Enough said. Your lack of a coherent response says it all." Mel giggled.

"Oh, whatever." Taylor pursed her lips, thinking about her new school. "We'll see what happens once we're at the same school. I don't even know if he has a girlfriend."

"Why don't you ask him? Don't you have another training session scheduled for tomorrow?" Mel asked.

"Well, yeah, but—"

"It's normal to be nervous. Just tell him how you feel, and see if he feels the same," Mel said.

"Sure, and let him stomp all over my heart if he doesn't like me in that way," Taylor snapped.

"Or not. Hey, it's your choice, kiddo. I'm offering some words of wisdom from my years of experience, but I'm not making you do anything," Mel said, putting up her hands in front of her body in a placating gesture.

Taylor flopped backward onto her bed. "It's hopeless."

Mel joined Taylor on the bed. "It will be okay, I promise. If it doesn't work out with Julian, I'm sure there will be lots of other cute students at Grimwood Magical Academy. Besides, you're going to love school, learning more spells, and practicing your magic so much that I bet you'll hardly have any time to think about romance."

"What are you going to do about the amulet?" Taylor asked, swiftly changing the subject.

"I met with Vanessa Ellis today. We were friends back at the academy. Although we grew apart over the years, she's always been kind. In fact, she was the only council member who voted against the amulet decision. Anyway, I asked for her help. She agreed, but she wants a favor in return.

"Apparently, her oldest child, Oliver, got involved with an unsavory group of demon hunters this summer. Demon hunters who didn't attend the academy because their parents don't agree with the idea of having a council make decisions for all of us. They also believe the academy 'brainwashes' demon hunters and that they should learn through experience and going on missions, not training in a safe environment and learning from textbooks, history, and experienced, talented professors.

"I'm not sure of the details, but Vanessa thinks Oliver had a curse placed on him by one of his new friends. She said he's been ill for weeks and has barely left his bed. He was asleep when I was there, but she promised that next time I could speak with him."

"I didn't know there were other demon hunters who didn't agree with the council and didn't attend the academy. I assumed it was like the human world and that everyone sucked it up and went to school and listened to the government. I didn't know there was a choice," Taylor said, perking up. "Does that mean I don't have to go to the academy if I don't want to? Can I go to school with Kylie instead?"

Mel chuckled. "There are always people who want to rally against the government, whether they're humans or demon hunters. Some people don't like following the law, even if it's for their own best interests. And yes, you're going to Grimwood Magical Academy. It's the best place for you since you're entering this world so late. You're already at a disadvantage. Not to mention the fact that you'll be safer there, learning magic in a controlled environment."

"I guess so. I didn't realize the demon hunter world had so many political issues too," Taylor said.

"Most of us grow up following the same path as our parents, never questioning the beliefs that are instilled in us. It's what we're expected to do. While there isn't anything inherently wrong with questioning things and wanting to form your own beliefs, it can be dangerous if you let the wrong people influence you." Mel put her arm around Taylor and squeezed her shoulder. "You'll be fine. And you can always come home on the weekends to visit."

Brody hopped up onto the bed, not wanting to be left out.

Taylor hugged him, and Mel wrapped her arms around her niece.

"Family cuddle time!" Taylor announced and giggled.

"I'm going to miss this. It's been nice having company in this big, old house."

Taylor's giggling stopped. "Oh, no. I can't bring Brody with me to the academy, can I?"

Mel pulled back slightly to look at her. "With everything else going on, I hadn't considered that. We can speak with the headmistress when I drop you off. She might make an exception."

"I can't leave Brody alone. If I can't bring him with me, will you take care of him?" Taylor pleaded, putting her hands together and pouting.

"Of course I will. We certainly aren't getting rid of him. He's part of the family. Isn't that right, Brody?"

Brody responded by licking Mel's face.

Taylor burst into laughter and fell back onto the bed. Then Brody licked her face too.

All three of them lay on the bed together in good spirits. Taylor could almost ignore the fact that soon she had to start over and her life would completely change . . . Again.

CHAPTER 17

TAYLOR

Squinting through the shining sunlight, Taylor gawked at the sprawling series of buildings that took up several blocks of Grimwood. The campus looked like an old college campus, similar to a fancy school like Harvard or Yale—all turrets, towers, and columns, with grand, awe-inspiring architecture that took her breath away.

Except instead of the stereotypical red brick on most campuses, the buildings at Grimwood Magical Academy were a light tan color. Mel had explained that it was enchanted to look like an abandoned shopping mall to non-magic users. Most humans didn't go to malls anymore, anyway. But as an extra precaution, to deter humans from loitering or breaking in, protection wards extended around the entire campus, encompassing up to several hundred feet on every side so humans couldn't get too close and accidentally glimpse something they shouldn't.

Taylor had to admit, she was impressed. She wasn't sure what she had expected, but it wasn't this.

"So what do you think?" Mel prompted, grinning from ear-to-ear and setting one of Taylor's suitcases on the pavement.

Brody sat back on his hind legs and stared at the campus, wide-mouthed in awe too. Or that might have been a yawn after the drive there.

"It's beautiful. I can't wait to see my dorm," Taylor said.

Mel hoisted the suitcase strap onto her shoulder. "Let's go to the headmistress's office first, then we'll find your dorm."

Mel led the way down a series of winding paths to a rectangular building that was considerably shorter and less stately than the others. Brody trotted after them, obediently following. The sign out front simply said, *Headmistress's Office.* Taylor supposed if that was the only purpose for the building, it didn't need to be spacious or impressive.

Mel pushed open the door and let Taylor and Brody enter first.

A secretary was seated at the desk in the center of the room. Her dark hair was swept back into a low bun, and she wore black rectangular glasses. "Hello, how may I help you?" Her eyes narrowed at the sight of the terrier trotting in after them. "No animals are allowed in this building. Unless they're service animals," she added, almost as an afterthought.

"Hi, I'm Mel Turner, and this is my niece, Taylor Windsor. I'm here to enroll her for classes. She's starting at the academy this semester. We would like to speak with the headmistress, please. It has to do with our dog."

The secretary typed on her computer and frowned. "Sorry. I don't believe that's possible today. Headmistress Lockwood is quite busy and—"

"Lockwood?" Mel said, her tone coated with disbelief.

Taylor turned to her aunt. "Do you know her? Is she the same headmistress as when you went here?"

A woman who appeared to be in her late thirties or early forties came walking out of the room on the right. "Well, considering we went to school together, no,

I wasn't the headmistress back then." She smiled at Taylor kindly and turned to Mel. "Hi, Mel. It's been a while." She shook Mel's hand.

"Blaire Lockwood? You're the headmistress now?" Mel asked.

"Yes, apparently their standards have lowered enough for me to finally take over here," the headmistress joked.

The secretary rolled her eyes. "You've been holding this school together for years, Headmistress Lockwood."

The headmistress chuckled. "I don't know about that, but I certainly try." She returned her attention to Taylor and Mel, sweeping her arms open wide in a welcoming gesture. "You must be Christa's daughter. Nice to meet you at last."

"Hi. Yeah, I'm Taylor Windsor." Taylor shook her hand.

"Come into my office, and let's see if I can help you."

They followed the headmistress into her office. Headmistress Lockwood widened her eyes when their terrier scampered into the room after them. Mel shut the office door.

"And who is this?" Headmistress Lockwood asked, bending down to let Brody sniff her hand.

"Brody," Taylor said, grinning as Brody jumped up to lick the headmistress's face.

"Oh my goodness," Headmistress Lockwood said, giggling. "Well, aren't you a cute little dog? I apologize for my secretary. She's a dedicated employee, and I would be lost without her. But Natasha can be a little . . . serious. I don't mind bending the rules sometimes, but she's a stickler for them."

Mel smiled at Taylor and turned back to the headmistress. "I was hoping you would say that. Brody is a . . . a rescue dog we recently adopted. I'm sure you've heard by now that Taylor lost her parents only a few short months ago. Brody has been a great source of comfort to her, and to me too. He's become a part of our family. While, of course, I'll keep him at home if necessary, I'm at work all day and can't run home frequently to take him out or look after him. Is there any way you can make an exception and—"

Headmistress Lockwood held out a hand, stopping Mel from proceeding. "I see where this is going. The answer is yes. You can keep Brody in your dorm. The only stipulation is that you must speak with your roommate about it first. As long as she isn't allergic to dogs and has no issues with it, then you have my permission. I'll write you a note in case anyone questions it."

"Really?" Taylor squealed, bending down to pat Brody's head.

He wagged his tail in excitement.

Headmistress Lockwood nodded. "Yes. I can already tell how fond you are of him, and it would be a shame to separate you two." She leaned back against her desk, still standing. "Are you planning on sticking around for the day, Mel? I would love to give you both a tour of the campus and show Taylor around."

"Oh, you don't have to do that, Blaire—uh, Headmistress Lockwood," Mel interjected. "I know my way around the campus. Besides, I'm sure you have more important tasks to focus on today, especially with the new semester starting in a few days."

Headmistress Lockwood brushed her off. "Of course you know the campus, but Taylor's a new student, and I want her to feel welcome here. The first-year students always go on a group tour before school officially starts and then they're given time to settle in. Taylor's circumstances are unusual, so I want to make sure she has time to adjust."

"Okay, that would be great. Thanks for the offer," Mel said.

Taylor chimed in, "Thank you. Can we go see my dorm first?"

"Absolutely," Headmistress Lockwood replied.

Headmistress Lockwood grabbed a sealed envelope that jingled when she picked it up. Then she turned to her computer and typed for a few seconds before papers started printing from the printer across the room. She headed to the printer and snatched up several sheets of paper. "Ah! There we go. I printed out your class schedule, your dorm assignment, a permission slip to keep Brody in your dorm, and a map of the academy." She handed a folder full of papers to Taylor.

"Oh, thank you." Taylor didn't have the heart to tell her that she had all the files—except the pet permission form—saved on her phone already. Old people and their need to print out physical copies was something Taylor would never understand.

"Shall we go, then?" Headmistress Lockwood asked with a bright smile.

"Sure!" Taylor replied cheerily, beckoning for Brody to follow as they exited the office. She tucked the folder under her arm as they proceeded outside.

"At least the weather is pleasant today," Headmistress Lockwood said.

"Yeah. Although I'm hoping it cools off soon," Taylor replied.

Mel laughed. "I hate to disappoint you, kiddo, but we have at least another month of this heat. Grimwood will start to cool off mid-September. Sometimes it doesn't happen until October."

"If we're fortunate," Headmistress Lockwood added with a chuckle. "You'll get used to it." She led them down a paved pathway toward a cluster of similar-looking buildings that were all several stories high. She gestured toward them. "These are the dorms. Yours is the Flamel building, I believe."

Taylor glanced at her dorm assignment on the printed sheet of paper, spotting the Flamel name. "Yup, it is," she confirmed.

"Great. Here you go. The larger key unlocks the building. The smaller one goes to your specific dorm room. After you get your photo taken and receive your student ID, you can scan your ID to unlock the dorm. The physical key is a backup. You wouldn't believe how many students lose their IDs." Headmistress Lockwood shook her head and handed the two keys to Taylor.

"Thanks," Taylor said, using the larger key to unlock the door. The door made a buzzing sound as it unlocked. Taylor spotted a camera above the entrance, with a red light flashing and monitoring them. She went inside first.

Her aunt and the headmistress followed, with Brody trailing in last.

"Which way to my dorm?" Taylor asked, turning to the headmistress.

The headmistress glanced down at the room assignment as Taylor held out the piece of paper toward her. "Room 305. On the third floor. The elevator and the stairs are this way." She pointed to the left.

"Oh, thank God there's an elevator," Taylor said.

"Well, of course there is. What kind of magical academy would we be without one?" the headmistress said.

Taylor bit her tongue from voicing her thoughts out loud that for a magical school, Grimwood Magical Academy sure didn't seem to have much going for it.

Taylor

After Taylor and Mel brought all of her belonging into her dorm room, Taylor set up Brody's dog bed.

"Bed, Brody," she told him, pointing to the bed.

Brody obeyed and jumped into his bed, tail wagging as he gazed up at her.

Taylor turned to the headmistress. "I guess we can't bring him with us everywhere, right?"

Headmistress Lockwood shook her head. "Unfortunately, no. I was planning to show you the dining hall first. No animals are allowed in there. It's a food service requirement."

Taylor nodded. "I understand." She turned to her dog, squatting so her face was level with his little snout and warm brown eyes. "We'll be gone for a few hours, okay, buddy? Be good."

Brody barked once as if agreeing and circled his bed multiple times before lying down.

Headmistress Lockwood led the way halfway across campus to the dining hall—a long, rectangular, single-story, tan structure.

When they entered the building, Headmistress Lockwood pulled an ID card out of her wallet and swiped it three times. "Lunch is on me," she told them with a wink.

With trepidation, Taylor followed her to the dining options. The food was spread out buffet-style, with employees serving the food. Taylor wasn't a picky eater, but she would be living on campus, so she hoped the food was decent.

Mel grinned and pointed to the soft-serve ice cream machine. "This was always my favorite."

Taylor giggled. "Ice cream for a meal?"

"Yup. No parents to stop you from eating whatever you want," Mel said, her smile disappearing as she realized the impact of what she had said to her parent-less niece. "Taylor, I'm so sorry. I wasn't thinking."

Taylor rolled her eyes. "It's fine." She grabbed a bowl from the stack next to the soft-serve machine and filled it with chocolate and vanilla swirl. She scoped out the toppings and added chocolate syrup, crushed Oreos, gummy bears, and Kit-Kats.

"Why did I mention that was an option?" Mel grumbled to herself. Then, in her normal tone, she added, "You better eat vegetables and fruit while you're here too."

Taylor smirked and asked one of the employees for a plate of steamed broccoli. "There. Now it's a balanced meal. Happy?"

Mel shook her head. "No, but it's my own fault."

Mel and Headmistress Lockwood selected their meals, while Taylor found an empty table. Taylor sat down and ate a huge spoonful of ice cream, making sure most of the toppings were in the first bite.

When they joined her, Headmistress Lockwood and Mel each set down a plate with a side salad, spaghetti, and a breadstick.

Headmistress Lockwood gestured to her plate. "This is a more typical meal here. Although, of course, we offer dessert options every day too, those aren't meant to be entire meals for growing teenagers."

"Mmm," Taylor said as she continued eating her ultra-healthy lunch.

"I should have known better than to tempt you. You're my niece, after all," Mel said, taking a bite of her salad and grimacing.

Taylor grinned. "Yup. We're definitely related."

Headmistress Lockwood looked between the two of them and smiled. "So it would seem the two of you are getting along well. I don't mean to pry, but I know Taylor has gone through a lot this summer. More than most people endure in a lifetime. I wanted to check in and make sure you're doing alright. We do have a guidance counselor on campus if—"

"I'm fine," Taylor butted in before Mel could answer for her. "I still miss my parents a lot, but I don't think that will ever change." She glanced at Mel. "But Mel has been a great parent, even during the worst summer of my life."

Mel's eyes glimmered with tears as she sniffled. "Thank you, Taylor. That means a lot. I won't pretend it's been easy, but I think we've both learned a lot already. Getting to know Taylor better and be there for her during such a difficult time has been the highlight of my summer."

"I'm glad to hear it. But keep in mind, Taylor, there are resources for you while you're grieving. We pride ourselves on wanting the best for our students, and that includes supporting their mental health," Headmistress Lockwood replied.

Taylor polished off the rest of her ice cream sundae and stood, ignoring the headmistress's offer. "I'm ready to go."

Chapter 19

Taylor

Taylor sat on her bed with Brody beside her. After their campus tour from Headmistress Lockwood, Mel had hung out with her for a few hours. Saying goodbye had been more difficult than Taylor anticipated. Mel promised to pick her up and bring her home in a few days, and Taylor was already looking forward to it. She didn't start classes until next week, but the headmistress had invited her to campus early to start adjusting.

Although it was low on her list of concerns, Taylor tried not to dwell on the fact that she didn't have a car and still hadn't practiced driving. Her birthday wasn't until October, but she wanted to get her driver's license as soon as she could. Then she could visit home whenever she wanted, and she wouldn't be stuck on campus all the time.

Being able to keep Brody in her dorm would be nice, though, as long as her roommate didn't have an issue with it. For whatever reason, her roommate hadn't shown up yet, but she would worry about that later. Mel was already gone, so Taylor could only hope having a dog live with them wasn't a problem.

Taylor decided she might as well use her free time to be productive. She unpacked her clothes and placed them in the dresser provided by the school. It was a gorgeous mahogany dresser with five drawers. There was a matching dresser for her roommate and a tiny closet they were expected to share. On top of that, there were two desks with drawers for storage. Two full-sized beds were set up on opposite ends of the room.

Taylor pulled out her clean set of sheets, a pillow and pillowcase, and a blanket, and then made the bed. She surveyed the room, wondering what else she could do before a thought struck her. She should stop decorating in case her roommate wanted a say in the appearance of their room. She didn't want to be inconsiderate, but she had never had a roommate before. Growing up as an only child meant she never had to share a room.

She shuddered as she imagined living in such close quarters with a complete stranger for the entire semester. She had endured worse, but it wasn't ideal. She reminded herself that she could always find a new roommate for the spring semester if the first one turned out to be terrible, but she hoped that didn't happen.

Taylor wanted to get along with her new roommate, even if they weren't best friends. And in general, she was excited about making new friends and learning more about magic. It was a fresh start for the first chapter in her new life as a demon hunter in training.

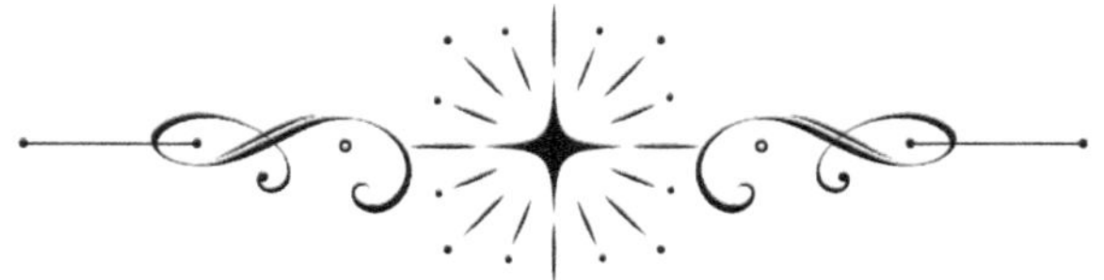

"Hellooo?" a soft voice called out from the doorway.

Taylor glanced up from the book she had been reading. Brody's ears perked up as he turned toward the redheaded teenage girl standing hesitantly by the door to Taylor's dorm.

"Are you Taylor?" the girl asked, balancing a box awkwardly in her arms. Her long red hair fell past her butt. She had striking green eyes, and there were freckles scattered across her face.

"Yup. Are you Grace?"

The girl nodded, her arms shaking with the weight of the box.

"Here, let me help you with that." Taylor jumped up from her spot on the bed and walked over to Grace.

Grace sighed in relief as Taylor grabbed the other end of the box and directed her to set it down against one of the walls.

"Ugh, thank you. That box was so freaking heavy I thought I was going to drop it," Grace said.

Brody leaped out of his bed and trotted over to Grace, sniffing her leggings and sitting patiently in front of her feet, as if waiting to be greeted.

Grace giggled and pet him. "Who is this? Do we have another roommate?"

Taylor hesitated. "If you're okay with it. My aunt and I already talked it over with Headmistress Lockwood and got her permission." She scrambled to find the note the headmistress had typed up and thrust it into Grace's face. "Do you like dogs?"

But Grace already seemed enamored with Brody, who had rolled over onto his back so Grace could rub his belly. "I've always wanted a dog, but my parents don't like having animals in the house." She sighed. "I'm fine with him living here. It will be nice to have him looking out for us."

"Thank you. I promise Brody is great company. You'll love him." Taylor peeked into the hallway, noticing Grace was alone. "Where's your family?" Taylor asked curiously. She had assumed most students at the academy would have parents or guardians helping them move in. She felt a glimmer of relief that she had Mel in her life.

Grace rolled her eyes. "My brother Oliver is 'sick.'" She did air quotes with her fingers to emphasize the final word. "I think he's faking it to get out of working this summer or doing anything productive with his life. He didn't want to help me move in today. Anyway, my mom is staying home with him. My dad drove us here."

"Us?"

"Yeah, me and my little sister, Molly. She's twelve, so it's her first year here. My dad is helping her move in and get settled first. He's supposed to help me, but"—she gestured toward the box—"he hasn't yet."

"So have you been going to school here since you were twelve? What year are you? What's the school like?" Taylor asked, bombarding her new roommate with questions.

Over the past few weeks, since she had found out she would be attending Grimwood Magical Academy, the questions had piled up. Granted, Julian had told her a bit about the academy, but she wanted to hear it all from someone else.

Grace giggled and put her hand over her mouth. "Don't worry. I'll tell you all about it. We're going to be spending a lot of time together during the next few months."

"True. Do you want help moving the rest of your stuff in?" Taylor offered, pointing to where she had already set up her stuff. "I'm done with mine."

"Sure, I would love that. Thanks." Grace turned to leave the room.

Taylor followed, dying to ask more questions, but Grace had barely responded to any of her original questions. She didn't want her to think she was weird or too talkative.

Grace led the way to a black SUV and popped open the trunk. "Here it is." She pointed out a few items that were hers.

They both grabbed whatever they could carry and headed back to their dorm.

"So, this might be weird, but . . ." Grace took a deep breath. "I know you're new here and new to magic. I'm sure most people in the demon hunter world have heard your story. I'm just warning you. People will already have their own ideas and opinions formed about who you are before they meet you. Be careful who you become friends with."

Taylor smiled uneasily. "Great. Just what I need."

"Sorry. I didn't mean to worry you. I thought you should know. Some of the students here can be really gossipy. And immature," Grace said, shoving open the door to their dorm room once again.

They both dropped their piles of Grace's belongings inside their shared space and headed back to the SUV for another trip.

"No, it's fine," Taylor said. "I guess I would rather know upfront, so I can prepare myself." She paused before grabbing another box and put her hands on her hips. "I am curious, though. What have you heard about me?"

She might as well get the rumors out of the way right off the bat. Then she could deal with them and try to dispel them before they spread like wildfire. At her old high school, she had a pretty large group of friends and acquaintances, but she wasn't popular. Most people at her school didn't know who she was, nor did they care. This was going to be a completely different school experience.

Grace folded her arms across her chest, hugging herself like she was nervous. "Um, I heard about what happened to your parents," she started softly. "That you moved in with your aunt and . . ." She hesitated, biting her lip and probably wondering how to word the next part. "And that you had a run-in with a powerful demon and you survived."

Huh. That wasn't so bad.

"That's it?" Taylor questioned, raising her eyebrows.

"Well . . . no. Also that your full powers awakened before you turned sixteen, and you banished the demon by yourself," Grace added.

Taylor groaned. "Okay, okay. It will be fine. It's not weird that I was able to do all that, right?" She looked imploringly at her new roommate, hoping she agreed.

Grace shrugged both shoulders and headed back to the dorm after locking the car. "Sorry, but it's super weird and unheard of. In our history, no demon hunter has ever been able to perform such a powerful banishment spell by themselves, and definitely not while only being fifteen."

"Fifteen and three-quarters," Taylor interrupted.

Grace gave her an amused look. "Your powers are unique. That's why I warned you to be careful who you spend time with. There are students here who like having powerful allies. They'll try to use you for your powers and take advantage of you. Don't let them," she advised.

"That won't be an issue. I don't even know how to use my powers," Taylor retorted.

Grace blinked at her several times before she could choke out a response. She sat down on the empty bed in their room. Apparently, they were done moving. "Wait, what?"

"I guess that wasn't part of the gossip, then," Taylor said, snickering as her face flamed in embarrassment.

Had she given away information she shouldn't have? Maybe she shouldn't have told anyone she was so inexperienced. Was it better if they assumed she had grown up like them, being surrounded by magic and demon hunters and whatever else this world involved? Would it have given her an advantage if they thought she knew what she was doing?

"No . . . I had no idea. So did you grow up as a regular human, then?" Grace frowned. "Why didn't your parents teach you magic? The Turners are well-known for what they accomplished. Everyone knows about them. They should have passed down all their knowledge to you, given you the family grimoire, started your training when you were—"

Taylor interrupted her. "I don't know. They died before they had a chance to explain any of it to me. If there's one question I want to ask them, it's why they hid this world from me. Why didn't they want me to know? What were they so scared of?"

Grace shook her head. "Hmm. They must have had a good reason to keep it from you. Most parents only have their kids' best interests at heart, even if their kids don't always understand the reasoning. I bet they planned to tell you when you turned sixteen, but then their accident happened."

Taylor's heart sank. "You might be right, but that doesn't change the fact that they hid it from me for all these years."

"You have a lot of catching up to do, then."

Taylor nodded.

Grace smiled. "It's a good thing I like studying. I'll help you."

"Thanks," Taylor replied, before she remembered that Julian was already her assigned mentor. Who was to say that she couldn't have two mentors, though?

If she was supposedly the most powerful demon hunter to ever exist *and* she couldn't control her powers, then she needed all the help she could get.

Chapter 20

Taylor

Mel had picked Taylor up from her dorm last night, and the two of them had hung out—or three if you counted Brody, which Taylor thought everyone should. But now Kylie was over, and soon they would be heading next door to meet her mom's new boyfriend, Seth. Sarah and Kylie had invited Taylor and Mel over for dinner.

"Kylie, I promise it will be fine. You're getting all worked up," Taylor said, becoming annoyed with Kylie's nonstop worrying.

Taylor had asked Mel what changed and why she was suddenly allowed to hang out with the Andersons again, but Mel had brushed it off, claiming she no longer cared since her magic was gone. Something about it didn't sit well with Taylor because she thought the reason for keeping distance from their friends was because of her own magic—and her lack of control over her newfound powers. Apparently, that didn't matter now, but she intended to figure out why. She just had to wait until she was alone with Mel. Taylor had promised not to involve Kylie in the demon hunter world again.

Kylie flopped onto Taylor's bed and groaned. "I can't believe he's invited to our get-together tonight."

"It's not that big of a deal. I think you should—"

"You don't get it. For years now, it's just been me and my mom. We're happy. She's my favorite person in the world, and we have a great life together. I don't want some random guy to wedge his way into our lives and ruin it," Kylie said.

Taylor sat next to Kylie on her bed, careful not to get too close and intrude on her friend's personal space. "I understand, but first of all, it's not like they're getting married. They're just dating. It might not last that long. For all you know, he'll be gone in a few weeks and you'll never see him again."

"And . . . ?" Kylie prompted.

"And . . ." Taylor struggled to think of more comforting words to add so Kylie didn't bail on the dinner tonight. She didn't want to go without her. "If your mom is happy, then don't you want her to be happy? I know you're close to her, but she could be lonely. She might not have dated someone sooner because she was worried about how you would react. Now that you're older, she might have thought it was okay if she started dating again. If you react negatively to her boyfriend, do you want her to give up on a chance for happiness?"

Kylie groaned and covered her face with her hands. "I hate it when you're right, but you might have a point."

Taylor grinned. "So you'll go tonight?"

"Fine."

"And you'll be on your best behavior? Minimal complaining?" Taylor asked.

"No promises," Kylie said with a sly smile.

"Whatever. Don't be too mean to the poor guy. I'm sure he's perfectly nice. I can't imagine your mom being with a jerk," Taylor said.

"My dad wasn't exactly the greatest."

Realization dawned on her. "Oh. Is that what you're worried about? That she'll get into a relationship with someone who isn't good for her?" Taylor asked.

"Yeah, but this time I'm old enough that I can help her. She won't be left alone to fend for herself and take care of me, like she had to after my dad left. I can take care of myself now." Kylie's green eyes flashed. "And I'll take care of her too."

A sad smile crossed Taylor's face. "Your mom is lucky to have you looking out for her. You're both lucky to have each other."

"And Mel is lucky to have you," Kylie added, hugging her tightly. "Thanks for the pep talk. Ready to head over?"

"Sure." Taylor hopped off her bed and left her bedroom, with Brody following close behind and Kylie bringing up the rear.

"I love how he follows you everywhere," Kylie said, bending down to pet Brody's head. "Is he coming to dinner too?"

Taylor hesitated with her hand on the mahogany banister before she set off down the grand staircase. She had gotten so used to Brody always being with her, even living with her in her dorm at school, that she assumed he was invited everywhere she went. Within reason, of course. "If that's okay?"

She hadn't considered it as a potential predicament, but she didn't like leaving Brody home alone for too long, even if they would only be next door. She wasn't sure if he remembered Camille or if he missed her, but she didn't want him to think he was being abandoned. He was a member of their family, and it didn't feel right to leave him home by himself all the time.

Kylie shrugged both shoulders. "I'm sure my mom won't mind. Bring him."

They entered the kitchen and found Mel carefully sliding a pie from one of their favorite local dessert places into a ceramic pie dish.

"Really, Mel?" Taylor snort-laughed. "You think that's going to fool Sarah into thinking your pie is homemade? She's known you for years."

"Nope," Mel replied lightheartedly. "But it might fool her new boyfriend." She winked as she tossed the box into the trash can.

"Hey, I don't care if it's homemade or not. Their pies are amazing," Kylie said, practically drooling as she gazed at the pie.

"I agree," Taylor said.

Mel wrapped some plastic wrap over the top of the pie. "Okay. Are you girls ready?"

"As ready as I'll ever be," Kylie said with a heavy sigh.

Mel glanced at her sideways. "You okay?"

Taylor laughed. "She's fine. She doesn't like Seth."

Kylie glared at her. "Ugh, why did you tell her that?" She turned to Mel, putting the palms of her hands together. "Please don't tell my mom. I promised Taylor that I would be nice to him tonight. For my mom's sake. I want her to be happy, but it . . . it's just hard."

Mel patted Kylie on the shoulder. "I understand. And don't worry. I won't say a word."

The three women headed next door, with Brody leading the way, almost as if he knew where they were going.

"He hasn't been to our house before . . ." Kylie started, sounding confused. "How does he know where to go?"

Taylor hitched a shoulder up toward her ear before lowering it. "I don't know. He's a smart dog."

"Hmm, interesting," Mel said.

"What?" Taylor asked as they approached the front door at the Andersons' house.

"Nothing. We can discuss it later," Mel replied.

Kylie burst in through the front door, with the others trailing after her. "Mom, we're here!"

Sarah's tall frame came around the corner, peeking in from the kitchen. "Hello! Come in here. I'm setting the table, but the pot roast is almost done cooking."

Taylor entered the kitchen, letting Kylie, Mel, and Brody go in first. Brody sniffed Sarah, and she bent down to scratch behind his ears.

"And who is this little cutie?" Sarah asked.

"Brody. We adopted him a few weeks ago," Taylor replied.

"Where did you get him from? Is he a rescue?" Sarah asked.

"Um, no. He—" Before Taylor could say something incriminating, like 'We took him in after his immortal owner, who served a powerful demon, died,' Mel cut her off.

"He's a stray. We found him running around the neighborhood. The poor dog was terrified of us at first, and so dirty. His fur was all mangy, and he was skinny.

We gave him a bath, then took him to the vet and got all his vaccines. He's adjusted quite nicely to living with us," Mel said, smiling at Taylor.

"Oh, poor dog. I'm glad you found him, and he has a good home now." Sarah turned toward the door as the doorbell rang. A wide, ecstatic grin took over her entire face. "That must be Seth. I'll answer it." Her grin cracked slightly as she narrowed her eyes at her daughter. "Please be nice, Kylie."

Sarah stalked off to the front door, leaving Kylie muttering under her breath after her mom. Taylor practically held her breath as she waited for Sarah to return with the newest visitor.

Mel smiled at both of them. "I'm sure tonight will be fine."

Sarah returned to the kitchen, with her arm looped through the arm of a tall, gorgeous man, at least several inches taller than her. He must have been over six feet because Sarah was pushing five foot ten. His chestnut waves fell down to his chin, with a few curls framing his green eyes.

"Hello," he said, waving to them.

Sarah turned to him, beaming. "Everyone, this is Seth." She pointed each of them out in turn. "This is Mel, her niece Taylor, and their new dog, Brody. Isn't he adorable?" She squeezed Seth's arm. "And, of course, you've already met Kylie."

"Oh, he is cute," Seth agreed, bending down to greet the dog. "It's nice to meet you all." Seth reached out his hand toward Brody as if he was going to pet him.

Brody bared his teeth and growled as Seth came closer to him.

Seth snatched his arm away, chuckled awkwardly, and backed up. "That's okay, little guy. I don't have to pet you." He held out his arms in a calming gesture. "We're all friends here."

Taylor heard Kylie whisper, "Are we, though?" and elbowed her in the side.

"Brody, what's wrong?" Taylor asked, moving closer to her dog.

But Brody continued growling, a low, guttural growl she had never heard from him before. His growling intensified, and he lunged for Seth's leg.

"Ahh!" Seth screamed, reaching down to extract the tiny dog from his leg.

Taylor and Mel both darted toward him and pulled Brody away.

Mel tapped him on the head as a warning. "Brody, no biting." She addressed Sarah and Seth with a wary expression. "He's never done that before. I'm so sorry. He's usually fine with strangers."

Taylor stooped to her dog's level, and she could have sworn he met her eyes and shook his head. Shocked, she gasped and stumbled, nearly falling onto the floor.

"Are you okay?" Kylie asked, the only one paying attention to Taylor.

"Yes." Taylor regained her balance and eyed Brody again. He had gone back to growling and creeping back toward Seth.

Seth winced and rubbed his leg where Brody had bitten him. His dress pants were torn at the knee where Brody had latched on and ripped off the fabric. Blood dripped down his leg.

"Oh, no, your pants!" Mel exclaimed. She glanced at Taylor. "Maybe you should bring Brody home? He'll be fine at home alone for a few hours."

Sarah raced to find a first-aid kit, while Seth took a seat at the kitchen table. He waved off their apologies and assured them he was fine.

Taylor scooped Brody into her arms and headed to the front door. "I'll be right back," she called out as she left.

Kylie hurriedly followed her. "I'll come with you. Any excuse to leave for a minute is fine with me!" She glanced at Brody, who had stopped growling once they were outside, and looked perfectly content in Taylor's arms as she carried him down the driveway. "What do you think happened? Did something set him off?"

Taylor shook her head, unsure of what had transpired. "He's met tons of people since we took him in, and he's never reacted like that toward anyone. Even on campus, he's friendly and loves when people pay attention to him and pet him. He soaks up all the attention. He loves people. I've never heard him growl like that before . . ."

She didn't want Kylie to worry, though, or for her to have yet another reason to dislike Seth, so she changed her train of thought. "Seth might own a dog or a cat. Maybe Brody could smell it. Dogs can react strongly to the scent of other animals."

Kylie crinkled her nose. "Is that really possible? Are dogs that sensitive?"

"Yup. I'm sure it was something like that. Besides, Seth didn't get mad. He seems like a nice guy."

"Oh, he's nice, alright," Kylie huffed as they crossed the threshold back into Mel and Taylor's house. She shut the door behind her.

"Are you going to be okay here all by yourself, Brody?" Taylor asked her dog.

He sat obediently in his dog bed, wagging his tail excitedly as if to say, 'Yes!'

"Okay, then. Let's head back over there," Taylor said.

Kylie eyed Brody again as they exited the house. "Do you think dogs can sense when people . . . aren't good?"

Taylor scoffed. "Don't be ridiculous. Seth is a normal guy, and Brody's a normal dog. What would he have sensed? You don't think he's like a serial killer, do you? Because not liking him is one thing, but—"

Kylie bit her lip. "Never mind. I'm being silly. I'm sure you're right."

But Taylor couldn't shake the looming sensation that Brody *had* sensed something off about Seth. After her demon encounter earlier in the summer, she felt on edge, alert to anything supernatural. What else existed in the world that she didn't know about? What if Seth was a threat? Something perhaps . . . not human.

Mel

As soon as the dinner was over and they were back in their home, Brody came running over to greet them. Taylor patted his head and followed Mel into the living room.

"Why am I allowed to hang out with Kylie again? And what do you think is going on with Brody?" Taylor asked, giving her dog a side eye.

Mel rubbed her forehead that suddenly ached. "Can we wait until tomorrow for this conversation?"

Taylor shook her head. "I'm going back to the academy tomorrow. I don't want you to put it off again."

"Okay." Mel sat in the armchair in the living room.

Taylor sat on the couch. Brody hopped up and joined her.

"I thought you were worried about me losing control of my powers and hurting someone," Taylor said, her forehead creasing in confusion. "Nothing has changed, right?"

"I'm still worried about that, but Kylie needs a friend, and so does Sarah. They'll be suspicious if we cut them out completely. I've known them for years, and we need to be careful," Mel answered.

"But you don't have your magic, so what if something happens? How are you going to stop me if I become overwhelmed or get emotional and my magic goes wild again?" Taylor asked.

"Not that I want to do this, but we could get the council involved and have them restrict your magic," Mel said.

"Um, I didn't think you wanted to see them ever again after what they did to you. Besides, won't they just take my magic away like they did to you?"

"You're probably right. I don't know, Taylor. I'm at a loss for what to do here. This is uncharted territory," Mel replied.

Taylor stroked Brody's fur. "Do you think Brody senses something off about Seth? Kylie seems to think he isn't a good person."

Mel smirked. "I don't think Kylie would like anyone her mom dated. It will take some getting used to. As for Brody . . . I'm not sure. Maybe he sensed the discomfort of the situation."

Taylor bit her lip. "Is it possible for dogs to have magic too? Could Brody know something we don't?"

Mel's eyes widened. "He was Camille's dog, so it's possible. He isn't like any normal dog I've ever been around."

Brody sat up straighter, and his ears perked up.

"Is it true, Brody?" Taylor asked, scratching behind his ears. "Are you a magic user too?"

Brody barked once.

Taylor giggled. "I think he's saying yes."

Mel came over to the couch and sat next to Taylor. She put her arm around her niece's shoulders. "I'm sorry for keeping you locked up in here for the end of your summer. I'm still learning. I want you to be safe, but I also want you to have fun. I don't want you to miss out and look back with regret about all the things you didn't get to do as a teenager. You can hang out at the Andersons', but the second something happens with your magic, call me and come straight home. We'll figure out what to do if it comes to that."

Taylor rested her head on Mel's shoulder. "Thanks, Mel. I guess I understand. I don't want to hurt anyone."

"I know, kiddo," Mel replied.

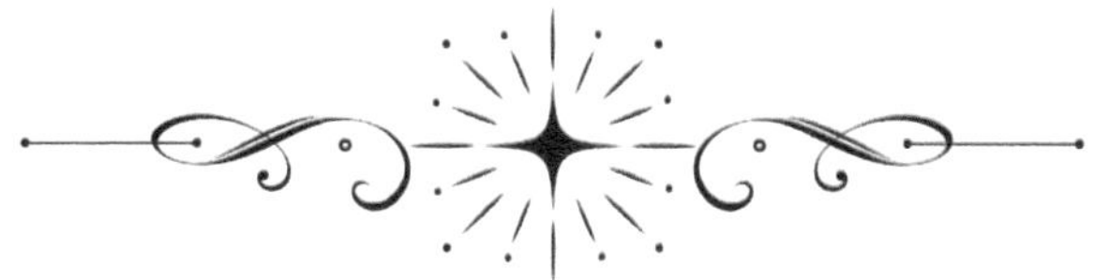

As soon as Mel had learned what was going on with Oliver, she had asked to see him. At first, Vanessa protested, but Mel insisted she couldn't help unless she saw him and spoke to him. She needed to know how bad it was. Vanessa seemed embarrassed, but after Taylor went back to the academy, she eventually agreed.

"I want to save my son," Vanessa said in a hoarse voice, clearly on the verge of bursting into tears.

"I know, and I want to help you," Mel told her.

"Thank you, Mel," Vanessa said. She led the way down the hall to a room with a sign on the door that read, *Danger. Keep out.* "Teenagers . . . so dramatic," Vanessa dismissed the sign before knocking softly on the door.

Vanessa waited a moment, then opened the door. "Ollie, you have a visitor," she said as she stepped into the darkened room. "Is it okay if I turn on the light?"

Mel couldn't make out much in the room. She hesitantly followed Vanessa inside, staying on guard. Although she trusted Vanessa, she was reminded that she didn't have her powers, and she was defenseless against any attacks. Maybe she should have told Taylor where she was going.

Vanessa flicked on the light, causing a hissing sound to emit from the human-like shape covered in a blanket on the bed.

Vanessa sat on the edge of the full-sized bed, patting the spot where her son's head must be. "Ollie? Can you take off your blanket and say hello?"

Slowly, the blanket pulled back, revealing a pale, emaciated face barely reminiscent of the Oliver in the framed photos proudly on display out in the sitting room. His bloodshot, green eyes had dark shadows under them, and his long black hair appeared greasy and unwashed.

"Hello," he said in a low, raspy voice.

Mel waved. "Hi, Oliver. It's Mel Turner. Do you remember me?"

Oliver nodded.

Mel glanced at Vanessa, who gestured her hand with a rolling motion, as if encouraging Mel to continue speaking to her son. The only problem was that Mel had no clue how to proceed, especially without her magic. She took another few steps into the room.

Vanessa chuckled and waved for Mel to come over. "Join us over here. He won't bite."

At that comment, Oliver chuckled darkly, which turned into a full-belly laugh. His razor-sharp teeth were exposed, fangs protruding from where his incisors should be.

Mel gasped, unable to contain her shock. She placed her hand over her mouth and turned to leave. "Oliver, what happened? What did you do?" she asked, backing out of the room.

Vanessa pulled the blanket back the rest of the way from the bed, then came over to Mel. "It isn't time for you to leave yet. I need your help, Mel. *We* need your help."

"Vanessa, I can't—this isn't what I signed up for. I thought—"

"Oliver needs blood, Mel. He needs fresh human blood. I've tried bringing him animal blood. You must know how much it pained me to kill those poor animals, but I had to. I would do anything for my son." Vanessa's voice remained calm and peaceful, despite the strength she exerted to wrap her fingers around Mel's wrist and drag her toward her eldest child.

"How could you do that? Why am I here?" Mel demanded, fighting to free her wrist from Vanessa's grasp. She didn't want to believe it, but the puzzle pieces were connecting, and she didn't like where this was going.

Vanessa shoved her into a kneeling position by Oliver's bedside, then pushed Mel's dark brown hair back from her face, exposing her neck. "Here you go, Ollie. Drink up."

Vanessa helped direct Oliver's mouth to Mel's neck, whispering encouraging words to him all the while. "That's it, sweetie. You'll be better soon. All you need to do is feed from a live human. You'll be better in no time."

The second the fangs pierced her neck, Mel screamed. Not only from the pain, but from the horrifying realization that Vanessa had tricked her. She didn't want Mel's help to reverse the vampiric curse that had clearly been placed on Oliver. All she wanted was to use the defenseless, magicless Mel to feed her son.

Chapter 22

Taylor

Taylor hadn't seen Julian yet since arriving at the academy. After their heartfelt moment during their last practice where she had revealed her feelings for him, she was a bundle of nerves and excitement at the possibility of seeing him again. She didn't want to be the first one to reach out, so she had patiently waited for him to text her.

"Wanna grab breakfast?" Grace asked, slipping her feet into a pair of tall, black wedges.

"I don't know how you can walk in those," Taylor teased.

"Lots of practice," Grace retorted as she struck a pose.

"Let me grab my purse." Taylor reached for her desk chair, which her purse was slung across the back of. "Kay. Ready."

“Do you have your keys or should I grab mine?” Grace asked.

“Got ‘em.” Taylor dangled her lanyard from two fingers, then locked the door behind them.

They walked side by side to the dining area.

They waited in line for breakfast and snagged a table by a window overlooking the gardens.

“Such a pretty view,” Taylor said, munching on her English muffin covered in strawberry jam.

The food at the academy was better than Taylor had expected, probably because she was used to nasty high school cafeteria food that was simultaneously unhealthy and disgusting.

Grace peered out the window too and smiled. “It is. I never get tired of it.”

“Beauty is something you shouldn’t get tired of. Ever.”

Grace rolled her eyes. “Okay, what are you now? A poet? Or a philosopher?”

“I haven’t decided yet,” Taylor retorted with a smirk.

Grace’s expression turned more serious. “You know, you’ll be expected to take over your family’s place on the council now that Mel doesn't . . .”

Even though Grace didn’t finish the sentence, Taylor knew what she meant. *Now that Mel doesn’t have magic anymore.*

“Crap. I hadn’t thought about it.”

Grace tilted her head. “Really? It’s all I think about, since I’ll be taking over my family’s council spot someday too. It’s a lot of responsibility. I don’t want to screw it up.”

“I don’t blame you. That sounds like a lot of pressure,” Taylor said. She bit into an apple.

“Yeah, but it will be worth it. The job is rewarding. Every council member impacts our society in a profound way. I can’t imagine a more important role or a better way to contribute to the future and help shape the next generation of demon hunters,” Grace said. She sat up tall with pride, her long red hair swishing back and forth as she vigorously explained the role.

“Yeah, well, I don’t know about all that. I’m not sure what I want to do,” Taylor admitted.

Grace nearly spit out her orange juice. “Um, what? You don’t have a choice. Your parents are gone. Your aunt doesn’t have her powers. You’re the only Turner left. It *has* to be you.”

Taylor stared at Grace, taken aback by her strong reaction. She set the apple core on her plastic tray. “I don’t know. I’m still coming to terms with all of this. It’s so new to me.”

“Taylor, you don’t understand how this works. You can’t just decide not to be involved with the council. Although your family’s already on thin ice, so maybe the other council members won’t want—” Grace seemed to realize she had said something she shouldn’t have. Her green eyes widened. She hurriedly scooped a bite of cereal into her mouth and became silent.

“They won’t want *what*?” Taylor asked, narrowing her eyes at her roommate.

Grace swallowed the cereal before replying. “I meant . . . it might be different with you. They might not want you involved.”

“Great. So first I didn’t have a choice about saying no to the council, and now it might not be an option? What about what I want? When do I get a say in any of this?” Taylor protested.

“I’m not sure.” A brief smile flickered across Grace’s face. “I’ll let you know when I find out.”

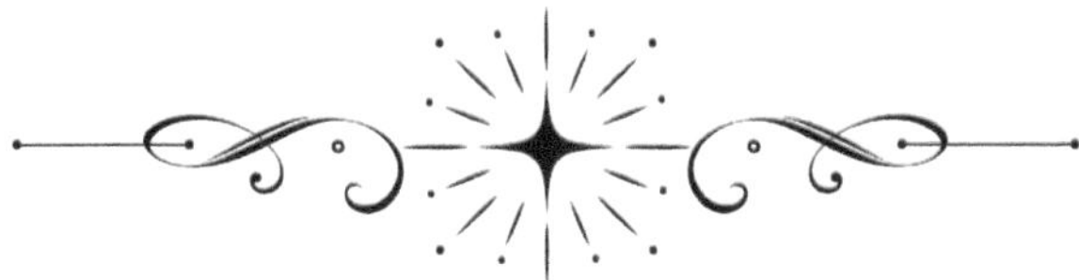

Taylor was walking across campus with Brody, getting to know the area her new home was located in. Since the campus was enormous, she was doing her best to memorize where the buildings were before classes started. She had never attended such a large school before, and she kept having nightmares about being late for class, or worse, not being able to find her classes.

Brody obediently trotted along in front of her, leading the way, like he preferred. Every once in a while, he stopped to sniff something, and Taylor tugged him along. She cringed when he lifted his leg to pee on a sign and promptly tugged the leash.

"Hey, Brody! Don't pee on that!"

She heard a deep chuckle from behind her and whipped around to see who had witnessed her embarrassing moment.

"Cute dog, but the owner's even cuter," the voice said, before Taylor registered it was Julian. He walked up to her, grinning.

"Oh, uh, hi," she stuttered, unable to come up with a witty retort—or any kind of logical response.

Julian stepped closer to her. "Taking a walk?"

"Yeah." Taylor gripped Brody's leash tighter as her dog attempted to jump up on Julian. She twisted the leash around her wrist again. "Brody, heel."

Brody whined, but finally relented, plopping his butt down onto the pavement and wagging his tail.

Julian laughed and bent down to pet Brody, who immediately lunged at him and licked his face. Julian turned to Taylor. "At least someone is giving me kisses," he said with a wink.

Taylor arched an eyebrow. "You want me to lick your face?"

Julian patted Brody on the head and gently pushed him away before standing up and moving closer to Taylor. "No."

Taylor's heart thudded uncomfortably in her chest as Julian leaned in. When she thought he was going to kiss her, Brody intervened, cutting in between them and whining, demanding attention.

A wave of relief washed over Taylor. She wanted to kiss Julian, but not here, in the middle of campus and out in the open where anyone could see them. Their first kiss had to be special.

"Sorry. Brody can be clingy," she apologized.

Brody barked indignantly, as if he had understood what she said.

Julian shook his head as a small smile played across his lips. "It's fine. Do you want to meet up later? Alone?"

"I would love to. Did you have something in mind?" Taylor asked.

Julian smirked. "I might. Which building is your dorm in? I'll pick you up at seven."

"Flamel."

"Ah. Mine's Pernelle. Right next to yours," he added with a mischievous grin. "I'm surprised we haven't run into each other yet."

"Lucky me," Taylor retorted in a huff. But Julian living so close to her was thrilling. She could already picture them hanging out all the time, and him sneaking into her dorm, or vice versa. Although she wondered how Grace would feel about a guy being in their dorm . . .

"Taylor?" Julian asked in a concerned tone, sounding as if he had already said her name once before.

"Oh, sorry. I was just . . ." Taylor started, her cheeks burning as she fumbled to come up with an excuse for getting lost in her thoughts.

"What were you thinking about?"

"Nothing."

"Right . . . That's why your face is redder than a tomato. Thinking about being alone with me later?" Julian joked.

"I'll see you at seven tonight?" Taylor asked, ending the conversation.

"See you then." Julian waved and headed toward the center of campus, leaving Taylor and Brody to continue their walk.

Chapter 23

Taylor

Taylor speed-walked around the rest of the campus until she felt like she had gotten more of her anxious jitters out. Then she turned around and took Brody back to the dorm.

Grace was sitting on her bed scribbling in a journal. She took out her earbuds when she noticed Taylor. "How was your walk?"

"Fine."

"Wanna grab dinner together later?" Grace asked, closing her journal.

"I'm not sure," Taylor said. She took off Brody's leash and poured some fresh water into his bowl.

"Why not?" Grace asked, scrunching her eyebrows together. "Not hungry? We only ate breakfast today, since we were studying for most of the day." Her stomach growled loudly, as if to accentuate her point.

"No, that's not it. I ran into Julian and—"

"Whoa. *Julian Cromwell*?" Grace asked, tossing aside her journal and leaning forward in interest. "Ooh, I want to hear all about it! Did you meet him today? What happened? Was it like a meet-cute?"

"No, I already knew him. He started training me over the summer. The demon hunter's council agreed that I needed someone to keep an eye on me, someone to act as a sort-of mentor and bodyguard. Although I hadn't even seen him since arriving on campus until today. Some bodyguard . . ." she muttered.

Grace's forest-green eyes widened. "You spent the summer hanging out with him?"

"It's not what you think. It was only the last three weeks of summer, and we spent most of our time together training," Taylor said.

Grace smiled knowingly. "So what else did you do, then? He's really cute."

"We hung out. It's not serious," Taylor said.

"Then why are you so flustered after seeing him?" Grace pried.

"He asked me out on a date. He wouldn't tell me where, but he's picking me up at seven tonight."

"*Tonight*? Oh my God." Grace glanced at her phone. "It's already almost five! What are you going to wear? Do you have enough time to get ready? Maybe you can ask him to push back the date?"

Taylor giggled, feeling less nervous after her roommate's barrage of questions. For some reason, it calmed her to see someone else acting so erratically.

"I think I'll be fine. He's already seen me at my worst, all sweaty and disheveled during practice. He's knocked me onto my butt a dozen times, and he's seen me with cuts and bruises. He never minded," Taylor said.

Grace made a sound that came out like a squeal. "Oh, this is so exciting! I'll have to live vicariously through you."

"You don't have a boyfriend or girlfriend? Anyone you're interested in?" Taylor questioned.

"Nah. I don't have time for dating. I need to focus on studying and preparing to take over my family's spot on the council someday."

"But don't you feel like you're missing out?"

Grace shrugged a shoulder. "Not really. I wouldn't want to get too close to someone when I have all this responsibility to handle. I would have to meet someone amazing to make me change my mind."

"Well, then I hope you do," Taylor said. "I love how you know exactly what you want out of life. I envy you."

"Most of it isn't my choice. I don't think my parents would like me dating, anyway. Not unless it was like a super powerful, affluent demon hunter. Someone whose family could help my family achieve a higher status."

"Yikes," Taylor said, thankful she didn't have to worry about that. Her mood deflated. Taylor's parents would never approve or disapprove of whomever she dated since they were dead. They would never get the chance to meet Julian or anyone else she dated. It was a horrible thing to consider, and it shattered her happiness about her date.

"Yeah, I've gotten used to it. My parents mean well. They want the best for me and my siblings. It's particularly annoying right now since they're so focused on Oliver and whatever he's going through. They barely paid attention to me all summer. I could have gotten away with murder, and I doubt they would have noticed," Grace said, uttering a harsh laugh.

"At least you have parents who care about you," Taylor retorted and instantly regretted snapping at her new roommate. "Sorry, I didn't mean—"

"No, you're fine. I wasn't thinking. Complaining about my parents like that when you don't—"

"It's okay." Taylor wandered over to her closet, hiding her face, which was now shining with tears. She cleared her throat. "What do you think I should wear? He gave me zero hints about where he's taking me."

"Hopefully not to, like, a sacrificial ritual or something creepy," Grace said.

"Um . . . what?" Taylor asked.

"I was making a dumb joke." Grace let out an awkward laugh. "Apparently it didn't work. Noted." She joined Taylor in front of their tiny closet. "What about a versatile outfit that would work for a variety of dates? Not too classy or fancy, but something that could be dressed up if necessary?" Grace suggested.

"Yeah, that sounds great." She stared blankly at her clothes. "But what outfit makes all that possible?"

"Hmm." Grace tapped her chin with her pointer finger and thumb. She pulled a lacy, short-sleeved, black shirt from a hanger. "This." She pointed to a pair of dark-wash jeans lying across Taylor's desk chair. "And those. What size shoes do you wear?"

"Um, seven. Why?" Taylor replied.

"I wear a seven and a half usually, but they should fit you." Grace retreated into the closet and came out a moment later with a pair of sparkly silver sandals. "Ta-da!"

Taylor stared dubiously at the pile of items as Grace set them all on her bed. "Are you sure about this?"

"Definitely. Fashion is one thing I know a lot about. Try on the outfit and see how it looks."

"Okay, fine. I'll trust your judgment. You *do* always look well put together," Taylor relented.

"Smart answer," Grace said.

CHAPTER 24

TAYLOR

Julian held her hand as they crossed the street, heading into the woods.

"You aren't taking me all the way out here to kill me, are you? I think I can take you," Taylor joked, lightly punching his shoulder.

Julian chuckled. "I love how that's where your mind went." He shook his head. "No, of course not. This is one of my favorite spots, so I wanted to show it to you."

"I feel honored," Taylor said sarcastically. She stared off into the woods.

"What are you thinking about?" Julian asked.

"Am I the first one you've brought here?" Taylor blurted out.

Julian's smile disappeared, his face becoming impassive. "No, but there was only one other girl."

"Who is she?"

Julian's face took on a hard, bitter look. "No one you need to worry about. We dated for a while until she cheated on me with my best friend."

"Oh . . . wow. I'm sorry." She squeezed Julian's hand. "That must have been difficult to go through."

"It was hard at the time, but I'm over it. It hurt for a while, but I moved on. And then I met you and . . . it's almost like she never existed," Julian said, turning to face her and gazing into her eyes.

Her breath hitched in her throat as he leaned in, gently brushing the stray hairs from her face.

As Taylor was certain they were finally going to have their first kiss, her cell phone rang, shattering the romantic moment. She pulled out her phone to see who was calling during her first official date with Julian. *Dang it, Kylie.*

"Do you need to get that?" Julian asked after clearing his throat and letting go of her face.

"No, it's just Kylie. I'll text her later," Taylor said. She already missed the warmth of his hand on her face and the feeling of their fingers intertwined.

"Okay, then. We're almost there." Julian gestured to the path in front of them. "Only a little further."

Taylor followed him for a few seconds, but stopped when her cell phone rang again. "Okay, maybe I should answer. She usually doesn't call multiple times in a row. It might be an emergency."

"I understand," Julian said, halting his footsteps to wait for her.

Taylor answered the phone, her apprehension growing about her friend. Something must be seriously wrong for Kylie to call her repeatedly. "Hello? Kylie?"

"Tay! Finally. Geez, I've been trying to reach you. Are you too busy for me now?" Kylie asked in a bitter tone.

"Well, I'm on a date, but I can talk for a minute. What's up?"

"A date? Oh my God. With Julian?" Kylie asked.

"Yes, I promise I'll tell you all about it later," she said with a sly smile at Julian. "Why did you call? Is something wrong?"

"Um, yes, horrifically wrong," Kylie responded.

Taylor's heart thudded in her chest uncomfortably loudly in the silent woods. Was it about Mel? Was she okay? Had there been another demon encounter? Her mind started running wild with all the possible scenarios.

"What's wrong?" Taylor finally asked when Kylie didn't elaborate.

"My mom's new boyfriend is over at our house like every day." Kylie groaned. "She claims it isn't serious, but he's always here, and it's gross."

Taylor's heart calmed at last. "That's it? I met Seth when I was home last time, remember? He didn't seem that bad, Kylie. I'm going to kill you! I thought something bad must have happened."

"It *is* bad, though! You have to help me break them up. There's something wrong with him," Kylie insisted.

"What?"

"I don't know yet, but I'm sure there's something. They only met a few weeks ago, and he's already brought up marriage. Isn't that strange to you?" Kylie prodded in an exasperated tone.

"I mean, kind of . . . but maybe he really likes her. Your mom is great, so would it be that strange if he wanted to marry her?" Taylor said.

"I don't want her to get remarried," Kylie replied in a sullen tone.

"I'll call you later when I'm back in my dorm. We'll talk more then, okay?"

"Oh, fine. Have fun on your date while I'm forced to hang out with my mom and my soon-to-be stepdad," Kylie said.

Taylor could imagine her pouting.

"You'll be fine. Talk to you later," Taylor said, ending the call and putting her cell phone back in her purse. She turned to Julian. "Sorry about that. Kylie is being dramatic about her mom's new boyfriend, Seth."

Julian squeezed her hand. "That's tough. Is Kylie okay?"

"Yeah, she'll be fine. She needs to get used to the idea of her mom dating. I met Seth the last time I was home. He seemed like a perfectly nice guy." Taylor smiled, eager to get back to their date. "So where were we?"

"Well, before our moment was ruined, we were about to head to my secret spot. Are you sure you're ready for this?" Julian teased.

"Of course. The suspense is killing me."

"Okay. Close your eyes and keep walking forward. I'll direct you," Julian said.

"Okay," Taylor agreed.

Taylor listened to him and shut her eyes tightly, letting him guide her forward, further into the woods for a few minutes. The eagerness and anticipation grew until she thought she was going to explode. She couldn't wait to see what they were doing on their first date.

"Okay. You can open your eyes now," Julian told her.

Taylor opened her eyes and gasped in awe as she gazed around the wooded area he had led her to. Slightly off the dirt path, there was a small, black folding table and two camping chairs. On top of the table were two plastic wine glasses, plates, silverware, and folded cloth napkins. A picnic basket sat next to the table. Sparkling twinkle lights hung from the surrounding trees, creating a magical atmosphere.

"Wow," Taylor said, finally remembering how to breathe again. "This is so sweet, Julian."

"I'm glad you like it." He smiled, pulling out one of the chairs for her. "Take a seat." He bent down to open the picnic basket and pulled out a warming tray.

The scent of the food wafted out as he pulled off the lid, revealing lasagna and garlic bread.

"That smells amazing. Did you cook it?" Taylor asked, slightly incredulous at the thought of Julian cooking such a delicious-looking—and what she assumed was complicated—dish for their dinner date.

Julian chuckled and served a portion of the lasagna onto their plates. "No. It's from my favorite Italian place. I told them I had a date with a special girl tonight."

Taylor's cheeks flushed. She grabbed a piece of garlic bread to distract herself from how warm and fuzzy he was making her feel. He had gone to all this trouble to make their first date memorable. *Although*, the thought snuck into her mind, *he brought his ex here too . . .*

"Enjoy. I hope you like lasagna. And if you don't, this probably won't work out, anyway," he teased in a lighthearted tone.

"I love lasagna," Taylor replied, spearing a piece of it with her fork. She blew on it a few times before taking a bite. The flavors of the perfectly cooked noodles, Italian sausage, cheese, and sauce hit her in layers, enticing her taste buds and making her want more. "This is so good. What's the sauce on it? It doesn't taste like marinara sauce."

"Oh, it's their special sauce they make in the restaurant." Julian shrugged. "They refuse to tell me what's in it, but whatever it is, it's good."

"Agreed."

They fell into a comfortable silence as they both ate.

Julian stopped eating and jolted upright. "Oh, crap! I forgot about the drinks. I'm sorry."

Taylor glanced at their empty wine glasses. "It's okay."

Julian bent over the picnic basket once again and pulled out a wine bottle. He poured some into his glass.

As he reached for her glass, Taylor grabbed his wrist to stop him. "Oh, uh, I don't really drink."

She felt lame for voicing it out loud, but she didn't want to compromise her values for a guy. It's not like she was waiting until she turned twenty-one, but she didn't see the appeal of drinking alcohol.

Julian smirked and turned the wine bottle around, so she could read it. *Welch's Sparkling Grape Juice.*

"It isn't wine," Julian confirmed, the bottle still in his hand hovering over her glass. "Do you want some sparkling grape juice, or are we breaking some kind of law that I don't know about?"

Taylor giggled. "Oops. I just assumed . . ."

Julian shook his head and poured some into her glass, then set the bottle back in the picnic basket. "I wouldn't know how to get any alcohol. I'm only sixteen. Besides, I don't want to get in trouble at the academy for drinking. If you're caught, that can be enough to get expelled. I'm not blowing my future over a stupid drink."

"Oh. Good to know," Taylor replied, fighting back a smile. He was too good to be true.

She sipped the sparkling grape juice and enjoyed the rest of the meal with Julian.

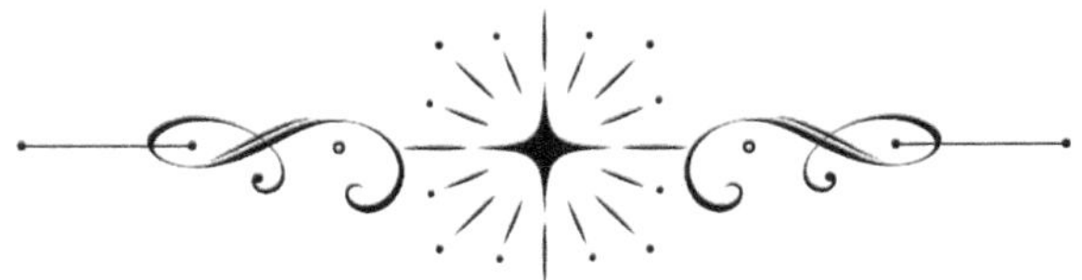

Later, he brought her back to her dorm and dropped her off in front of the Flamel building.

"I'll see you tomorrow," he said, holding both of her hands and tugging her closer to him. His arms wrapped around her in an embrace.

Taylor hugged him back, resting her head on his shoulder and soaking in the contentment. It had been a wonderful date.

"Wanna meet up after classes tomorrow?" Taylor offered, thinking it was her turn to initiate a hang-out.

He pulled back slightly to gaze into her eyes, then his lips brushed against her cheek. "Sounds good. Tomorrow can't come soon enough."

She smiled and turned to head into her dorm. "Bye, Julian."

Chapter 25

Taylor

Taylor tugged on her dark gray pleated skirt and straightened her short-sleeved purple polo. It was still warm enough for her to go without tights or leggings, so her bare legs were exposed. She stared at herself in the floor-length mirror Grace had attached to the closet door.

"How are you feeling? Nervous?" Grace asked.

Taylor finished fixing her clothes and turned to her roommate. "Yeah. Kind of. I hate starting over."

"Don't worry. It won't be as bad as you think. Most of the students here are really nice. Just avoid the ones who aren't."

"Great advice," Taylor teased.

"I try," Grace commented with a curtsy. "What's your first class?" Grace picked up her backpack stuffed full of books and school supplies.

Taylor pulled out her class schedule and scanned the list for the dozenth time. "Introduction to Demon Hunter History with Professor Storia."

"Ah, that's right. You're going to be taking all the beginner demon hunter classes since you're behind," Grace said.

"Wait. Really?" Taylor asked, re-reading her schedule in horror.

Grace shrugged. "Yeah. What other classes do you have?" She bounced off her bed and went over to Taylor to check out her schedule.

8:00 A.M. – 9:30 A.M. - Introduction to Demon Hunter History with Professor Michael Storia

10:00 A.M. – 11:15 A.M. - Basic Spells with Professor Helena Magos

Lunch

2:00 P.M. – 3:00 P.M. - Self-Defense with Professor Alice Bellum

3:40 – 4:40 P.M. - Demon Hunter Missions 101 with Professor Catie Caldwell

Dinner

6:00 P.M. – 7:30 P.M. - Tutoring

Taylor snuck a look at her roommate to see her reaction to the schedule.

"Yup, those are all classes for first-year students," Grace replied.

Taylor's posture slumped downward. She hadn't expected to be in all the classes for her age group, but she was disappointed upon finding out she would be stuck in classes with a bunch of twelve-year-olds.

"Hey, it's fine. I know you have Julian helping you practice magic already, but I can help you with studying. That's what I'm best at. Plus, look on the bright side. My little sister, Molly, is really sweet. She'll be in most of your classes."

Taylor groaned and put her head in her hands. "I'm going to stand out so much at this school."

"Is that what you're worried about?" Grace sat next to Taylor on her bed. The mattress squeaked as she sat down. She put her arm around Taylor's shoulders. "It could be worse. At least everyone will know who you are."

"Is that a good thing, though? I'm more of a 'blend in with the crowd' kind of girl," Taylor said, lifting her head from her hands.

Grace bit her lip before smiling sympathetically. "You might have to get used to being the center of attention. Whether you like it or not, you're already notorious at the academy. You might as well embrace it."

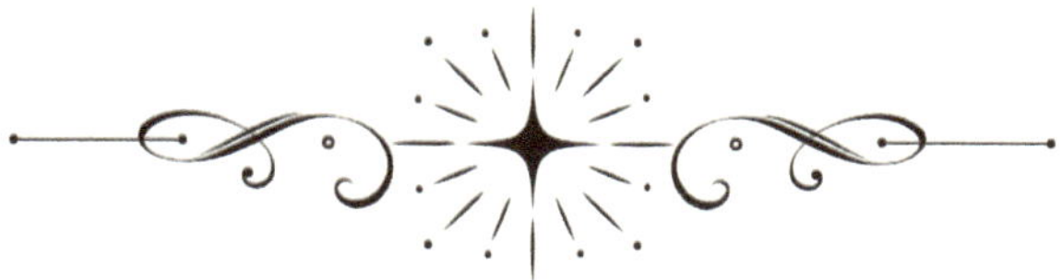

Taylor paused in the doorway of her first class, Introduction to Demon Hunter History with Professor Michael Storia. She was excited to learn more about their history, but catching up on three years' worth of classes and studying was daunting.

"Come in, come in," a middle-aged man with slicked-back, blond hair and blue eyes welcomed her into the classroom.

Taylor entered the classroom, eyeing the rows of desks. Only a few students were seated. Taylor had arrived fifteen minutes early, worried about being late for her first class and making a bad impression.

"Hello. I'm assuming you're Taylor Windsor?" the man asked her in greeting.

"Yup, that's me," Taylor said, holding out her hand to shake.

"Nice to meet you, Taylor. I'm Professor Storia." He shook her hand and smiled brilliantly. "Welcome to Grimwood Magical Academy! Feel free to take a seat anywhere."

"Thanks, Professor."

Taylor chose a seat near the back and dropped her backpack on the floor. She scanned the classroom and pulled out her cell phone, sending a quick text to Mel.

Taylor: Hey. I made it to my first class. Wish me luck!

She waited a few minutes, but Mel didn't reply. Taylor had expected a good luck text or a phone call on her first day of classes. *Hmm. Maybe she's busy at work.*

Taylor slid her phone back into her pocket and waited for class to begin. A few minutes later, the classroom was nearly full.

Professor Storia called the class to attention. "Hello, everyone. I'm Professor Storia. This is Introduction to Demon Hunter History, so if that doesn't sound right, I suggest you check your schedule and figure out where you're supposed to be."

A nervous-looking young boy, about twelve or thirteen and wearing round glasses, scrambled to gather his belongings and raced out of the classroom.

"There's always at least one," Professor Storia said in a lighthearted tone. "Since that's out of the way, everyone, please get out your textbooks. We're going to start by going over the basics. This will be old news to most of you, but I promise it's essential to understand where we came from and how we got here before we move on to more complicated matters." He cleared his throat and rifled through his own worn copy of the textbook. "Your assignment for this week is to read the first three chapters. You all know there were five original demon hunter families. Two hundred years ago, when the demon population started to grow out of control, the demon hunters were created to take care of them. Killing demons is the only way to stop them. They can also be banished, but that usually takes a group of experienced demon hunters, and it shouldn't be attempted by anyone inexperienced." Professor Storia paused and eyed Taylor.

Taylor felt all eyes on her at the comment. Everyone must have heard by now about what happened this summer. She sank down in her seat, wanting to disappear.

When the bell rang an hour and a half later, Taylor leaped to her feet and practically ran out of the classroom.

A small girl with shoulder-length red hair and freckles kept pace with her. "Hi, I'm Molly Ellis," the girl said, sticking out her hand for Taylor to shake.

Taylor halted to talk to her. "Grace's little sister? I'm Taylor. Nice to meet you."

Molly threw her arms up in the air. "Why is that the first question everyone asks? Yes, I'm her sister, but I'm my own person."

Taylor laughed nervously. "Sorry, I didn't mean it like that."

"It's fine. So I guess we'll have some classes together since you're behind. What do you have next?" Molly asked.

"Um, Basic Spells."

"Cool. Me too. Wanna walk there together?"

Taylor smiled. "Sure."

"So what do you think of Grimwood Magical Academy so far?" Molly asked. "Pretty impressive, right?"

"Yeah, the campus is beautiful. I'm excited to learn more spells and continue my demon hunter training," Taylor said.

Molly tilted her head. "I heard you've been training with Julian Cromwell." A mischievous smile snuck across her face. "I'm jealous. He's one of the cutest guys on campus."

"Is he? I hadn't noticed," Taylor said.

"I bet he's a great teacher." Molly sighed dreamily.

"He's okay," Taylor replied, not wanting to give too much away about their relationship.

"Really? Just okay? That's all I get?" Julian interrupted, coming up behind them. He planted a kiss on the top of Taylor's head. "Gotta run. I'm almost late for my next class, but I'll text you later."

"Sounds good. Bye," Taylor called after him, her face a bright red from the unexpected public display of affection.

Molly turned to her, smirking. "Uh huh. That's what I thought."

"Oh, whatever. Come on. We'll be late for our next class," Taylor said.

Chapter 26

Taylor

Taylor entered the classroom with Molly. "Where do you want to sit?"

"In the front," Molly replied, choosing a seat in the center of the front row.

Taylor sat next to her. "I can't wait to start practicing spells."

"Me too. But I think Demon Hunter Missions 101 is the class I'm looking forward to the most." Molly grinned.

As they chatted, more students filed into the classroom. Eventually, a woman with curly, reddish-brown hair entered the room and started writing on the chalkboard.

Taylor glanced at Molly curiously. "That's the professor?" she whispered.

Molly shrugged a shoulder. "I guess so."

"She looks really young," Taylor replied.

The woman turned around to face the class. "Hi, students. I'm Professor Helena Magos. I've only been teaching at Grimwood Magical Academy for three years, but I was a demon hunter for five years before I started teaching. Today we'll begin with a basic spell since, after all, that's the name of the class. I'm assuming you're all familiar with *aeris*. Who knows what this spell is used for?"

Professor Magos looked out at the students and called on Molly.

"The *aeris* spell, or air spell, can be used to manipulate wind and even create storms for more experienced demon hunters. It can be used to lift heavy objects, breathe in high altitudes, and bring forth bursts of speed and larger leaps," Molly recited, as if reading directly from the textbook.

Taylor stared at her new friend in awe. The Ellis sisters were incredible. She wondered if their older brother, Oliver, was as smart as they were.

"Very good, Ms. Ellis. I taught your older sister, Grace, my first year here. I expect you'll be just as impressive in this class as she was," Professor Magos said.

Molly's cheeks flushed. "Thank you, Professor."

Professor Magos pulled out a large cardboard box from behind her desk. She opened it and started taking out objects. Since Taylor and Molly were in the front row, they leaned forward to see better. Professor Magos lined up flat stones on her desk.

"Everyone should have their textbook for the class with them. You can reference that for the *aeris* spell. After you have the spell memorized, come up here and choose a stone. We're going to practice making the stones float today. If you're able to master that, then move on to practicing with your textbooks. Those are quite a bit heavier, so I imagine that will take up the rest of the class period." Professor Magos eyed Taylor. "If anyone needs further instructions, please come see me. I'll demonstrate first, so you can see how it's done."

Professor Magos picked up a stone and set it on the ground in front of her desk. She cleared her throat and gestured with her right hand at the stone. "*Aeris*!"

The stone floated up toward the ceiling until Professor Magos reached out her hand to grab it. "And that is how it's done." She set the stone back with the others.

The students all clapped.

"Keep in mind that as your magic grows more powerful and you become more experienced, you will no longer need to recite the spells out loud. Focus and intent are everything," Professor Magos told the class.

Murmurs filled the room as everyone recited the spell.

Taylor opened her textbook to the basic spells section. "*Aeris . . . aeris . . . aeris . . .*"

Molly stood and walked to the pile of stones, then went back to her desk. Taylor turned toward her to watch her perform the spell.

Molly set the stone on her desk and stood up straight with her shoulders pulled back. In a clear, sharp voice, she said, "*Aeris.*" The stone floated into the air. Molly jumped up and down, clapping.

Taylor grinned. "Good job."

Molly grabbed the stone and set it back on her desk. Then she shot a smile at Taylor. "Thanks. I'm sure you'll get it too."

At this point, most of the other students were attempting the spell. Molly was the quickest one to successfully make the stone float, while the others had varying degrees of success. Taylor stood slowly. She couldn't waste the entire class period without even attempting the spell.

She carefully selected a stone and returned to her desk, setting the stone in the center of the desk. She flexed her fingers and mimicked Molly's perfect posture as she recited the spell. "*Aeris.*"

Nothing happened.

Taylor hadn't felt the magic like she had before when attempting spells. She flexed her fingers again and gestured to the stone. "*Aeris.*"

She rolled her shoulders back a few times and cleared her throat, willing the magic to travel through her body to her fingers. She concentrated on the stone, letting the world around her vanish. She flicked her wrist toward the stone. "*Aeris!*"

The stone shot up into the air, hitting the ceiling and causing a chunk of the plaster to come down. The stone fell back down at an alarming speed, causing nearby students, including Molly, to disperse.

Whispers surrounded Taylor as she picked up the stone and set it back on Professor Magos's desk. Her cheeks burned as she caught snippets of the other students' conversations.

"Do you think it's really her?" one student asked.

"It can't be. She didn't grow up in our world."

"Yeah, but look what she did to the ceiling! New demon hunters don't have that kind of power."

". . . the prophecy talks about it . . ."

"We didn't know when or who it would be . . ."

"The Chosen One . . ."

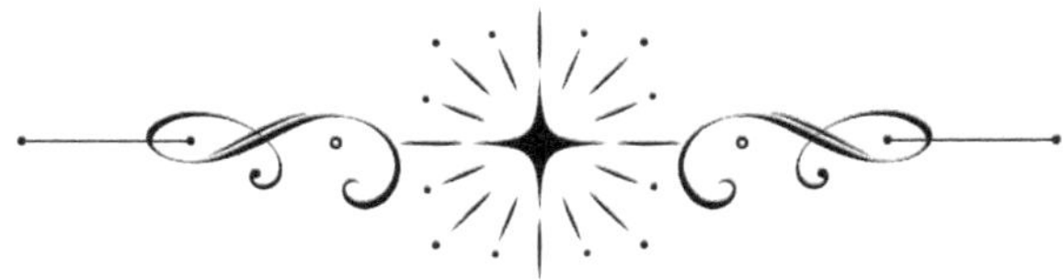

When the bell rang, Taylor sprinted out of the classroom without waiting for Molly. This time, she was able to make it to the next building before she caught up.

Molly fell into step beside her. "Geez, you're fast. You should consider trying out for the track team."

Taylor rolled her eyes. "Funny. I wanted to get out of there."

Molly put her hand on her shoulder. "Hey, it's okay. I'm sure it's hard with everyone at school knowing who you are and judging you for what happened this summer."

"No, that's not it. I mean, sort of, but . . . Did you hear what they were saying about The Chosen One? Apparently, some people think it's me," Taylor said.

Molly raised her eyebrows. "Yeah, I heard it, but they don't have any proof. So you sent a stone flying up to the ceiling? It's not a big deal." She gave Taylor a brief hug. "Come on, let's go to our next class."

Taylor smiled, thankful for Molly's presence. Even if some people at school didn't like her or were spreading rumors about her, she was glad Grace and Molly had her back.

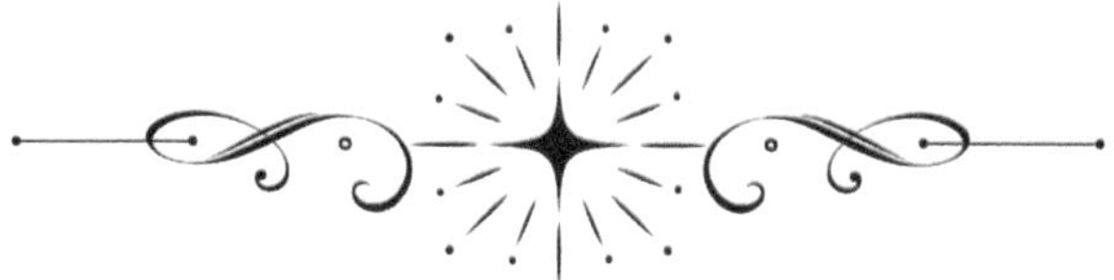

Julian had texted her to meet him in the cafeteria for lunch. She had eagerly agreed, especially since her first day of classes hadn't been going at all how she had hoped.

As soon as his striking blue eyes and smirk turned in her direction, she felt a flutter in her stomach.

"Hi, Julian," she said, walking up to him.

"Hi, Taylor," he replied, wrapping her in his arms.

She put her hand on his chest, relaxing almost immediately.

"You okay?" he asked, pulling back slightly to look at her. His eyebrows were drawn together.

"Yeah, it's just been a rough day," Taylor replied.

"Well, maybe eating and talking to me will help," Julian said, lacing his fingers through hers and leading her to the food line.

After they had selected their lunches, they found a quiet table near the back of the cafeteria and sat down.

Julian took a bite of his chicken Caesar wrap. "So what's wrong?"

Taylor shook her head, feeling silly. "It's nothing. How's your day been?" she asked, changing the subject.

Julian peered at her, his blue eyes piercing through her. "Are you sure? I'm here if you need to talk. I can only imagine how hard it must be starting at the school when you're already fifteen."

"I'm fine," Taylor said.

"You should eat." Julian nudged her.

Taylor took a few half-hearted bites out of her wrap and then nibbled on her pasta salad.

Julian demolished his food and stood. "I'm ready for dessert. What about you? I think I saw cookies today."

"Sure."

Julian narrowed his eyes at her. "I've never seen you so indifferent about food before, especially sweets." He glanced at the clock on the wall. I have to get to my next class soon, but wanna meet up for training tonight? We can talk then."

"Sounds good," Taylor replied. She stood too and walked out of the cafeteria with him.

He snagged two cookies on the way out and handed her one. "They're almost as sweet as you." Julian kissed her on the cheek.

Taylor smiled, feeling slightly better. "Thanks." She bit the cookie. "You're right."

Julian laughed. "Don't forget about training later. I hope your day gets better. And if not, I'll make sure it ends on a good note." He waved as he headed off to his next class.

Taylor finished the cookie, then went to her next class—Self-Defense with Professor Alice Bellum.

Chapter 27

Taylor

Self-Defense was one of the classes Taylor had been looking forward to the most. She couldn't wait to learn more about how to defend herself as a demon hunter. This seemed especially important after Mel lost her magic.

Once again, Taylor and Molly sat beside each other in the front row, eagerly waiting for class to start. A petite woman entered the room. Her short, black hair curled at the ends, and her brown eyes shone with a mischievous edge.

"Hello, students. My name is Professor Alice Bellum. I'm the professor for Self-Defense for beginners. We're going to start off today by learning about the basics of self-defense. This class won't only include defending yourself against demons, but also against other supernatural creatures and even other demon hunters. You never know when you'll need an evasive maneuver to get yourself out of a sketchy situation. Magic is powerful, and we're blessed to have such gifts, but there may come a time when your magical energy is depleted or, for some reason, you can't tap in to your powers. So what do you do in those instances?"

Most of the students shared uneasy glances at this statement and muttered to each other, but Taylor merely nodded at Professor Bellum's words. She knew all too well how useful self-defense skills were in life-or-death situations. If she had known some self-defense moves when she encountered Ammitt and Camille over the summer, she could have stopped the demon lord sooner. Maybe she could have saved Camille.

Taylor tuned back in to Professor Bellum's lecture about a basic self-defense move they would be practicing in class tomorrow. She hastily opened her textbook and skimmed the first chapter as the professor spoke. She was eager to learn how to defend herself, not just with magic, but with physical strength and finesse too.

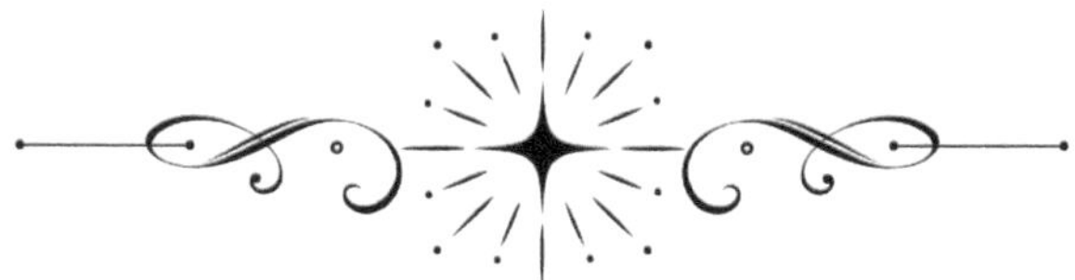

By the time Taylor got to her last class of the day, Demon Hunter Missions 101 with Professor Catie Caldwell, she was already getting used to all the whispers and sideways glances from her classmates. She hadn't anticipated how embarrassing it would be for everyone to know who she was and what she had done. The whispers were only compounded by the fact that everyone assumed she was The Chosen One. Taylor still wasn't entirely sure what that meant. She only knew it couldn't be true. She hadn't grown up with magic or demon hunting in her life. There was no way she could be the one to save humanity from the demons. The idea was laughable.

Professor Caldwell stood at the front of the classroom, her dark brown hair streaked with gray and held back with a large, sparkly purple scrunchie. She cleared her throat, and the classroom immediately devolved into silence.

"Hello, students," she greeted the class. "I'm Professor Catie Caldwell. You can call me Professor Caldwell or simply Professor."

"What about Catie?" a boy with short blond hair asked as his friends all snickered.

Professor Caldwell surprised Taylor by smirking. "Ha ha. Very funny. Today, we're going to start by discussing the basics of demon hunter missions. Does anyone know what the three basic rules are?"

Taylor slouched in her seat, hoping the professor didn't call on her, as she had hoped in every class that day.

Professor Caldwell met her eyes. "Ms. Windsor?"

"Um, the three basic rules are . . ." Taylor cleared her throat, stalling for time.

Molly shot her a sympathetic look and raised her hand eagerly, waving her arm around in the air.

Professor Caldwell smiled and acknowledged Molly. "Yes, Ms. Ellis?"

Molly sat up straight in her chair. "The three basic rules of demon hunter missions are: one, stay vigilant; two, assess the situation; and three, retreat if necessary."

"Very good," Professor Caldwell said. "For those of you who don't yet have the basic rules memorized, I suggest some extra studying to catch up. Anyone who needs more help, please stay after class to speak with me." She turned back to the whiteboard and grabbed a dry erase marker. "Now, who knows the list of supplies demon hunters should bring on every mission?"

Several hands shot up.

Taylor sank lower in her chair, as she realized how far behind the other students she was. This was going to be a long semester.

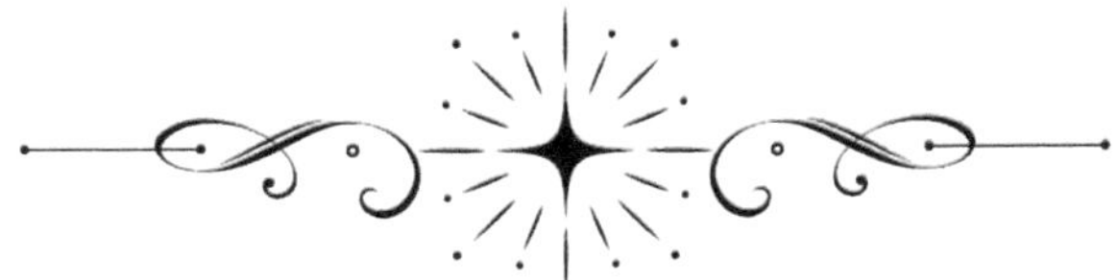

Time crawled by for the next hour, but eventually, it was 4:40 and class was over. Taylor had a break for a little over an hour to eat dinner before her first tutoring session. She left the classroom without waiting for Molly, not wanting to deal with the embarrassment all over again.

As she strode down the hallway, a voice called out, "Taylor, wait for me!"

Taylor turned around to see Molly scrambling to catch up to her, her backpack slipping off her shoulders and her red hair flying wildly around her face. She sighed and stopped walking.

"Where are you heading? Do you want to get dinner together?" Molly asked.

"Sure. I have my first tutoring session at 6:00, though," Taylor replied.

"That's fine. There shouldn't be too many people in the dining hall right now, since it's still early. Maybe Grace can meet us there too," Molly said, pulling out her phone, presumably to text her older sister.

When they reached the dining hall, it was mostly empty, with only a handful of students eating an early dinner. Taylor and Molly scouted out their meal options. They both chose lasagna, breadsticks, and mixed veggies, agreeing they would get ice cream afterward.

As they sat down at a table near the windows, Taylor spotted Grace coming their way.

"Hey! I just got out of my last class. I'll grab some food and join you," Grace said.

"Sounds good." Taylor smiled at her roommate.

"We're not waiting for you to start eating," Molly said, shoving a large forkful of lasagna into her mouth.

Grace rolled her eyes and headed toward the hot meal options.

Taylor started eating too and was enjoying the meal until Molly interrupted. "What did you think of all the classes today?"

"They were fine," Taylor replied.

"Fine? Aren't you excited to learn more about the demon hunter world and expand your abilities?" Molly asked.

"I would be happy with learning how to keep my abilities in check," Taylor lamented.

"Hmm, good point. Sorry about answering the question about the three demon hunter mission rules in Professor Caldwell's class, by the way. I didn't mean to—"

"No, it's fine. I didn't know the answer. Thanks for jumping in," Taylor said.

"No problem. My older brother Oliver graduated last year, and Grace is always studying, so it's impossible for me not to pick up on this stuff at home. Being the youngest demon hunter in a family full of successful demon hunters is never dull," Molly said.

"What does Oliver do now that he's a full-fledged demon hunter? Like, what are your options after graduation?" Taylor asked curiously, scooping up a serving of mixed veggies.

"Oh, well . . . I guess you could say Oliver hasn't taken the traditional path. After graduation, most demon hunters team up with an experienced demon hunter and go on missions with them for a while. He didn't want to do that. He's mostly been sitting at home in his room. I think he only went on one or two missions before he gave up." Molly shrugged. "I don't know what his problem is. I can't wait to go on missions!"

Just then, Grace joined them. She set her tray on the table and straightened her purple polo before sitting down. "Are you talking about Oliver?"

"Yup," Molly replied, tearing off a piece of her breadstick and dipping it into marinara sauce.

"Have you heard from Mom and Dad lately?" Grace asked her sister.

"Not much," Molly said through her mouth full of breadstick, then finished chewing it. "I thought it was weird because they seemed so worried about their 'youngest baby' going off to the academy."

Grace narrowed her eyes, still not touching her food. "Hmm. I think something might be going on with Oliver."

Molly didn't have much of a reaction. She simply continued eating her dinner. "Like what? Besides the usual, I mean. Ha."

"I'm not sure yet. Maybe drugs or . . . or something really bad," Grace elaborated.

"What other ways are there to get into trouble in the demon hunter world?" Taylor asked. "What do teenagers do when they rebel here?"

Molly snickered. "Oh, all sorts of things. Attempting advanced spells while being underage or without adult supervision from an experienced demon hunter. Going on dangerous missions or trying to confront a demon or supernatural creature underage. Then, of course, there are the normal things most human teenagers do. Drinking, drugs, sneaking out . . ." Molly listed the illicit activities one by one on her fingers.

"That isn't all, though," Grace interjected. "There are some demon hunters who don't believe in sending their children to schools like Grimwood Magical Academy. They train their kids themselves. There are rumors of dark magic and deals with demons. But the worst part of it all is that they aren't Shadow Bound."

"Shadow Bound? I think I've heard of that before. What does it mean?" Taylor squinted, trying to recall where she heard the phrase. Then it struck her. The Demon Lord Ammitt had mentioned it in the clearing before he killed Camille.

Grace took a deep breath before answering. "It's a ceremony that happens after graduation. Only demon hunters who have successfully completed their training go through the ceremony. I only know what my parents have warned me about, which is that if you're a demon hunter and you turn eighteen without being Shadow Bound, you won't live to see your nineteenth year."

Mel

"Please . . . please. You have to let me go. Taylor will be so worried when she doesn't hear from me," Mel begged.

She was chained to a pole in the Ellises' basement, where she had been kept for two days. Without her magic, the situation was hopeless. Her only chance to escape was to plead with Vanessa to let her go.

But Vanessa was relentless. She only cared about one thing, everyone else be damned. "I wish it didn't have to be this way," was all she said as she started up the stairs. She had left a tray of food and a water bottle for Mel. "Be sure to eat every last bite. We don't want you going hungry. You need your vitamins and nutrients for Oliver."

The door shut a moment later, leaving Mel alone once again. She stared forlornly down at the tray—steak, a baked potato, asparagus, and a chocolate chip cookie. It smelled delicious, but she wasn't sure she could make herself eat any of it. Her stomach was in knots as she obsessed over ways to escape.

Constant worry filled her mind about Taylor and what she would do when she realized Mel was missing. They had made plans for Mel to come to the academy for a visit this weekend. They were going to celebrate Taylor getting through her first week of classes. That meant Mel had three days to escape. Three days to find a way out before Taylor guessed something was wrong. Maybe a little longer if Taylor didn't panic right away.

The main problem was whom Taylor would go to if she thought Mel was in trouble. If she told Kylie or Sarah, they would contact the police. While that would be helpful in a normal missing-persons scenario, Mel didn't think a human police officer would react very well to the sight of a vampire. Besides the Andersons, Taylor seemed to have gotten closer to Julian during their training sessions. In fact, Mel suspected Taylor had a crush on him, which was fine—but would she ask for his help in finding her? If Julian told his parents, who knew how they would react? They might say good riddance and let it be. After all, the Cromwells weren't exactly her biggest fans.

As unlikely as it was, Mel hoped Taylor told Headmistress Lockwood or one of her professors. That would be the best solution. Last time she heard from Taylor, she hadn't started her classes yet, but she should have met her professors by now. The headmistress or any of the professors were powerful and intelligent enough to track her down if they were alerted to the situation.

Mel adjusted her position on the cool, polished concrete floor, touching the silver chain around her ankle again. It was no use. Besides, Vanessa was right. She needed to keep up her strength. Not for Oliver to feed on her again . . . but so she could get the hell out of here.

TAYLOR

Taylor had survived her first day of classes. She was on her way to meet Julian for a training session. After meeting some of her classmates and finding out how much they already knew about the demon hunter world, their history, and magic, she knew she still had lots of catching up to do. Thankfully, her training with Julian over the summer had helped prepare her a little. She wasn't mad about needing more lessons with her cute new boyfriend. Although she worried it might make training more difficult.

Julian had requested that Taylor meet him in the gymnasium. It wasn't being used for any events that evening, so the giant, open room was all theirs. Taylor had left Brody in her dorm room under the care of Grace, who had been all too happy to have a cuddly study buddy for the night.

After walking across campus, Taylor entered the gymnasium. She hadn't seen this building yet because she wasn't involved in any sports and she wasn't taking any fitness classes this semester. She would have to in the spring semester, though, so getting in shape was important.

As she entered the building, Taylor spotted Julian in the corner, laying down some practice mats.

"Hey," she called out softly.

"Hey," Julian replied, placing the last mat on the floor and greeting her with a kiss on her cheek.

Taylor flung her arms around his neck. "We don't have to train, you know. We could practice other things instead."

Julian's blue eyes smoldered at her. He pulled her to his chest and held her tightly in his arms for a minute before replying. "We could, but you need to train. We can't have The Chosen One being taken advantage of or shown up by some regular old demon hunter."

Taylor leaned her head against his chest, hiding her face. "So, you heard the rumors . . ."

"Yeah, everyone's talking about it."

Taylor stepped back from him with a hard glint in her eyes.

"Sorry. They are. I'm just being honest. And they're probably right, you know. Who else would it be?" Julian asked.

Taylor's gaze dropped to the ground as she backed further away from Julian's warm embrace. "But how can it be me? I don't know the first thing about being a demon hunter! I only learned about this world a few months ago. I'm years behind you and all of our classmates. I already feel like I'm struggling in my classes, even though they're all introductory classes. I can't control my magic, much less use it the way I want to, yet everyone thinks I'll be the one to save the world from demons. How can that be possible?"

Julian brushed his fingers against her cheek softly. "Because I believe in you. You're powerful. Even if you don't know how to fully use your powers yet, you'll get there eventually. And I'll be there every step of the way. I'm sure Grace and Molly will too. And Mel, of course. You have people who care about you, people who want to help you succeed. Not everyone is blessed enough to have people like that in their lives."

Taylor's stomach plummeted. "I know what you're trying to say, but I would give all of this up"—she waved her hand around the gymnasium—"if it meant getting my parents back."

"What are you saying? You wouldn't . . ." Julian gulped loudly. "You wouldn't use dark magic to try to bring them back from the dead, would you? Because it's never been done successfully before, and I don't know if it's possible, even for someone with as much power as you."

"No, no. Of course not." Taylor shook her head. "I'm not interested in dark magic. I just miss them." Taylor wrapped her arms around herself as a slight chill grew in the air. The air conditioning must have kicked on in the gymnasium.

Julian brushed a few stray hairs away from her face and gently pressed his lips to her forehead. "I know. I'm sorry. I shouldn't have said—"

"It's fine." Taylor cleared her throat and moved toward the practice mats, tightening her ponytail. "Are you ready?" she asked with a faux grin, masking her sadness.

"Are you okay, Taylor? We don't have to train today if you aren't feeling up to it. There's always tomorrow. We can go back to my dorm and watch a movie and eat popcorn."

"As tempting as that offer is, I need to train. If I really am The Chosen One, I need to prove I'm worthy," Taylor said. "I need to be prepared for anything."

Julian smiled at her. "I can help with that."

He lunged toward her with a jab of his fist, but Taylor quickly side-stepped away from him. Taylor faked to the left, then swung hard to the right and managed to punch Julian's shoulder. He grinned and shot forward, sweeping her legs out from under her, so she fell on the mat, landing on her butt.

"Ow. Why are you always making me fall on my butt?" Taylor groaned, lying down on the mat on her back.

Julian lay down next to her and entwined his fingers in hers. "Because you look so cute from this angle."

Taylor laughed and squeezed his hand, then jumped back onto her feet. "Come on. Let's go again. I'm just getting started."

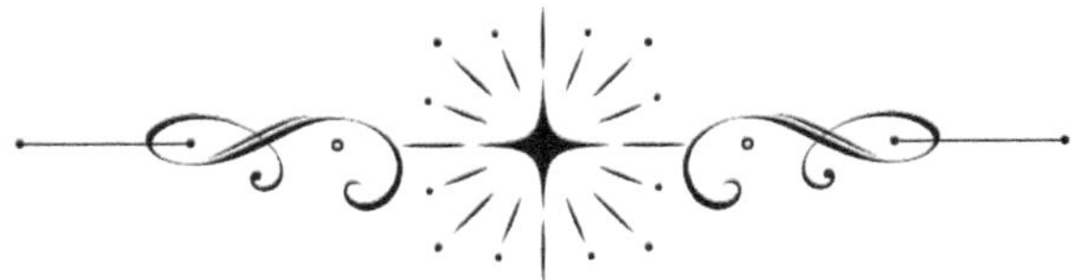

An hour later, Taylor was sprawled out on her bed with Brody curled up near her feet and Grace sitting in front of her desk across the room.

"Still studying?" Taylor asked her roommate.

Grace closed the textbook she had been reading. "I think I'm done for the night. How was training with Julian?" she asked with a smirk, drawing out the way she said his name.

"It was fine. Exhausting, though." Taylor covered her mouth with her hand as she yawned. "I think I'm going to go take a shower before bed. I'll be back in a bit."

"Okay. I'll be here," Grace said.

Taylor selected a pair of pajamas and her shower supplies, then headed to the bathroom down the hall. Sharing a bathroom with so many other girls hadn't been fun to adjust to. In fact, she couldn't say she was used to it. It was a pain.

She set her clothes and shower supplies down on the bench outside one of the shower stalls and reached inside the stall to turn on the water, letting it heat up before slipping into the stall and shedding her dirty workout clothes.

As Taylor scrubbed her hair with shampoo, she heard footsteps scampering across the tile floors of the bathroom. It wasn't that late, so someone else must be showering or brushing their teeth. But then she heard what sounded like someone pacing right outside her shower stall. Clutching the shower curtain closed in her hand, she called out, "Hello?"

The only answer was a swishing sound against the floor.

"Hmm, weird." Taylor shut off the shower and reached her hand outside the curtain to grab her clean clothes. She didn't feel anything.

She peeked her head out, not seeing anyone, and realizing with a sinking sensation that her clothes weren't there either.

"Seriously?" she muttered, searching under the bench and spotting her clothes. *Maybe they fell under the bench. How would they have fallen, though?* That didn't make sense unless someone had moved them there.

She bent down to grab her clothes as a snake with glowing red eyes slithered out from underneath the bench, its tongue darting out of its mouth as it hissed.

Taylor screamed and jumped back into the shower stall. She hurriedly put on her clothes.

She gathered up her shower stuff and slowly pulled the shower curtain back again, checking for the snake. It was gone. Taylor darted out of the bathroom and hurried down the hallway to her dorm. Once she was safely inside, a sob wrenched its way out of her throat.

Grace turned to her with widened eyes as Taylor entered their dorm. "Everything okay?"

A few tears slid down her cheeks, but Taylor nodded. "While I was showering, I heard someone in the bathroom. When I was done with my shower, I found my clothes underneath the bench, and . . ." She paused. "There was a snake."

Grace gasped. "What? Why was there a snake in the bathroom? What kind of snake was it? Should we tell the headmistress?"

Taylor shrugged a shoulder. "I don't know. After I got dressed, the snake was gone."

"But where did it go? It could have slithered down the hall and gone into someone's dorm. If it's poisonous, someone could get hurt."

As Grace spoke, Taylor thought through the situation. An unusual animal with glowing red eyes . . . It was there one minute and then disappeared shortly after. Was it possible that Ammitt had another form? He appeared as a crow before, but could he turn into a snake too? But how would he have re-entered the mortal realm after the banishment spell? He shouldn't be able to return.

Taylor said, "I must have pissed off the wrong person."

Grace frowned, scooting forward on her bed. "Girls can be mean, but I don't know why someone would mess with you like that. We've only been on campus for a week and a half, so it's not like you know that many people yet. And to find a snake and put it in the bathroom while you're showering . . ." Grace shook her head. "That's so dangerous."

"Unless . . . Do you think Julian's ex, Sophie, would do something like that? Maybe she's jealous that Julian has a new girlfriend," Taylor hypothesized.

"Hmm, I don't know about that. Sophie is pretty confident and self-assured. She cheated on Julian with his best friend, so I don't know why she would be mad about Julian moving on. She moved on first, or at least she pretended to."

"Who else would already hate me so much this early in the school year?" Taylor asked, fear flitting across her body as the answer sounded in her mind. All signs pointed to one thing.

It had to be a demon.

Chapter 30

Mel

Two days until Mel was supposed to visit Taylor at Grimwood Magical Academy. Two days left for her to find a way to escape. Or a way to convince one of the Ellises to let her leave. All she needed was for one of them to see the error of their ways and let her go. So far, she had only seen Vanessa and Oliver, though, which had made her contemplate if the others even knew she was being held captive in the basement. And she wasn't sure Oliver counted, considering he was a newborn vampire, devoid of any emotion or thought besides his relentless thirst for blood.

Grace and Molly—the other two Ellis children—attended Grimwood Magical Academy, so they might not be aware of the situation. Mel had the feeling that their parents had hidden Oliver's condition from them, not wanting to take the chance of Oliver feeding on one of their daughters. As far as Randall went, Mel wasn't sure if he knew about Vanessa's actions. Mel hadn't seen him since being locked in the basement. If Randall found out she was there, she might be able to convince him to release her.

"Come on. Feeding time," Vanessa commanded, startling Mel from her plans of escape. "Did you eat all of your dinner?" Vanessa glanced down at the mostly empty tray and made a *tsk*ing noise.

A pile of green spears remained on the tray. Mel hated asparagus.

"You really need to eat *every last bite*, Mel. It's important for—"

"For what? For me to let your bloodsucking son feed from me? You need to tell the council what happened to him, Vanessa. You can't hide this forever. They might be able to help, and you can't keep me down here—"

"Don't you think I've thought about that already?" Vanessa hissed, her dark eyes flashing in the dim light from the single bulb hanging in the basement. "Don't you think I've contemplated every possible scenario to save my son? You have no idea what I would do for him, the lengths I would go to. You couldn't *possibly* understand because you aren't a parent."

The comment stung in more ways than one. Especially since Mel had taken in Taylor two months ago and had taken responsibility as her guardian after her parents died. She was Taylor's legal guardian. At least for a little over two years until she turned eighteen, but she would be there for her after that too. She thought of herself as more than just Taylor's legal guardian; she was her parent.

Mel did all the things a parent would do—she bought her clothes, school supplies, and a new laptop. She provided her a home, a safe space to live. She fed her; although she was a terrible cook, Taylor never went hungry. She was there for her after the grief of losing her parents. Mel hung out with her and took her on adventures—whether it was watching scary movies, hiking, trying rock climbing for the first time, or confronting a demon she had accidentally been tricked into a deal with. She did her best to protect Taylor and look out for her. She had Taylor's best interests at heart, even if it meant she sometimes screwed up. All parents screwed up sometimes, and Mel was new to this. But most importantly, Mel loved Taylor so much that she couldn't handle thinking about what would happen to Taylor if Mel was dead.

She knew, without a doubt in her mind, that she would do anything for Taylor to give her the best shot at life. Vanessa was wrong. Mel might not have been Taylor's parent biologically, but that didn't mean she loved her any less.

If Taylor wanted to stay with her, even after she was an adult and had graduated from the academy, Mel would be more than happy to agree to it. Wasn't there more to being a parent than being pregnant and giving birth? Or simply letting a kid live in your house? Or raising a child from being an infant to an adult? Wasn't it possible to be a parent without physically having anything to do with the child being born? There were all sorts of families. Blood meant nothing if your parents didn't love you and look out for your wellbeing. Mel was Taylor's parent in all the ways that counted.

Vanessa unlocked the chain from around Mel's ankle. She was allowed a daily twenty-minute walk around the basement. Mel spit into Vanessa's face and scratched her eye with her sharp fingernails.

Vanessa jerked back and screamed. Mel shot for the stairs. She sprinted up them two at a time. Then she flung open the door. She raced down the hallway, her feet bare and dirty. She hoped the dirt stained the beautiful hardwood floor. She stumbled into the kitchen and glanced around. She must have gone down the hallway too far.

She heard a door close. Before she could hide, she spotted Randall near the entryway. He froze at the sight of her, his stocky legs halting in their path. He stared down at her, his hook nose prominent as he stared in disbelief.

"Mel?" he questioned, as if he couldn't believe his eyes.

"Randall, you have to let me out of here. Please." Mel closed the gap between them, grabbing his shirt sleeve in desperation.

"What are you talking about? What's going on? Why are you here?" Randall asked, eyeing her disheveled appearance.

"I don't have much time before Vanessa comes up here. She's been holding me hostage in your basement and making your son feed off of me. Please help. Please let me—"

"Oliver?" Randall questioned, clearly struggling to piece together what was going on. "Something happened to my son. He's been sick . . ." his words trailed off.

"*He isn't sick*. He's a vampire, and Vanessa's been hiding it from everyone. Please. I need to leave before she lets him kill me," Mel said.

"Oh no. We have to get you out of here."

It seemed that Randall hadn't known the fate of his son yet, either. Vanessa must have acted on her own.

"Thank you. You're a good person, Randall." Mel edged around him, clasping the doorknob.

As she was opening the door, a cold voice came from the basement stairs. "Where do you think you're going, Mel? We aren't done with you yet."

"Vanessa, what's going on?" Randall asked, confusion painting his features.

Mel fully opened the door, preparing to bolt, but she was yanked back the second she stepped foot outside. The gentle giant pulled her back into the house and shut the door softly.

"I'm sorry, Mel, but I need to hear my wife out," Randall said, imploring her to understand with his kind brown eyes.

Mel's soul deflated like a balloon losing the rest of its helium. She had held out hope that Randall would let her go. But she wasn't going anywhere.

Mel

One day left until I'm supposed to visit Taylor at Grimwood Magical Academy. Only one more day to escape this hellhole before this situation gets interesting. Although there's a chance Grace and Molly will come home for the weekend. I might be able to convince one of them to let me out. Surely, they won't go along with their parents' scheme . . .

Mel resisted the urge to scratch her forearm, particularly around the wrist. Bite marks pierced her skin, adding to her blemishes and freckles. Of course, the bite marks stood out more, as they were unnatural. She hoped her arm wouldn't get infected from all the bites. It was possible, although it wasn't the worst thing that could happen after a vampire fed on a person. The worst scenario would be if they got carried away, couldn't stop feeding, and ended up killing you. She knew a decent amount about vampires. It was required at the academy to take a basic class or two to learn about the other types of supernatural beings. The demon hunters viewed vampires the same way they viewed demons—and most other supernatural beings—as evil.

The main difference was that demons tended to be the most powerful beings besides demon hunters, and vampires were a rare occurrence now. Most of them had been killed about fifty years ago, when Mel's parents were two of the most powerful demon hunters and had been at the top of their game. They had helped vanquish most of them.

Not for the first time, Mel wondered how Oliver's new "friends" had found a vampire. They weren't common in this area. They preferred cooler climates with minimal sunlight and a more robust human population—or at least a higher murder rate—so they could feed easily without being noticed. Not to mention the fact that they were so rare.

Mel had only encountered a vampire once, and the memory was burned into her mind forever, since she and Christa had both nearly died.

When she was seventeen, her sister Christa, Taylor's mom, was nineteen and had already been a full-fledged demon hunter for over a year. Christa was requested on a mission deep in the mountains. She had asked Mel to tag along since she was close to graduating.

"It will be good experience," Christa had told her.

Mel groaned and rolled her eyes. "What's the mission? Something boring, like watch duty for supernatural beings?"

Christa smirked, pulling on her warm puffer coat and zipping it up all the way. "Nope. We're going to capture a vampire."

Mel gasped. "A vampire? But they're rarely seen around Grimwood."

"This one isn't in Grimwood. It's further north, deep in the mountains, where it's colder. In fact, there's probably snow there, so make sure to wear warm clothes and layers," Christa advised.

Mel pursed her lips. "Yeah, yeah. Fine, I'll come with you."

Mel hid her sudden excitement about encountering a vampire from her older sister. She didn't want to seem like the naïve teenager that she was. She wanted to prove herself to Christa, to show her that she was going to be a powerful demon hunter someday too. Not to mention, she was excited about what sounded like a cool, unique mission. Most students Mel's age didn't get many chances like this. But Christa told her that she had vouched for her to the council, and their parents had agreed.

Christa drove them to the section of the mountains where the vampire had last been spotted. She parked the car a little way away, not wanting to scare it away if it noticed them. All it would take was the vampire realizing there were two demon hunters close by for it to flee and go into hiding somewhere else. That would be good for the people here, but not for the humans wherever it went next. It was better to get rid of it as soon as possible.

Christa left the car and went to the back to open the trunk. Mel joined her sister.

Christa handed Mel one of the backpacks, while putting the other one on her own back. "Be quiet and follow me."

"Whatever you say, sis," Mel said cheerily.

Christa glared at her younger sister. "What did I literally just say?" she whispered.

"Sorry," Mel whispered back.

Christa locked the car and set off down the road. Mel followed her for what felt like hours, but logically, she knew it probably wasn't that long. Her legs ached from climbing up the steep incline of the mountain, the air becoming more frigid and harder to breathe in as the altitude increased. Her teeth chattered, gnashing together uncomfortably, despite the warm beanie on her head, her thick socks, fur-lined boots, and the multiple layers of clothes she wore underneath her warmest winter coat.

"We're almost there. It was spotted in one of the caves up here. We need to catch it off-guard and stab it with a stake through the heart," Christa whispered.

Mel huffed and nodded, not wanting to utter a word in case her sister yelled at her again. She wasn't dumb. She had taken the class about supernatural beings during her first year at Grimwood Magical Academy, so of course she knew how to kill a vampire. A stake through the heart. Holy water. Or burning it and destroying the ashes.

Breathing heavily from the cold and the exertion of hiking up the mountain, Mel hoped Christa was fit enough to take down the vampire by herself. Being a demon hunter was hard work.

"Ready?" Christa whispered as the trail curved around a corner.

Mel couldn't see what was around the corner, but she assumed it was the vampire's hideout. She squeezed her sister's shoulder to confirm she was ready.

Christa unzipped her backpack and pulled out a wooden stake. She hid it in her jacket pocket and crept around the corner, slinking into the cave. Mel followed her, her heart thundering in her chest as it never had before. As she began to question if they had picked the right cave, red eyes flashed in the darkness, maybe twenty feet further back.

"Christa!" she yelped, grabbing her sister's sleeve to get her attention. She pointed to the spot where she had seen the glowing red eyes. "I see it!"

"What did I tell you about staying quiet? Damn it, Mel," Christa chastised her, shoving her hand into her jacket pocket, then frantically into the other pocket. A look of complete and utter terror crossed Christa's face. Her older sister was always calm and collected. She was fearless, but just then, she looked terrified.

"What's wrong?" Mel asked, fear coating her throat and making it difficult to speak. She swallowed.

"My wooden stake! I must have dropped it. It isn't in either of my pockets."

The vampire must have seen them by now. It must be biding its time.

"Crap," Mel responded. "Hold on. I think I can help." She quickly yanked her backpack off and unzipped it. She didn't have a stake, but she had brought a vial of holy water as a backup. She held out the vial to Christa, but Christa was shaking and she could hear her sniffling.

"What— Are you crying?" Mel asked. She glanced back to where she had seen the vampire, but it was gone. "Christa! We don't have time for this. The vampire is—"

Christa screamed, a bloodcurdling scream riddled with fear and horror, as the vampire lunged toward her.

Mel darted forward, further into the cave, clutching the vial of holy water in her right hand. Red eyes flashed again. She didn't think or hesitate. She popped the cork off of the vial and splashed the holy water in the general direction of the floating red eyes, wishing she had better night vision.

She heard a horrific screeching sound and then the sound of something falling to the ground. "*Lux*," she muttered. A ball of white light appeared in her palm, and she used it to locate her sister.

Cowering against the wall, Christa was huddled next to a pile of ashes with her eyes shut tight.

Incredulous and wide-eyed, Mel stared at the ashes. Was that the vampire . . . or what remained of it?

"Did it work?" Mel whispered.

Christa opened her eyes and blinked, staring up at her. She examined the pile of ashes next to her, then stood on shaky legs. "I think so. C'mon. Let's leave."

"Wait. Don't we need proof that we killed it?" Mel asked.

"Oh. Right." Christa pulled a glass vial out of her backpack and a pair of gloves. She put the gloves on and scooped some of the ashes into the glass vial and placed it in her backpack. "Okay, we can go."

As they left the cave, Mel squinted from the sudden appearance of light, although it was nearly dusk. Compared to the suffocating darkness of the cave, it felt blindingly bright. Light and warm and welcoming.

"Are you okay?" Mel asked, pausing outside the cave.

Christa nodded. "Yeah. Sorry, I wasn't honest with you."

"About what?" Mel asked.

"I overheard Mom and Dad talking about the vampire. They were planning to send a team out tomorrow. I wanted to take it down by myself to prove I'm ready to go out on my own. I only asked you to come with me so I had proof. But now I'm glad you were with me. I don't know what I would have done if I had been alone." Christa clasped her gloved hand in Mel's as they headed back toward the car, walking side by side. "Thank you," Christa said, squeezing Mel's hand.

"You're welcome," Mel replied automatically, but she couldn't help but wonder what had made her strong, capable sister freeze in a life-or-death situation. Christa had been on dozens of missions during the last year, so why had she reacted like that? If it hadn't been for Mel's quick thinking, they would both be dead.

Mel felt someone roughly shake her, and she was brought back to the present, where she was in another life-or-death situation. If this was the end, well, she certainly couldn't say her life had been boring.

Mel

It was the final day. She was supposed to meet Taylor on campus this evening and bring her home for the weekend. Mel imagined Taylor might already be panicking a bit, assuming she had tried to contact her. It was the last day of the first week of classes, so Mel knew how stressed Taylor must be, especially considering she was still new to this life. She only hoped her niece was making friends and that her peers were nice to her. Mel wanted the best for Taylor, and that meant she had to find a way out of this stupid basement.

Footsteps sounded near the door, and Mel sucked in an anxious breath. Vanessa had taken her phone away when she abducted her, so she had no way of telling time. Did the footsteps belong to Vanessa, who was about to bring her dinner for the evening . . . so she could then be dinner for Oliver? Or was it someone else? If she had another chance to talk to Randall, she might be able to convince him to let her go. She had been so close before, her freedom just within reach . . .

She heard the door swing open and moved about restlessly, her chain rattling as she adjusted her position. Mel considered knocking Vanessa unconscious and waiting for another family member to come searching for her. It might not have been a great option, but it was an option. The longer she was stuck in their basement, the more desperate she became.

Footsteps tapped down the stairs, lighter and more graceful than Vanessa's. They reached the bottom of the staircase, and the light flickered on, revealing a teenage girl with red hair that fell to her butt and freckles scattered across her face. She hadn't seen her in years, but Mel guessed this was the Ellises' middle child.

"Grace?" Mel called out softly.

Grace blinked slowly at her, her green eyes appearing to not register the sight of a woman chained to a pole in her basement. She remained at the foot of the stairs. "I thought I heard something down here. Who are you? Why are you here?"

"Grace, please listen to me. Your parents are keeping me captive—"

"What?" Grace snapped. "They wouldn't do that unless you were being punished."

Mel hesitated, almost too scared to ask what she meant, but what did she have to lose at this point? "Punish me? For what?"

Grace took a step toward her. "For not obeying the council."

"Do you know who I am?"

Grace shrugged. "No. Does it matter?" She turned to leave, heading for the stairs again.

"I need to get out of here. I have plans to meet with Taylor today, and—"

Grace turned back around. "Taylor *who*?"

Mel jumped at the potential opportunity to capitalize on her niece. Grace might have met her. "My niece! Taylor Windsor, although she's from the Turner bloodline. Her dad was a Windsor. Do you know her?"

Grace paused before continuing toward her once again. "She's my roommate."

Mel's heart nearly leaped into her throat. That was the best possible news she could have heard. Taylor got along with most people, so she assumed they were friends. "I'm glad to hear that. I'm supposed to pick Taylor up from campus today, so she can come home for the weekend. How is she?"

"She's fine, just stressed about classes. She already feels like she's falling behind. Julian is still practicing with her, though, and I told her I would help too," Grace said.

"Thank you. I'm sure she appreciates the extra help." Mel smiled warmly, hoping it was enough. "Are your parents home?"

"No, they went grocery shopping or to run errands or something. I don't remember exactly where they went."

"Can you please let me out of here before they get back?"

"Are you going to tell the council what they did?" Grace pried, glaring at her. "And get them taken away from me and my siblings?"

Mel's tone softened. "No, I promise I won't tell a soul. I just want to get out of here and go home. I need to be with my niece. She must be so worried after not hearing from me for almost five days. She lost her parents, and she's . . . She's still very fragile . . ."

"Fine," Grace said, closing the remainder of the distance between them. She kneeled to touch the end of the chain. "*Magicae uptis.* Please come forth and allow me to harness my magic to break this chain."

The chain snapped where Grace had touched it, clanging onto the polished concrete floor.

Grace raised an eyebrow. "Well?"

Mel extended her hand and clasped Grace's hand in hers. "Thank you, Grace. Truly. You have no idea what it's been like . . ."

"You're welcome. You owe me. But for now, let's get you the heck out of here before one of my parents gets home."

Mel shoved away the idea of owing Grace a favor. The last time she owed someone a favor, she ended up locked in their basement. She could worry about what Grace wanted later.

What could the daughter of such twisted people want as a favor?

Chapter 33

Taylor

Bounding down the steps to the front hall, Taylor practically skipped as she left her dorm, with Brody trotting along beside her. His tail wagged with excitement, seeming as thrilled as her, as if he knew they were going home for the weekend. Taylor couldn't wait to spend the next few days with her aunt and tell her all about her classes. The weird thing was, she hadn't heard from Mel since classes had started, but she had brushed it off as her aunt being busy. She still didn't understand much about Mel's job, but she knew it was stressful and often demanded long hours. With Taylor gone, Mel must have thrown herself into her work as a distraction.

Taylor smiled at the thought of being reunited with her aunt. She had missed her so much the past week, but Mel had told her it would be good for her to get used to being independent. As much as Taylor hadn't liked the idea at first, Mel had been right. Taylor was forced to figure things out on her own, and she felt more like a responsible adult than ever. She hoped they could get in some practice driving this weekend. Her sixteenth birthday inched closer every day, and Taylor wanted to get her driver's license as soon as possible. Not to mention, turning sixteen in the demon hunter world meant something entirely different than it did in the human world.

Waiting outside the building, she commanded Brody to stay.

He plopped down on the sidewalk, pouting.

Brody probably wanted to run across campus or go on a walk since the weather was nice, but Taylor didn't want to miss Mel arriving at her building, especially since she had been so hard to reach lately. Grace had already left hours ago, since she had been called home for a family emergency. Once Taylor was on her own, she had quickly grown bored.

Taylor slunk down to sit beside Brody and leaned against the building. Brody shoved his head into her lap, peering up at her with his eyes wide and pleading.

She laughed and ruffled his fur. "Okay, come here," she relented, patting her lap.

Brody jumped into her lap and curled up, letting out a little sound of contentment.

A familiar voice came from down the sidewalk. "Well, isn't that the cutest thing I've ever seen?"

Julian came toward them, a broad grin stretching across his face. He sat down next to them and petted Brody as a greeting, then kissed Taylor on the cheek. "Hi."

Taylor blushed furiously and tried to hide her warm cheeks from him by turning away. "Hi, Julian."

"Why are you out here? Done with classes for the day?" he asked.

"Yeah. I'm waiting for Mel to pick me up." Taylor glanced at her phone again, frowning. "I thought she would be here by now, and she hasn't responded to my texts or phone calls."

Julian's giddy expression vanished. He leaned in close and gripped her shoulder. "How long has it been since you last heard from her? What did she say the last time you talked to her?"

Terror gripped Taylor in an icy chokehold. What if something was wrong with Mel? She hadn't wanted to consider it, but after everything they had gone through this summer and Julian's questions . . . How could she not assume the worst?

"Five days ago," Taylor choked out. "Do you think she's—"

Julian averted his eyes, clearly avoiding eye contact. "I'm sure she's fine." He loosened his hold on her shoulder and squeezed gently. "Did you try calling her?"

Taylor rolled her eyes. "Oh. Of course, why didn't I think of that?"

When Julian huffed in response without saying a word, Taylor added, "Yeah, I called her multiple times."

"Okay, then this might be an emergency."

"What kind of emergency?" Taylor questioned, gently pushing Brody off her lap and getting to her feet.

Julian stood too, placing his hand in hers and intertwining their fingers. "I'm not sure yet. Let's go talk to Headmistress Lockwood and see what she thinks. She'll know what to do."

Taylor nodded, swallowing past the lump in her throat. Where was Mel, and was she okay?

"Do you think Mel got involved with another demon? She doesn't have her magic anymore, so she's more vulnerable than before. What if—" Taylor ran through all the worst-case scenarios.

"Hey, slow down. We'll get this sorted out. Mel's tough, even without magic. I wouldn't mess with her," Julian joked, clearly trying to lighten the mood.

Taylor cracked a small smile. "I know, but still . . . What if something happened to her? I should have told the headmistress sooner. Or I should have asked you to take me home to check on her. I don't know what I was thinking. I just—"

Julian kissed the top of her head. "You didn't want to jump to the worst-case scenario after losing your parents, right? You didn't want to consider something like that happening again to someone you love."

Taylor swallowed uncomfortably, her heart pounding hard in her chest. She was just getting to know Mel. Her aunt wasn't a replacement for her mom, but she was a parental figure, all the same. Taylor couldn't imagine losing her now.

"She has to be okay, Julian. If she's not . . ." Taylor didn't dare finish the rest of her sentence.

A blue Subaru Outback pulled up to the administrative building they had been walking toward, where Headmistress Lockwood's office was.

Mel scrambled to get out of the car and slammed the door shut, racing into the building.

Taylor glanced at Julian before grabbing his hand and quickly following her aunt into the building. Why was Mel so late and ignoring her calls and texts? And why was she going to speak with the headmistress? Something was definitely wrong.

Chapter 34

Taylor

"Mel?" Taylor yelled in a voice much too loud for the professional setting of the headmistress's office.

Natasha, Headmistress Lockwood's secretary, glared at her and raised a finger to her lips. "Shh. Headmistress Lockwood is in a meeting."

"With who? My aunt? I need to speak with her," Taylor said, slightly out of breath from her sprint across campus.

Natasha adjusted her black, rectangular glasses, then rubbed the bridge of her nose as if Taylor was the most annoying person on the planet.

Why did she work at the school if she was so averse to loud noises and didn't like teenagers?

"Miss Turner, please be respectful in the headmistress's office. You can't come barging in here whenever you—" Natasha berated her.

"Actually, it's Windsor," Taylor corrected.

"Wh—what?"

The door burst open again, this time with Julian and Brody entering the building.

Brody ran to Taylor, jumping on her legs and wanting confirmation that she was okay.

She patted his head in reassurance.

Natasha threw her arms up, looking like her head was about to pop off because she was so angry. She pointed a finger at Julian and then the dog. "You can't bring an animal in here. Please take it outside. Now!"

"*It*?" Taylor said indignantly, putting her hands on her hips and standing her ground. "First of all, his name is Brody, and second—"

The door to the headmistress's office opened.

Out came Aunt Mel and Headmistress Lockwood.

Taylor rushed to her aunt and wrapped her arms around her in a tight embrace. Brody joined them, jumping up on his hind legs repeatedly, demanding attention.

Mel laughed. "It's nice to see both of you too. What's with all the commotion out here?"

Headmistress Lockwood raised an eyebrow. "Did you need something, Taylor?"

"I saw Mel come in here when Julian and I were walking across campus. I was waiting for her to come pick me up for the weekend, so I wanted to see what she was doing. I hadn't heard from her in five days, and I was worried," Taylor explained, her cheeks heating after making a scene.

It had all been for nothing. There must be a reasonable explanation. Mel was clearly fine.

Mel wrapped her arm around Taylor's shoulder. "Come on. Let's go home. We can talk more during the drive."

Taylor glanced at Headmistress Lockwood, wanting to know what Mel had been discussing with her, but she decided to let it go for now. Mel would tell her if it was important. "Okay," she agreed.

Brody trotted after them as they exited the building and headed to the guest parking lot nearby, where Mel had parked her SUV. Julian helped load her bag into the trunk. He had grabbed it after she sprinted to the admin building. She was thankful he hadn't left it outside her dorm, where anyone could have stolen it.

"I guess I'll say bye to you now, then. When are you coming back to campus?" Julian asked.

"On Sunday afternoon," Taylor said.

"Okay, I'll see you then." Julian hesitated and glanced at Mel before hugging Taylor.

Taylor giggled. He probably felt awkward about showing her any affection in front of her aunt. "Bye, Julian."

"Bye. Have a good weekend," Mel told Julian.

He let go of Taylor and waved to them, then turned toward the student parking lot to walk to his car.

Mel turned to her, dangling the car keys in two fingers. "Do you want to drive home? After we make the first turn, it's pretty easy because we're on that road for most of the drive."

Taylor grinned, snatching the keys from her aunt's hand. "Yes!"

Mel climbed into the passenger seat and beckoned for Brody to jump onto her lap. He did so, and Mel helped him get settled. She turned to Taylor. "Ready?"

Taylor buckled her seatbelt and turned the key in the ignition. "As ready as I'll ever be!"

"I'm sure you'll be fine. Try not to be too nervous. Pay attention to your surroundings, and assume everyone else on the road isn't paying attention . . . Because they usually aren't," Mel said.

Taylor used the turn signal and turned left out of the parking lot. She stopped at the stop sign on the road that led off-campus, checked both ways, and went straight.

"Good job," Mel told her. "You're already doing better than most people twice your age."

Taylor glanced at her incredulously. "Are there really that many bad drivers?"

"You would be surprised. A lot of people don't have common sense, or they simply don't care about following the law," Mel said.

"Where do I go after this?" Taylor squinted, trying to remember the route, but this was only her second time going home for the weekend. She had never driven the route, so she didn't have it memorized yet.

"Oh, sorry, I'm getting distracted." Mel pointed. "Turn right after the gas station up there, and then you're on that road for about fifteen miles."

"Okay."

Silence ensued as Taylor concentrated on driving. But she was still curious about why Mel had been late to pick her up and why she had sprinted into Headmistress Lockwood's office. What had been so urgent? And why hadn't Mel contacted her in five days?

"Um, Mel . . ." Taylor cleared her throat, unsure about how to ask her aunt the dozens of questions looping through her mind.

"Yeah?"

"Were you busy this week? I texted and called you a bunch of times, but I didn't hear back from you. I'm sure you had a lot going on at work, but I was getting worried. I thought something bad happened." Taylor snuck a quick peek at her aunt's face.

Mel's cheery demeanor disappeared. "I'm sorry, Taylor. I knew you would be worried, and that wasn't my intention at all. In fact, I didn't have a say in it. I was . . ." Mel concentrated on petting Brody for a moment, inhaling deeply. "For the past five days, I was being held captive in the Ellises' basement."

Chapter 35

Taylor

Taylor gawked at her aunt for a few seconds before returning her gaze to the road. She knew she couldn't drive if she was distracted. "You . . . in the Ellises' basement . . . What?!"

Mel tucked her dark brown hair behind her ear, avoiding eye contact as she delved into her explanation. "It isn't easy to tell you this. I went over there five days ago on Vanessa's request that I help her eldest child, Oliver, with a predicament. He got involved in dark magic. I didn't see how I could help, since I no longer have magic, but she insisted that I had to be the one to help. After I arrived and she introduced me to Oliver, it started to make sense."

"Why? Is he cursed or something? Or does he have an affliction that demon hunters can't help with? Something you have knowledge of that other demon hunters wouldn't?" Taylor asked, glancing at her aunt in confusion.

"Not exactly." Mel paused, clearly mulling over how to tell Taylor the truth. "Oliver is a vampire."

Taylor gasped, the shock causing her to inadvertently slam on the brakes in the middle of the road. Thankfully, no one was behind them.

"Taylor, be careful!" Mel screeched, holding on to Brody, so he didn't go flinging from her lap and hit the windshield.

"Sorry! Sorry," Taylor said, swerving the car off to the side of the road and onto the shoulder. Her arms were shaking, and her pulse had shot up. After she put the car in park, she took her hands off the steering wheel. "I don't think I can drive anymore. Can you . . . can you drive the rest of the way home?"

"Of course."

Mel and Taylor switched seats, and this time, Brody sat on Taylor's lap. Taylor stroked his soft fur, allowing his soothing presence to calm her frayed nerves.

Before Mel pulled back on to the road, she squeezed Taylor's arm. "I'm sorry for scaring you, but you deserve to know the truth. I can drive us home, so you have time to let this sink in. I know you must be shocked right now."

"Yeah, that's an understatement," Taylor managed to say, still reeling. "I didn't know vampires were real too," she blurted out a minute later, after Mel had been driving for a mile or two.

"There are a lot of things you don't know yet. You'll learn about some of them at Grimwood Magical Academy. For starters, vampires are rare, so they aren't talked about as much. That's why you haven't heard about their existence until now. There used to be a lot more of them, but the demon hunters banded together and got rid of most of them. The only ones that remain are hiding out in faraway places, unreachable even for demon hunters."

"Wait, then why are we called demon hunters if other supernatural beings like vampires exist? The 'demon hunter' name doesn't make sense then. What else is out there that I don't know about?" Taylor asked, fear crawling over her skin like a light breeze.

Mel chuckled. "Demons were the first supernatural being we encountered. They were and still are, the most powerful and the biggest threat to humanity. They're our top priority. We banish them or kill them at whatever cost necessary. Vampires and other supernatural creatures exist, but in much smaller quantities, and they're almost always easier to defeat. So, although demon hunters do encounter other beings, demon hunting is still their primary job."

"That's kind of dumb. They could change the name," Taylor said, mulling it over.

Mel shrugged. "I think they like how powerful it makes them sound. Plus, it brings some clout to the job, so even demons know who to look out for, who to fear. If they know they're our main target, they'll be less likely to try to encroach on an area with demon hunters residing there."

"Hmm, okay. I still have more questions, but I'm curious about the Ellises. Why did Vanessa bring you to Oliver if he's a vampire? Wouldn't he—" Taylor stopped talking as she realized what they could have gotten out of Mel, especially without her powers. "He fed off of you? Ugh, never mind." Taylor shivered delicately, rubbing her arms from the sudden chill that had crept across her body. She couldn't stop the image of a vampire sucking on Mel's neck from entering her mind.

Mel interrupted her grotesque imagination at the right time. "Yes, he did. For five days. I was beginning to lose hope of ever escaping. Your roommate, Grace, came home today. She's the one who let me out."

Taylor scratched her arm. "My roommate . . . ? So her mom is crazy? Great, just when I was starting to like Grace and thought we were becoming friends. I met her sister Molly this week, and I thought we might be friends too."

"Please don't hold this against Grace or Molly. They've always been perfectly nice kids. As far as I'm aware, they didn't have any part in this. Their mom is . . . misguided. She's trying to help her son in what she thinks is the best way possible. At least she wasn't harming an innocent human. Although I'm not sure what he's going to do for a blood supply now that I'm gone . . ." Mel contemplated. "We can worry about that later."

When Taylor remained silent, Mel spoke again. "I rushed out of the Ellises' house so fast that I didn't have time to look for my phone. Vanessa took it from me after I was taken down to the basement. We need to stop somewhere so I can buy a new phone. Then we need to get home and figure out the best course of action. I think we need to tell the council what's going on."

Taylor gulped loudly. After their last interaction with the demon hunter council, Taylor was surprised Mel wanted to see them again. One of the council members had held her captive in their basement for five days and forced her vampire son to feed off of her. Another council member had assaulted Mel, then forced the amulet on her and stripped her of her magical abilities. To Taylor, it seemed like there had to be another path. A better option for someone who could help. Who knew what else the council members were capable of?

CHAPTER 36

MEL

Mel strode into the council headquarters with her shoulders pulled back and head held high, full of purpose and faux confidence. She didn't have a clue how the other council members would react to the news about the Ellises. She had requested that Vanessa not be present at the meeting, but the others had vehemently objected to that proposition. So now Mel had to present her concerns with Vanessa there to refute her claims. Mel hadn't wanted Taylor involved, but Taylor didn't want to leave her defenseless, so she was waiting in the parking lot with Julian, ready to intervene if necessary.

Mel stood in front of the council for the second time in a month—the most she had seen them in years.

Vanessa greeted her with an icy smile. "Mel, it's so good to see you. I hope you've been well."

Mel snorted. "That's rich, coming from you."

Vanessa dug her long, manicured nails into Mel's arm and snarled into her ear in a low voice. "You better watch what you say to them. Remember, I'm the one in control here, not you. I've been a loyal council member for decades. They'll back me up. Besides, no one will believe you. They have no reason to."

Mel shook Vanessa's grip off and backed away, but not before retorting, "Then I guess you better find somewhere to hide Oliver, so you don't have any proof."

And somehow get rid of these scars on my arms and bite marks on my neck . . .

Vanessa's face paled as she slithered away to her rightful spot behind the dais, joining the other council members.

Mel scanned the rest of the dais, where the council members were seated. Everyone was accounted for. But one seat was empty.

Wait. Mel scanned the dais once again.

Alastair wasn't there.

Clarissa's long black hair was pulled back into a low ponytail, with several strands elegantly framing her pale face. Her green eyes focused on Mel. "Hello, Mel. What a pleasure to have you here again." She paused and cleared her throat. "I wanted to apologize on behalf of everyone on the council for what happened with Alastair." Clarissa gestured to the empty spot next to her. "As you can see, he has been temporarily asked to step down from his position while we determine our next steps. I know how much of a pain it is to not have access to your magic, but I promise we are incentivizing Alastair to reverse the enchantment."

Mel nodded brusquely, not willing to fall for their fake apologies and niceties. "Thank you."

"Now, for the reason we're meeting today," Clarissa continued. "You mentioned it was an urgent matter regarding the security and safety of demon hunters?"

"Yes. I went to the Ellis household six days ago. Vanessa was one of my old friends from the academy, as I'm sure you all know. I thought she might be able to help me get my magic back. Instead, she tricked me into helping her son and letting him feed off of me," Mel replied.

Gasps echoed throughout the large, circular room. Lavender covered her mouth with her small, delicate hand.

"Yes, Oliver Ellis is a vampire. I'm not sure when he was bitten, but I was held captive in their house for five days, while Vanessa let him feed off of me. Without my magic, it was impossible to escape. Until the fifth day, when Grace—"

Vanessa cut her off. "How can you allow her to speak such vile things about me and my family? This is slander! Lies. All of it. She has no proof."

Lavender eyed Mel, then addressed Vanessa, her big blue eyes becoming round and questioning. "Mel is making a serious accusation. Why would she lie about that?"

Clarissa waved her hand. "Because she's desperate without her magic. Perhaps she thinks throwing out a wild accusation will somehow get her magic back, or that she can take over her family's spot on the council."

Mel massaged her suddenly aching forehead. "I know none of you trust me, but all I'm asking is for you to go to the Ellises' house and find Oliver. If you see him for yourselves, then you won't be able to deny it. He's a vampire."

"Of course we can do that. We must investigate the accusation and ensure it isn't true. If we discover Mel is right, then we will, of course, take action," Lavender agreed.

"It isn't true!" Vanessa screamed, beating her fists against the wooden dais and stalking out of the council headquarters.

"And what if it turns out I'm right?" Mel questioned.

"Then Vanessa and Randall will be punished accordingly," Clarissa replied in a cold tone.

"What about Oliver?" Mel asked.

"If Oliver is a vampire, then you know we can't allow him to exist. If he's been turned, then he's not a living being. He can no longer be considered a demon hunter, so we have no obligation to protect him. Our laws state that all vampires must be killed. No exceptions," Clarissa said.

Mel swallowed hard. She didn't want Oliver to die. She had only wanted Vanessa and Randall to pay for what they did to her and how terribly they treated her.

Had she taken things too far? Was she on the right side anymore?

Lavender cut into her thoughts with an announcement. "We must get to the Ellises' house immediately. Vanessa stormed out of here. If what Mel said is true, then I can only assume she's trying to hide Oliver or mask his vampirism. We need to go. Now."

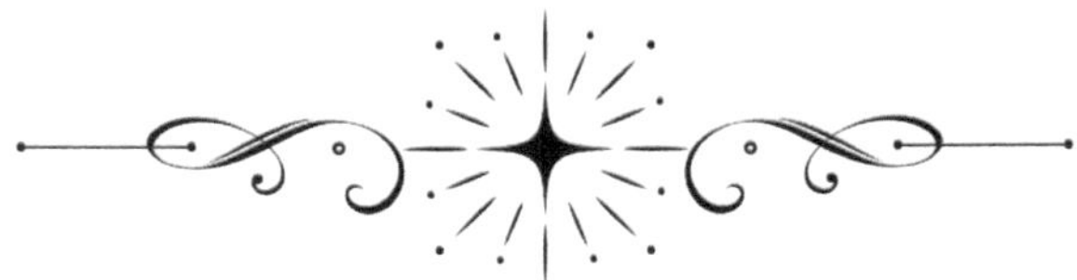

Mel showed up at the Ellises' after everyone else. They must have used magic to get there faster, but she didn't have that option anymore, so she drove her car. When she arrived, she noticed the front door was open. She ran inside.

"Hello?" Mel called out, reaching for the pocketknife in her jacket pocket. She heard shouting and the sound of a heavy object being thrown or slammed into the wall.

"Shit," she muttered, attempting to summon her magic.

Nothing happened. She sped down the hallway before remembering she didn't have her magic anymore.

If there was an altercation, what could she do?

She reached Oliver's bedroom, finding it empty. Mel continued down the hallway to the door that led down to the basement. The door stood ajar, and she could hear raised voices. They were down there.

She stared at the stairs, gulping uncomfortably. She placed her foot on the first step, and her breathing became ragged. Mel couldn't make herself go down there and relive one of the worst times of her life. It was too recent, too fresh. Shutting the basement door, she leaned against it, gathering herself. She took in slow, deep breaths and counted to ten.

Mel went back outside and sat in her car, automatically locking the doors. She wasn't proud of herself for leaving, but she had to consider Taylor. Was it worth risking her life when she had her niece to worry about? Taylor had already lost her parents. Mel didn't want her to lose anyone else. It would be devastating.

Taylor needed her, so Mel drove home, trying to convince herself she had made the right decision.

Taylor

"Thanks for coming," Taylor said.

Julian's blue eyes crinkled as he smiled at her. "You're welcome."

Brody came running out from the living room and jumped up on Julian.

Julian laughed and patted the dog's head. "Hello to you too, Brody."

Mel hovered behind her in the doorway. "Hi, Julian. Good to see you again."

Julian snuck around behind Taylor and shook Mel's hand. "Good to see you too. So should we get started? The sooner we reinforce the protection charm, the better."

Mel clapped her hands together. "Right. Thanks again for offering to help, Julian. What should we do first? Set up a perimeter around the outside of the house?"

Julian nodded. "That's what my dad and I did over the summer after I had my . . . uh, I mean, after we heard about the demon encounter."

Taylor scrutinized Julian, pondering the first time they met in her dream. "How did you know about the demon? You dreamwalked that night, right after it happened. But no one knew yet."

Julian scratched the back of his neck, stepping out onto the doorstep. "My mom is on the council, remember? They have systems in place to keep an eye on all the demon hunters."

"Okay," Taylor said, letting it go for now. But she was burning with unanswered questions about how Julian's powers worked and how he always knew when something was going to happen. It was almost as if he—

"Ready?" Julian asked, striding down the front steps.

Taylor and Mel followed him outside, with Brody trotting along too.

"Like I said, my dad and I already set up a protection charm here a month ago. But since you asked, I can reinforce the charm and show Taylor how to do it too," Julian said.

"What's the spell?" Taylor asked eagerly, bouncing on the balls of her feet.

Julian held his right hand out, palm up. "*Praesidium*. Please create a barrier around this home. Keep the inhabitants safe from danger, and don't allow anyone who intends harm to enter." Pale blue and green bursts of magic came out of Julian's hand and flew up into the air, dispersing around the outside of the grand house she now called home.

Taylor watched in awe as Julian performed the spell once again.

"Now it's your turn," he told her.

Mel stood back with her arms crossed over her chest, her face impassive. Taylor could only imagine how she must feel not being able to contribute in this situation.

Taylor held out her right hand with her palm up, as Julian had moments ago. She recited the spell, "*Praesidium*. Please create a barrier around this home. Keep the inhabitants safe from danger, and don't allow anyone who intends harm to enter." Purple bursts of magic came out of her hand and followed Julian's blue sparks, creating a dazzling, colorful display for the three demon hunters.

Taylor surveyed the house, searching for any changes. It looked the same. Julian walked around the side of the house, toward the backyard. The others followed him.

"Did it work?" Taylor asked, unable to contain her question.

Julian smiled. "It should have worked. It's an intermediate spell, but it's one I've used many times. We keep a constant protection spell up at our house. I have one on my dorm room too."

"How will we know for sure?" Mel asked.

"You'll know if someone tries to break in. The alarm will go off, and you'll feel the magical energy of whoever tries to break through. You'll be able to tell if it's another demon hunter or someone intending harm," Julian said. "Hmm, speaking of that, we should put a protection charm on Taylor's dorm room too. Just in case."

Mel agreed eagerly. "Yes, please do that as soon as you two are back on campus. Thank you for all of your help, Julian. You've been there for Taylor so much during the past month. She needed a friend. You really followed through, even though you didn't have to do anything more than help her with training."

A mischievous smile flitted across Julian's face. "It was my pleasure, I promise. I was having a boring summer, anyway. Mostly training and studying." He turned to Taylor, and his face softened. "Hanging out with you, practicing magic, teaching you about the demon hunter's history . . . That was the highlight of my summer."

Taylor's cheeks warmed. "Me too," she said quietly.

Mel glanced between the two of them and smirked. "I'll leave you two to say goodbye. Unless you want to stay for dinner, Julian? I'm going to order pizza."

Julian smiled. "Definitely. Thanks for the invite."

Mel went back into the house and called Brody to come inside too.

He whined before Taylor told him to go ahead.

"Well, now that I have you all to myself . . ." Julian started, moving closer to her.

Taylor raised her eyebrows. "Yeah?"

Julian pulled her against him for a hug, wrapping his strong, muscular arms around her waist. Taylor placed her arms around his shoulders, leaning into his chest.

"This is perfect," he muttered, nestling his face into her hair.

"I agree. I wish it could always be like this," Taylor said in a melancholy tone.

Julian pulled back from her a bit to kiss the top of her head. "Should we go inside before Mel starts to worry about what we're doing?"

Taylor giggled and laced her fingers through his. "Sure. What kind of pizza do you like?"

"Whatever you like. I'm fine with any toppings," Julian responded.

"I knew I liked you for a reason," Taylor said.

Chapter 38

Taylor

Taylor and Mel were meeting the Andersons—and Seth—at a nice Italian restaurant called Rossi's Fine Dining. It was Sarah's birthday. Taylor had no idea how old she was, and she was smart enough not to ask. Mel pulled up in front of the restaurant and parked, then got out of the car, waiting outside for Taylor. Taylor slowly extricated herself from the seat. She was wearing black boots with a slight heel, a black, flowy skirt that fell past her knees, and a maroon-colored, short-sleeve shirt with lace around the neckline. She felt awkward dressing up with the new outfit Mel had let her pick out, but it was expected for them to dress nicely to dine at a place like this.

"Ready?" Mel asked with a cheerful smile.

"I guess so," Taylor groaned.

"The food here's really good. I've eaten here a few times," Mel said, heading toward the front door and holding it open for her niece.

"That's one thing to look forward to, I guess."

"And you get to hang out with Kylie," Mel reminded her.

"Yeah," Taylor said in a glum tone.

"What's wrong?" Mel asked, pausing in the entryway before going all the way inside.

"Kylie is convinced something is off about Seth. At first, I thought she was making things up, but now . . . I'm not so sure."

"What are you implying, Taylor?"

"I don't know. That's the problem. If you want to help me figure this out, keep an eye on Seth tonight and look out for anything out of the ordinary," Taylor said.

Mel chuckled and beckoned Taylor inside the restaurant. "Okay, kiddo. Let's get in there before they order lunch without us. I don't know about you, but I'm starving."

Mel wrapped her arm around Taylor's shoulders and steered her into the restaurant, where they spotted Kylie and Sarah already sitting at a table.

Kylie stood and waved enthusiastically at them. "Hey!"

Mel glanced at Taylor and grinned. Taylor followed her aunt to the table.

"Happy birthday, Sarah!" Mel said, greeting Sarah with a hug.

"Thanks, Mel," Sarah replied.

"Happy birthday," Taylor told Sarah. She glanced around, not spotting anyone else. "Where's Seth?"

Sarah's smile disappeared. "Oh, he's running a bit late." She pulled out her phone to check the time.

"I'm sure he'll be here soon. Maybe an emergency came up," Mel said, comforting her.

"It worries me. This isn't like him. He's always punctual. Always kind, always says and does the right thing . . ." Tears glimmered on Sarah's mascaraed lashes. "He's probably getting tired of me, isn't he? I knew it was too good to be true."

Kylie surprised everyone there by reassuring her mom. "Mom, if he doesn't see how amazing you are by now, he's an idiot. Besides, he's only a few minutes late.

That doesn't necessarily mean something is wrong. He could have lost track of time, or he's stuck in traffic or something."

Sarah nodded, holding her head up high. "You're right, Kylie." She chuckled. "I'm being silly. Look at me, in my forties and falling head over heels in love with someone . . . I never thought this would happen for me again. After your dad, I—I couldn't allow myself to get hurt like that again. And raising you on my own was hard enough without adding dating into the mix. I know you aren't the biggest fan of him, but Kylie, please try to be nice today. At least on my birthday."

"Fine." Kylie sat back down and crossed her arms over her chest. "But I'm only doing this for you."

After a few more minutes, a waiter came around to take their drink orders. Taylor and Kylie asked for sodas, while Mel and Sarah ordered wine.

"Should we wait for Seth?" Mel asked, eyeing Sarah.

"No, it's fine. Go ahead and order," Sarah said.

Taylor scanned the menu and saw chicken parmigiana, one of her favorite Italian dishes. "I know what I'm getting," she announced.

"Me too," Kylie said.

The waiter came back shortly with their drinks and then took everyone's meal orders.

Seth came running into the restaurant wearing a black suit with a white dress shirt underneath, his wavy hair tousled and messy. "Sarah, I'm so sorry I'm late. There was a bad car accident, and I got stuck behind it. The highway was down to one lane, and it took much longer than anticipated to drive here." He leaned down to kiss Sarah's cheek before taking the seat next to her. "Happy birthday."

"Thanks," Sarah said, clearing her throat. "We already ordered. Sorry. I didn't know if you were going to show up."

"Oh, that's fine," Seth said, grabbing a menu and scanning it.

The waiter returned with everyone's meals, then turned to Seth. "And for you, sir? Do you know what you want?"

"I would like a steak with a baked potato and asparagus, please," Seth said, shutting the menu and handing it to the waiter.

"Very well, sir. How would you like your steak cooked?" the waiter asked.

"Ah . . ." Seth hesitated. "Rare. Cook it as little as possible. In fact, bring me the cow right now."

Everyone shot him strange looks.

Seth chuckled. "I was kidding, of course. Rare is fine."

The waiter nodded and left.

"We can wait for your food to arrive before we start eating," Sarah said, glaring at her daughter.

Kylie paused while shoveling pasta into her mouth. "Seriously, Mom?" she said through a mouthful of food.

Seth grimaced. "It's fine. The kids are hungry. Let them eat."

"I'm not a kid," Kylie grumbled as she resumed eating her meal.

Taylor didn't need to be told twice. She cut off a piece of chicken, twirled the noodles around her fork, and enjoyed the first bite of her delicious meal.

"I didn't eat breakfast," Mel said with a shrug, picking up her fork to eat too.

Fifteen minutes later, everyone was nearly done with their meals, except Sarah, who had patiently waited for Seth's meal, even though it was her birthday. Her food must have been cold by then.

The waiter set the steak in front of Seth. "Here you go, sir. Enjoy." He turned on his heel to leave.

"What the hell is this?" Seth said in a raised voice.

Sarah's warm brown eyes widened. "Seth, honey, what's wrong?"

"This steak isn't rare! It's well-done! This is absolutely ridiculous." Seth slammed the fork down onto the plate, and the plate cracked in half. "I demand to speak with the manager."

Sarah raised her hand to her mouth.

Mel jumped in, trying to resolve the situation. "Seth, it's okay. Calm down. We'll get this sorted out. It's not a big deal."

"Yes, it is. I took my girlfriend here for an extravagant birthday celebration. If I'm going to pay this much money, I expect to receive high-quality food. This isn't even close to what I requested." He shoved the cracked plate away from him, then stood. "Sarah, let's go."

"But Mel and I haven't finished our drinks. And I was going to order dessert since it's a special occasion," Sarah added in a small voice.

"Come on, we're leaving," Seth ordered, grabbing her arm.

Sarah shot a hopeless glance at them. "I'm sorry, everyone," she mumbled. She handed her credit card to Kylie. "Pay for everyone's meal, Kylie. I'll see you at home later."

Sarah and Seth left the restaurant. Kylie had a smirk on her face. Mel's lips were set into a thin line. Taylor was simply wondering what the heck had just happened.

Chapter 39

Taylor

Exhaustion weighed Taylor down. The weekend had been the opposite of relaxing, and not at all what she had in mind when she had planned to come home for a few days. She was looking forward to seeing Julian again and being back at school. She still wasn't sure if she was going to tell Grace that she knew what her mom did, or if she should wait to see if Grace brought it up. Either way, the roommate situation was going to be awkward for a while. Even if Grace was the one who had rescued her aunt, Taylor didn't know how she could live with someone whose parents were so . . . evil.

Before Mel drove her back to Grimwood Magical Academy, they were going over to the Andersons' house for lunch. Sarah had invited Seth over again.

Seth was trying to make up for the birthday lunch fiasco yesterday. Kylie wasn't happy about it, but Taylor hoped Kylie got over it. Seth might have been having an off day after being stuck in traffic. Seth was always polite to Taylor and Mel, and as far as she could tell, he was absolutely smitten with Sarah. Nothing had jumped out at Taylor as a red flag, so she stood by her original belief that Kylie was overreacting about her mom's new boyfriend.

They entered the Andersons' house at noon. Taylor wanted to allow enough time for the drive back to campus and to unpack and relax a bit after she returned. And the idea of seeing Julian that night might have also entered her mind . . .

They left Brody at home this time, since he had reacted strangely to Seth when he met him. At first, Taylor assumed it was something to do with him being a male or a stranger, but then she remembered how much Brody loved Julian and every other person he had met since she adopted him. So it must have been something else.

"Hi, Taylor!" Kylie greeted when they came inside the house. "Hi, Mel."

"Hi," Taylor replied, hugging her friend.

Mel waved and smiled, then headed into the kitchen to find Sarah.

"We didn't get to talk much yesterday. How's your new school?" Kylie asked. "Is it weird having a roommate? I don't think I could handle sharing such a small space with another person. I like my privacy and my routine."

Taylor shrugged. "It's fine. Grace is nice."

She left it at that, hoping Kylie wouldn't pry further, but she should have known better.

"*Nice*? Do you have anything in common? Does she like horror movies? Hiking? Shopping?" Kylie asked.

"I think she likes to shop," Taylor replied, after thinking about it for a moment. "She's pretty stylish. She has an older brother and a younger sister. Since she's the middle child, she's used to being the one who gets overlooked. We get along well."

"Oookaaaay," Kylie said. "Anyway, school here has been terrible. I wish you didn't have to go to that private boarding school. We would both be better off if we went to the same school."

Taylor's tense facial expression softened. "I'm sorry. Has the first week been that bad?"

Kylie rolled her eyes. "Not any worse than it's always been. I wish I had someone to eat lunch with and meet at my locker after school. Just to help, so I didn't feel as lonely. After we met earlier this summer, I thought school would be different this year." She forced a smile. "It's not a big deal. I'll be fine."

A spasm of guilt stabbed her in the gut. Here she had been worrying about Kylie's questions about Grace and her secret magical boarding school, but she hadn't considered that Kylie was so curious about her new life because she didn't have any friends besides Taylor.

"Of course you'll be fine. You're Kylie Anderson! You're unique, and you should continue being yourself, even if people don't always understand you," Taylor encouraged her.

"Yeah, okay." Kylie lowered her voice. "Did you hear about Mrs. Fritz?"

Taylor shook her head. "No. Who is that?"

"She lives a few houses down the street. She's a super sweet older lady. She always bought Girl Scout cookies from me when I was younger. Apparently, one of her sons came by to check on her because they hadn't heard from her in a few days. She passed away," Kylie said.

"Aww, that's sad. Sorry, Kylie." Taylor hugged her friend.

"Thanks. That's not the worst part, though. We heard from another neighbor that when they found her body, she was all shriveled up. What could cause something like that?" Kylie asked with wide eyes.

Chills slid down Taylor's spine. *Another demon in Grimwood?*

Hurriedly, Taylor changed the subject. "I'm not sure. Maybe she was dead for longer than they thought. Do you know what we're eating for lunch today?"

"Yeah, Seth is already here. He cooked this time, so I guess we'll find out if he's worthy of my mom soon enough. He's trying to make up for the birthday disaster yesterday."

Taylor giggled and placed her hand over her mouth, relieved Kylie had moved on from the conversation about Mrs. Fritz. "I don't know about that. No one is a better cook than your mom. Seth is going up against some tough competition."

"Yup, but he offered, so that's his bad decision," Kylie replied with a snide grin.

"At least try eating whatever he made. It can't be that bad," Taylor said.

As they entered the kitchen, the pungent smell of food burning assaulted her. Seth pulled a covered dish out of the oven, waving his other hand around to disperse the smoke that was spreading throughout the kitchen. The smoke alarm blared.

"Oh no," Sarah said, staring worriedly at Seth and the ruined dish. She stood on a chair, fanning the smoke around.

Kylie opened the kitchen window, chuckling and failing to hide her amusement.

Seth set the dish on a potholder on the counter and sighed. "Sorry I ruined lunch, everyone." He paused, pulling out his cell phone. "Is pizza okay?"

Mel smiled sympathetically at him. "Don't worry, Seth. I've been there many times, my friend. You're still new to this family, but Sarah is the designated cook. There's no use in going up against her. I usually bring takeout or dessert to these get-togethers."

"I thought I had it right. I guess it didn't need to cook for as long as the recipe said," Seth responded with a frown.

Kylie lifted the lid from the dish and peered inside. "What is this supposed to be?" She coughed as she inhaled some smoke.

"A baked chicken casserole," Seth replied. He scrolled on his phone and stepped away to order pizza.

Kylie turned to Taylor with a smug expression. "At least we know lunch will be good now."

"Stop gloating. You wouldn't have done any better," Taylor chided.

"Whatever. You're thankful we don't have to eat that thing too," Kylie said, pointing to the still smoking casserole dish.

Sarah eyed the dish and grimaced before picking it up with potholders and dumping it into the trash can. "Sorry about lunch. Good thing we all like pizza!" she said cheerfully as Seth returned.

"Okay. Pizza's ordered," Seth told them. "Lesson learned. Don't cook for the Andersons."

"I hope you didn't get any weird toppings on the pizza," Kylie mumbled.

Seth's face visibly paled. "Oh . . . I'm sorry. I should have asked. What do you like on your pizza?"

Sarah chimed in, “It’s fine. Kylie can pick off the toppings she doesn’t like.”

Kylie crossed her arms over her chest and stared him down. “I only like cheese pizza. Sometimes pepperoni, but only if it’s from Giordano’s.”

Sarah pursed her lips. “Kylie, Seth ordered pizza for us. Tell him thank you. You’ll eat whatever he ordered, or you can eat leftovers,” she ordered with a pointed look at her daughter.

“Fine. Spaghetti and homemade meatballs it is, then,” Kylie said, going to the refrigerator and pulling out a plastic container. “Want some?” she offered, holding it out toward Taylor.

Taylor shook her head. “No thanks. I love pizza, and unlike you, I’ll eat it with almost any toppings.”

Kylie heated the leftovers, and soon, the pizza arrived.

“I promise I’ll get a plain cheese pizza for you next time,” Seth told Kylie. “I won’t forget your preferences. I never forget anything.”

Sarah smiled and wrapped her arm around Seth’s shoulder. “He’s right. He remembers everything I tell him. It’s a nice change from your dad who couldn’t even remember my birthday.”

“Fine with me, but I’m not complaining. Mom’s spaghetti and meatballs are delicious, so I’m not missing out,” Kylie said.

The rest of the meal passed uneventfully. When they finished eating, Taylor said goodbye to Kylie.

“When will you be home again?” Kylie asked, staring at her with such bright hope in her eyes that Taylor couldn’t bear to crush her.

“I’m not sure, but I’ll let you know.”

“Soon?” Kylie asked.

“Promise,” Taylor said.

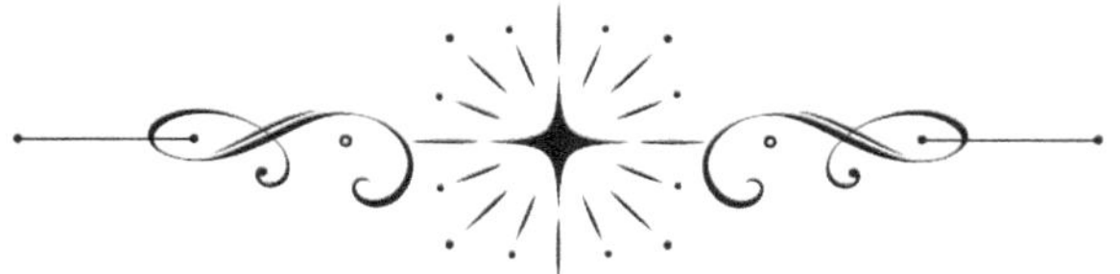

"When are you going to visit next?" Taylor asked Mel during the drive back to campus. After the scare on the way home, Taylor hadn't wanted to drive this time.

"Want me to come next weekend?" Mel offered. "Or is that too soon to see your old aunt again?"

Taylor smirked. "You are *not* old. At least, not that old." She giggled. "But I'm sure classes are going to pick up this week, so maybe the week after that?"

"That works for me. Let me know if anything changes. I can be here in about twenty minutes, okay?" Mel said.

"Don't worry. I'll be fine." Taylor bit her lip. "But don't get locked in another basement while I'm gone."

"Julian enhanced the protection wards around our house, so I should be fine. He's talented, so the wards should hold for a while."

"Yeah, but if you leave the house, you're vulnerable. I know you aren't going to stay home twenty-four-seven. You have to go to work. And you should leave the house sometimes, anyway. Hang out with people. Have fun. It isn't good for you to be home alone all the time," Taylor said.

"Taylor, I'll leave the house, but I need to be more careful than before. It isn't just demons we're up against this time. After Oliver fled and there wasn't any proof of what happened to me, now the other demon hunters are against us too."

Chapter 40

Taylor

Taylor rushed into Julian's arms the second she saw his smiling face. He wrapped his arms around her and held her close.

"I missed you," he whispered, kissing the top of her head.

"I saw you two days ago," Taylor teased.

Julian pulled back from her, holding his hand to his chest and miming being stabbed. "Ouch."

"I missed you too," Taylor admitted.

Julian smirked. "That's better. How was the rest of your weekend?"

Taylor laced her fingers through his and led him toward her dorm. "Let's wait until we're alone to talk about it." She glanced around the campus, spotting multiple people strolling by or hanging out on benches near them.

Julian raised an eyebrow. "Did something else happen after I left?"

"Sort of, but I can't talk about it now," Taylor whispered urgently.

"Julian?" a high-pitched female voice said.

Taylor and Julian both whipped around to see who had called his name. Taylor still only knew a handful of people on campus, and she recognized even fewer faces, but she did know this person. Glimmering blonde hair that framed her face like the halo of an angel, sparkling blue eyes, a curvy body, and only the newest and most stylish clothes.

Sophie Price, one of the twin daughters of Alastair Price. A year older than Taylor, she was a beautiful, talented student with lots of potential as a demon hunter, but worst of all, she was Julian's ex-girlfriend. The one who cheated on him with his best friend and broke his heart.

"Hi, Sophie," Taylor squeaked out.

"Sophie," Julian acknowledged with a slight nod.

"Is she your new girlfriend or something?" Sophie asked with a snide glance at Taylor, then at Julian.

Julian grasped Taylor's fingers firmly in his. "Yes, she is."

Taylor's heart hammered in her chest. They hadn't discussed their relationship status yet, so this was news to her, although not unwelcome news. She liked Julian. A lot. And she wanted to see where their relationship was headed.

"Oh. I thought you would want to be with a *real* demon hunter. Someone whose family hasn't betrayed our kind and nearly put all of humanity at risk by making stupid decisions . . ."

Julian interrupted Sophie before she could continue her hurtful tirade. "Sophie, that's enough! You cheated on me. That was your decision to end our relationship. I've healed and moved on, and I think you should too."

Sophie tossed her long, shimmering blonde hair over her shoulder. "Trust me, I have moved on. Blaze is hotter, anyway." She stalked off after her retort, not waiting to see their reactions.

Taylor turned to Julian with disbelief clouding her eyes. "So that's Sophie . . ."

"Sorry about that. Don't listen to her. You're a real demon hunter as much as any of us are." Julian grasped both of her hands in his. "I really like you, Taylor. I want to ask you something. Will you—"

A loud crack sounded nearby, reverberating across the campus. Before Taylor had time to react, an ear-piercing, shrieking noise sounded shortly after.

Taylor turned to Julian with a lump in her throat. "What is that?" she asked, raising her voice and fighting to be heard over the noise.

"It's the campus's security alarm. The entire campus has a magical perimeter around it. It's magically enchanted to keep humans away. Someone must have gotten too close." He tugged her toward the center of campus. "Come on. We should make sure it isn't a false alarm. Let's go see what's happening."

But something didn't feel right to Taylor. People screamed as they rushed toward the center of campus, where the auditorium was, and the spot where Julian and Taylor were headed.

"Julian . . ." she said slowly as an idea entered her mind.

"Yeah?"

"Could the alarm be triggered by something other than a human? Like . . . a demon?" Taylor asked.

Julian hurried even faster to the auditorium, with Taylor rushing to keep up with him. "Yes."

As they sprinted to the meeting spot, a slew of questions flooded Taylor's mind. Was a demon trying to get into Grimwood Magical Academy? And if so, what did they want?

Taylor hoped it had nothing to do with her.

Taylor

After they entered the auditorium, Taylor's phone rang.

Julian glanced at her. "You might want to silence that or turn it off. When they call an emergency meeting, they tell us to meet in here so they can let us know what's going on. If your phone goes off during the meeting, Headmistress Lockwood won't be happy."

"But what if it's important?" Taylor slipped her phone out of her purse and checked the caller ID: *Kylie.*

She groaned and silenced her phone before putting it back in her purse. "It's Kylie. She probably wants to complain about her mom's boyfriend again." Taylor rolled her eyes. "I'll text her later."

"Good idea. You might want to call Mel too after the meeting, since she's your guardian. Let her know what's happening, since she isn't in the loop anymore," Julian replied.

"Yeah, I will."

They found seats in one of the front rows and sat in the plush, padded seats. Julian leaned back against his seat, the picture of relaxation, but Taylor couldn't stop her racing thoughts. What if there was a demon on campus? What sort of protections did the headmistress and the academy have in place? How safe were they here? Was there a backup plan in case the demon managed to get onto campus?

"What if the demon breaks through the wards?" Taylor asked, unable to stop herself from voicing her fears.

"Grimwood Magical Academy is one of the safest places in the world to be during a demon attack. Not only is Headmistress Lockwood one of the most powerful demon hunters of the century, but the professors are all extremely powerful too. I don't know what it's like in the human world, but here, they don't let just anyone teach. The school only hires the best. Most of them don't want to go on missions or put themselves and their families in danger anymore, so teaching is often their second career."

That explained why most of the professors were middle-aged or older.

"Are you sure?" Taylor dug her nails into the cushy armrest on the seat.

"Trust me. We have nothing to worry about," Julian promised, smiling at her.

As they talked, more students and professors had entered the building and sat around them. The auditorium was about halfway full now. Chatter and gossip filled the room as people hypothesized about what was going on. Taylor attempted to tune it out, but she heard her own name whispered more than once.

Her classmates shot idle glances her way. Taylor shrank down in her seat, wishing they weren't seated in the third row. She stuck out too much, and people could spot her. She didn't want to be accused of setting off the alarm. It wasn't like she did something wrong. She wasn't involved in the infiltration. Or whatever it was. She had been talking to Julian outside of her dorm when the alarm went off. Not anywhere near the protection wards.

Soon, Headmistress Lockwood appeared onstage, coming out from behind the black, velvety curtains. She cleared her throat and stepped up to the microphone, raising it to her mouth. "Hello, students and professors. I'm sorry to interrupt your Sunday. I'm sure you all heard the alarm for the protection wards go off. And if you missed it, well, what the heck were you doing?" She paused to allow a few awkward chuckles. "The campus security team is investigating as we speak. For now, please sit tight and stay in the auditorium. We're going to conduct a headcount to make sure everyone is accounted for. We'll let you know as soon as we have more information, but please, remain calm. The professors, campus security, and I have no reason to believe this is a dangerous situation. The protection wards were most likely triggered by a curious human who got too close. It isn't completely out of the ordinary, although it is rare. Again, please stay seated, and remain inside the auditorium until further notice."

Julian turned to Taylor. "See? Nothing to worry about." He wrapped his arm around her shoulder and nestled in as close as possible, with the armrest in between them as a barrier.

Taylor felt slightly comforted by his presence, but a nagging sense of unease had been steadily creeping over her. When she realized what was causing it, she abruptly flung Julian's arm off of her and stood, causing the people nearby to glance at her or raise their eyebrows.

"I left Brody out there!" she screamed. Her mouth gaped wide open as she stared down at Julian. "I have to go get him."

Taylor abandoned Julian and marched down the center aisle of the auditorium, causing an eruption of whispers around her. Everyone stared at her as she proceeded to the exit.

"Taylor, wait!"

A hand grabbed her shoulder, and she spun around to face Julian.

"Let me come with you," he said.

Headmistress Lockwood stalked toward them, her sensible black boots pounding against the tile flooring. "Ms. Windsor, Mr. Cromwell, what are you two up to?"

Julian hesitated, so Taylor spoke first, "I'm sorry, Headmistress Lockwood, but my dog, Brody, is out there alone. In the panic of the alarm going off, I accidentally left him by my dorm."

The headmistress frowned. "Which building do you live in again?"

Taylor heaved a weary sigh, not liking where this was going. "The Flamel building."

The headmistress nodded briskly. "All right, then. I'll go fetch him."

Julian snickered at the unexpected dog pun. "Nice one."

A brief smile flickered across Headmistress Lockwood's lips. "Just because I'm in charge of this school doesn't mean I don't have a sense of humor. You may find it hard to believe, but I used to be a teenager too." She paused, scouting out the room. "I'll grab one of the campus security staff members and have them accompany me." She headed off, leaving Taylor flustered.

"Thank you, Headmistress Lockwood!" Taylor called out in a belated reaction.

As she turned to Julian, her stomach became queasy with nerves and anxiety about Brody. He hadn't been in her life for long, but she already couldn't imagine existing without him. He was like the best friend she hadn't known she needed, her constant companion, her buddy. He always knew when she was feeling down and needed to be comforted. That was more than she could say about most humans.

"Julian, what if he's—"

"Hey, he'll be okay. He's a smart dog. Smart enough to run off and hide if he has to," Julian said. "Do you want to go sit down?"

Taylor shook her head, but an intense feeling of dizziness and warmth was spreading across her body, as if she had been blasted by a wave of heat. Sweat dripped down her back. "Julian," she said, grasping for his hand to steady her. "I don't feel so gr—"

Swaying on her feet, a surge of electricity shot up both of her arms. Purple bursts of magic, larger than any she had ever seen before, blasted out of both hands. Unable to control it, Taylor was helpless as the purple bursts continued spraying out of her hands, uncontrolled and unstoppable. Two security staff members came over almost immediately and tackled her, pinning her down. Either they were wearing bulletproof vests—*wait, could those protect against magical attacks?*—or they were tough enough to endure her errant powers. Taylor lay on the ground with her eyes closed, as her emotions overwhelmed her. Tears trickled down her cheeks in a continuous stream until the magic finally stopped exploding out of her body. Her body that had betrayed her.

Taylor opened her eyes to see that Julian had backed away from her with a look of fear in his blue eyes.

Taylor

"Taylor? Taylor, are you okay?" a voice asked.

She slowly opened her eyes. Had she fallen asleep or passed out? Taylor rubbed her aching head and winced, struggling to recall the events that had led to her being unconscious. Her forehead felt warm.

"Yeah, using powerful magic like that causes side effects like headaches, nausea, fever, dizziness . . . It can be a real pain if you don't have it under control," Julian said, gazing down at her with a smile.

"Wh—what happened?" Taylor asked, searching the vicinity to figure out where they were. Taylor noticed the clothing rack on wheels and a small, white table with a curved mirror on top of it. They were no longer in the auditorium, that was for sure. "Where are we?"

"We're in a spare room in the auditorium. I think they use it to get ready before events. After the headmistress went outside to find Brody, you lost control of your powers. I think when your emotions overwhelm you, any sense of restraint on your magic flies out the window. Your worrying about Brody must have triggered it this time," Julian hypothesized.

Well, that makes sense. Sort of.

"Where's Brody? Did they find him? Is he okay?" Taylor asked, not caring about her powers until she knew her dog was fine.

A huge smile flashed across his face. "He's fine. They stepped outside, and he was waiting right outside the doors of the auditorium. Like he knew where you were. I guess he barked at them, and they let him come inside."

"Oh, thank God. Where is he?" Taylor attempted to sit up, but her arms shook. She just wanted to see him and make sure he was okay. She wouldn't believe it until she held his furry little body in her lap and petted his soft fur.

Her little white terrier with spots of brown and black dotted randomly across his fur came sprinting into the room and practically launched himself into her lap.

"Someone couldn't wait any longer to see you," Headmistress Lockwood said with a grin as she entered the room.

Taylor laughed as tears sprang to her eyes at the sight of him. "Brody! Oh, I missed you, buddy! I promise I'll never leave you again. Stay by my side, okay?"

Brody barked once, as if he understood, and stood on his hind legs to lick her cheek.

She laughed again and held him close to her chest, petting him in silence for a moment before she brought up the next pressing question. "So . . . what happened? What triggered the alarm?"

Julian's playful expression vanished, and he scratched the back of his head sheepishly. "Um, yeah . . . So it was triggered by a human, but not a random person who stumbled across our campus by accident."

Taylor's eyebrows shot up in confusion. "What do you mean? Who was it?"

"She's being questioned in the headmistress's office right now by the campus security officers, and the headmistress is going to join them too. They promised they would deal with it, which most likely means wiping her memories and sending her home safely. Taylor, this isn't good for you or Mel. They might expel you from Grimwood Magical Academy for revealing our existence and one of our secret locations to a human," Julian said.

"What? Who set off the alarm?" Taylor asked.

Taylor's heart plummeted as she recalled the phone call earlier from her next-door neighbor and friend. The call she had ignored because she assumed it wasn't important. The call that might have cost her future as a demon hunter.

She managed to sputter out one word, "Kylie . . ."

Taylor

Taylor stared at the headmistress with her teeth clenched, waiting for her to speak.

"Julian is correct, Ms. Windsor. I need to go to my office to interrogate the human we caught sneaking onto our campus. I realize that you most likely aren't feeling up to joining us, so I'll let you rest here for a bit longer with Julian to supervise," Headmistress Lockwood said, turning to leave the room. She paused in the doorway, adding over her shoulder, "But there will be consequences if you told a human about the existence of our world and, more importantly, if you revealed the location of Grimwood Magical Academy. Crimes don't go unpunished, Taylor. We've been very lenient with you thus far, but a lack of knowledge and experience only lets you get away with so much. We can't allow such reckless behavior from our students. We can't risk the safety of everyone on campus because you're unable to keep our existence a secret or control your powers. But we'll discuss this more later. In the meantime, try to get some rest. You'll need it."

After the headmistress left the room and closed the door, Taylor felt the weight of the world on her shoulders. "I can't believe it. I finally get accepted into the academy and start to feel like I belong, and then this happens? Maybe I'm not meant to be a demon hunter, after all." She was quiet for a moment before she uttered her deepest, darkest thought out loud to Julian. "Maybe my parents were right to hide all of this from me. I can't handle this pressure. I'm not meant to be a part of the demon hunter world."

Julian sat on the floor near her, since she was lying on a skinny couch—more like a chaise lounge than an actual couch, and there wasn't enough room for him to sit next to her. Especially not with Brody sprawled out on her chest.

He spoke in a soft, gentle voice. "You don't talk about your parents much, but I bet they would have told you the truth eventually. Based on what I know about them, they would have wanted you to decide for yourself. I think they would be happy with whatever decision you make. Whether it's embracing a new life as a demon hunter or choosing to live in the human world as they did."

"What are you saying? You don't think I should be a demon hunter?" Taylor struggled to shift her position, moving Brody off her chest so she could sit up. "You don't believe in me anymore?" Her hazel eyes were wide and dull, their sparkle dimmed. Every ounce of hope and excitement about her future as a demon hunter had been extinguished.

"No, that's not it at all! I only wanted you to know that if you don't want this life, then it's okay. I'll stand by your side no matter what you choose. I believe in you. I think with more training and time and patience, you'll master your powers. You'll be able to control your magic. I bet you'll be even stronger than your parents were. They would already be so proud of you and all that you've accomplished," Julian promised.

Taylor huffed in annoyance. "I haven't accomplished anything yet. I still have so much to learn." Taylor frowned. "Besides, we haven't known each other very long. Why would you want to be with a regular human? Without my magic or the academy to help me refine my powers, that's all I'd ever be. What if they take my powers away and expel me from the school? What if I don't have a say in it and I don't get to decide my own future?"

"Then we'll make the best of it, whatever that looks like." Julian leaned forward so their foreheads pressed together.

"But I won't be special. I won't be different from any other human," Taylor said quietly, voicing her deepest fears out loud about living a mundane existence. The very existence she had always feared.

"Taylor, I highly doubt your life would be boring as a human. And you are special, powers or no powers. I think you're incredible," Julian said.

She closed her eyes, inhaling his musky scent. She sighed deeply, comforted by his presence, his words, his overall being. Everything about Julian screamed calm and peaceful. He was everything she strived to be—her complete opposite in so many ways. He made her feel like it was okay to be herself, and she hoped she did the same for him. They balanced each other out. She had only known him for a few months, but he was already such an irreplaceable part of her life. She had grown to rely on him so much.

"Okay," she finally replied, pulling slightly back to gaze into his ocean-blue eyes.

"Okay," he repeated, beaming at her.

Brody inserted himself in between them, licking Julian's face this time.

"I think Brody's jealous," Julian said, laughing as he petted the terrier.

Taylor wrinkled her nose playfully. "Of what?"

Julian scoffed, standing and walking over to a mini-fridge she hadn't noticed before. He opened it and pulled out a white takeout container. As he popped the container open, the scent of meat and cheese hit her nostrils.

Her stomach grumbled loudly. She put her hand on her stomach and groaned.

"Hungry?" he asked. He brought the container over to her.

Inside was a sandwich piled high with meat, cheese, lettuce, tomatoes, and mayo.

"I got it from the cafeteria after they gave the all-clear on campus. I figured you would want dinner," Julian elaborated.

"You're a lifesaver," Taylor replied, taking the container from him and instantly tearing into the sandwich. "This is the best sandwich I've ever eaten in my life."

"Did you hear the part where I said it came from the cafeteria?" Julian teased.

"Yup, and I don't care. It's a million times better than the food at a human high school."

"Really? What types of meals do they serve there?" Julian asked, appearing curious. "I don't know much about human high schools. Or any type of human school, really."

"Um, like chicken nuggets and greasy pizza. Stuff like that. Never anything nutritious and it's so overpriced."

"Wait, so you had to pay to eat? Lunch wasn't included in the cost of tuition?" Julian asked.

"Not at a public school. You pay for everything there."

"Wow." Julian shook his head. "The human world needs some work. They could learn a thing or two from us."

"Yeah, well, demon hunters could benefit from humans too," Taylor said.

Julian bit back a smirk. "Yeah? How so?"

"I can't think of anything specific right now, but—"

"I'm sure you'll let me know when you do. After you finish your sandwich, I'll bring you back to your dorm. You should rest more and wait until Headmistress Lockwood is ready to talk to you," Julian replied.

Taylor took another bite of the delicious sandwich. "Mmm, this really is good. I don't know how I'll ever survive eating chicken nuggets for lunch again every day."

"What do you mean?" Julian questioned, leaning down to pet Brody again, who looked like he was feeling left out.

"If I'm expelled from Grimwood Magical Academy, I'll be forced to go to the human high school in Grimwood. The one Kylie attends. I guess that's one good thing. I'll have one friend there. Unless they erase her memories after this mess is over," Taylor mused, setting the empty takeout container on the ground.

"Please don't say that. We don't know what's going to happen yet. I might be able to talk to Headmistress Lockwood and see if she'll change her mind. Getting expelled is a bit extreme for your first broken rule. There must be some other type of punishment she would agree to. Something not as harsh."

"I don't know. Technically, I broke multiple demon hunter rules. It's not like I didn't know what I was doing. I shouldn't have told Kylie where the school .

. . ." Taylor trailed off, focusing in on what she had said. "Julian, I just realized something. I never told Kylie the location of the academy. I admit I told her about demons and demon hunters, but that was months ago, before I knew how serious all this stuff was. I swear I never gave her the address or any specific information about the school. I lied to her and said it was a private boarding school because I was scared of something like this happening."

Julian stared at her for a heartbeat, his beautiful blue eyes gazing at her in deep thought. "If you didn't reveal Grimwood Magical Academy's location to Kylie, then who did?"

Taylor

Taylor knocked on the door of Headmistress Lockwood's office. She was glad it was after hours, so Natasha wasn't working the front desk. In her current state of mind, she couldn't deal with someone who didn't like her.

"Come in," Headmistress Lockwood called from inside her office.

Taylor entered the office and hovered in the doorway. "Um, hi." She darted a glance at Kylie, whose face was scarlet.

"Hello, Taylor. Please have a seat." The headmistress gestured to the empty seat next to Kylie.

Taylor sat down and fidgeted with her hands in her lap as she waited for her punishment. Since she was new to the school—and to the demon hunter world—she had no clue what her punishment would be. Her mind churned out the possibilities. A slap on the wrist, like community service or being confined to her dorm? Or something much worse, like being expelled or having her powers taken away like Mel? If they were both devoid of magic, they would be left defenseless against any demons.

"I hope you understand how serious this matter is, Ms. Windsor. At Grimwood Magical Academy, we have rules. Normally, I would expect a student of your age to have the guidebook memorized, but since you're new . . . Are you familiar with it at all?" Headmistress Lockwood asked, pushing a binder toward her.

Taylor shook her head. "No, sorry. I haven't had time to look it over."

"Take this copy and make sure you study it until you know it forward and backward. One of our most important rules, not only at Grimwood Magical Academy, but anywhere in the demon hunter world, is that we must never tell anyone outside of the demon hunter community about our existence. And that goes double for revealing a hidden location, such as a demon hunter training school. Because I know you've been through a terrible ordeal this summer . . . well, more than one ordeal, I suppose . . . I've decided to allow you to remain at Grimwood Magical Academy for the time being."

Taylor straightened up in her chair, listening eagerly. "Thank you, Headmistress!"

Headmistress Lockwood nodded. "Now, you understand that you're on thin ice at the moment. One toe out of line, and I won't have a choice but to expel you. I can't have the other students and their parents accusing me of playing favorites. I was friends with your aunt Mel back in our school days, and many people remember that."

"I understand. Thank you for giving me another chance. I promise nothing like this will ever happen again," Taylor said, glancing at Kylie, who was unnaturally silent. She scrutinized her friend. "Kylie?"

Kylie turned to her and blinked slowly. "Yeah?"

"How did you get here? I mean, how did you find out where my school was? I never told you," Taylor said, searching for an explanation.

Headmistress Lockwood frowned. "Is that the truth, Ms. Windsor? You didn't tell your friend the location of our school?"

"No, of course not. I may not know all the rules yet, but I assumed we weren't supposed to tell anyone, especially after you mentioned the school has a protective barrier around it to deter mortals from coming too close. I really don't know how Kylie got here," Taylor said.

Kylie interjected at last. "I followed you here when you left home this afternoon. I was bored and sick of being at home alone, while you were out having a new and exciting life with all your new friends. I wanted to know what it was like at your new school and why you didn't let me visit."

Taylor turned to her friend with a sympathetic expression. "I've come home multiple times already, though. We hung out this weekend. I promise I didn't invite you here for your own good. For one thing, I didn't want to get into trouble, and it isn't safe for you to keep getting dragged into things like this."

"Hmm. The real puzzle has been solved then," Headmistress Lockwood said. "In any case, we'll have to erase Kylie's memories."

Taylor took a sharp intake of breath. "Does that mean she'll forget everything? Even meeting me and becoming friends? Or just the memories related to magic and demons?"

Headmistress Lockwood's lips set into a straight line. "Unfortunately, there isn't a spell precise enough to differentiate between the memories, so I'll have to erase any memories of you from her mind. I'm sorry, Taylor. It's for your own good, and Kylie's too. She and her family will be safer if you distance yourselves from them. It isn't easy to have human friends as a demon hunter. Someone always ends up getting hurt." She opened her desk drawer, pulled out a spellbook, and flipped through the pages until she settled on a spell toward the back of the book.

That must mean it was an advanced spell.

Taylor caught a glimpse of the spell name. *Retinentia.* She had never heard of it.

Headmistress Lockwood cleared her throat. "You can leave if you would like to, Ms. Windsor. Go back to your dorm and rest. I'll ensure Kylie gets home safely."

Taylor hesitated before standing and heading toward the door. "Wait." She turned back around. "Headmistress Lockwood, is this the only option? Is there nothing else we can do?" In a gentle tone, she added, "I'm Kylie's only friend, and she was my first friend after moving to Grimwood. She was there for me when I didn't have anyone else.

"When Mel and I were fighting, and I didn't understand what was going on because she was hiding the demon hunter world from me, Kylie and her mom were there for me. Their house was a safe place that I knew I could always go to, a place where I was always welcome. After losing my parents and the home I grew up in, it was one of the first places that felt like home again. Eventually, Mel told me the truth about our family's history, and as we grew closer and learned to trust each other, her house became my home too. But after weeks of feeling displaced, depressed, and alone, Kylie was the first one to make me feel like I belonged." Tears fell down her cheeks as she spoke. She turned to Kylie to see her face shining with fresh tears too.

"Oh, Taylor, I don't want to forget you! You're the best friend I've ever had." A sob wrenched its way out of Kylie's throat. "I don't know what I'll do without you. I guess I'll go back to being a loser and having no one to talk to or hang out with."

Taylor began sobbing and lurched forward, wrapping her arms around Kylie in a fierce hug. Kylie hugged her back, sobbing too.

Headmistress Lockwood pushed back her chair and stood from her desk. She sighed deeply and pinched the bridge of her nose. "I suppose I can do my best to detangle the memories Kylie has of you that aren't magic-related or demon hunter-related. It will take some time, though. And I must warn you, Kylie, it will be very painful."

Kylie pulled back from the hug. "I wish I could be a part of this world too, but it doesn't seem like that's possible. If this is what I have to do to keep Taylor in my life, then I can endure some temporary suffering. I'll do it."

Taylor squeezed her friend's hand. "Don't worry. I'll stay with you the whole time."

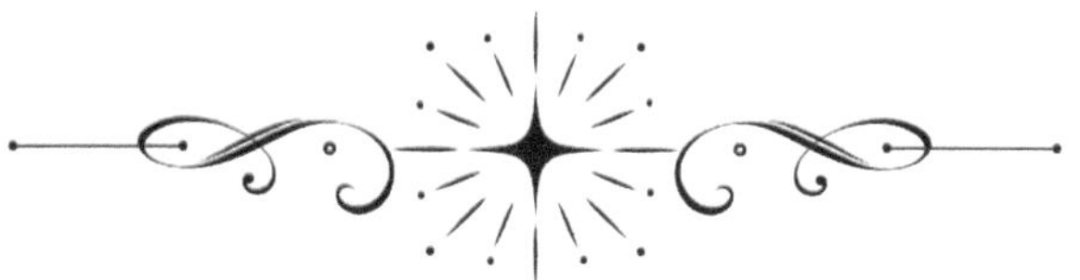

"*Retinentia*," Headmistress Lockwood said.

Silvery wisps of magic floated from Kylie's head and into the glass vial in front of the headmistress. She had explained that she would label the vial and keep it locked away in an enchanted storage room on campus where others like it were stored.

Taylor's mind raced as she thought of all the stolen memories that must be locked away in that room. What kinds of things had people lost forever because it was deemed unsafe for them to remember? There had to be others who had gone through something similar. Taylor couldn't be the only one who had told a human about their existence. It was highly unlikely.

Kylie screamed, an ear-piercing shriek that tore through Taylor, making her chest seize at the sound of her friend's pain. Kylie squeezed Taylor's hand, digging her nails into her palm, but Taylor didn't let go. She couldn't abandon Kylie. Taylor wanted to be there for her. No matter what.

"*Retinentia*," Headmistress Lockwood repeated.

Once again, silvery wisps of magic floated from Kylie's head and into the glass vial. This time, less of them came out.

"*Retinentia*," Headmistress Lockwood said.

Nothing happened.

"Is that it?" Taylor asked, daring herself to hope it was over. She couldn't bear to watch Kylie suffer anymore.

"Yes, I believe so," Headmistress Lockwood said, corking the glass vial and then shutting her spellbook. "I'll allow you to say goodbye to Kylie, and I'll bring her home as promised."

"What about my punishment?" Taylor asked, although part of her hoped the headmistress had forgotten about it. The realistic side of her knew there should be repercussions for what she had done and how she had exposed the demon hunters to a human. Even if it was only Kylie, who wasn't planning to exploit them or reveal their existence to others. In fact, Kylie thought the demon hunter world was cool and had expressed her jealousy at not being part of it.

Headmistress Lockwood's expression turned stern. "I think you've been punished enough for now, Ms. Windsor. Please go back to your dorm and only go to your classes this week. No extracurriculars and no trips home for two weeks."

Taylor nodded, hopping up from her chair. "That seems more than fair. Thank you, Headmistress. For everything." She turned to Kylie. "Kylie, I'll come home in a few weeks and we can hang out then, okay?"

Kylie stared at her, blinking her green eyes slowly, as if in a daze. "Taylor?" Her gaze darted around the enormous office. "Where am I? What are we doing? And who is she?" Kylie pointed to Headmistress Lockwood.

Taylor cleared her throat, grasping for a reasonable explanation.

Thankfully, the headmistress jumped in to smooth things over. "I'm Headmistress Lockwood, the one who oversees Taylor's boarding school. Do you remember what happened, Kylie?"

Kylie's eyes dropped to the carpet, and she shook her head. "No, I just feel really confused. And my head hurts."

"You came here to visit Taylor for the day. You two were out in one of the common areas playing fetch with Brody, and you tripped and fell down several steps. You hit your head pretty badly, and you've been unconscious for a while. We already had the school nurse look you over. She recommended that you go home to rest," Headmistress Lockwood lied deftly.

"Oh, geez. I think I remember that. Or at least part of it," Kylie said, rubbing her forehead. "I should get going, then. I bet my mom's worried and wondering where I am."

"I'll drive you home," Headmistress Lockwood offered. "To make sure you get there safely."

"Oh, that's nice of you, but I drove my car here, so I'll drive myself home. Or . . . actually, I don't remember driving here. But Taylor can't drive, so how else would I have gotten here?" Kylie asked.

"You drove your car," Taylor cut in. "You followed me and Mel here when she dropped me off."

"Temporary memory loss is common after a head injury. You'll be fine, Kylie," Headmistress Lockwood promised. "I'll wait outside while you two say goodbye." She exited her office, leaving them alone.

Kylie shook her head. "What a weird day. I guess I'll see you soon?"

"Yeah." Taylor hesitated, wanting to say something else to comfort her. "Are you sure you're okay?"

Kylie rubbed her head again. "I think so. My head really does hurt, though, so I think going home to rest is a good idea. Maybe a good night of sleep will help."

"Sounds like a plan. I hope you feel better." Taylor hugged Kylie and led her out of the office and to the parking lot, where Headmistress Lockwood was waiting beside Kylie's car.

Kylie waved and got into the passenger side of the car.

Taylor's forehead scrunched together. "Wait, Headmistress, if you're driving Kylie's car, how will you get back to campus?"

"Don't worry about that, Ms. Windsor. I have my ways," the headmistress said before winking.

Chapter 45

Taylor

Back in her dorm, Taylor snuggled up with Brody in her bed. Julian had left her alone to rest, promising he would come by later to check on her. It was 6:30 p.m., so not too late, but there was no sign of Grace yet, which worried Taylor. She sent her roommate a quick text, asking when she was coming back to campus or if she was back already. Grace had a lot of stuff, so Taylor couldn't tell if she had stopped by the room to drop anything off yet.

"What are we going to do for the rest of the night, Brody?" Taylor asked her dog, who was curled up near her feet.

His little head perked up at his name, and he stared at her intensely, as if trying to communicate with her.

After a brief staring contest, Taylor broke away, laughing. "You win this time, buddy."

As Taylor contemplated if she should find a show to stream on her TV or doomscroll social media, a tapping sound came from outside her window. Brody lurched toward the window, barking furiously.

"Shh, Brody, it's fine! It's probably just a tree branch scraping against the window."

Taylor ignored the sound, and it stopped. She turned on the TV and selected her favorite streaming service to find a movie to watch.

The tapping returned.

"Taylor!" a familiar voice said. "Taylor, let me in."

Taylor turned toward the window again, but the blinds blocked her view of the outside world. Who would be outside her window? Julian? But why wouldn't he have come to the front door and texted her to let him in?

A sickening feeling hit her.

Her dorm was on the third floor. No one could be outside her window, unless they were floating. She paused. Although Julian was a talented demon hunter, so he might know a spell for that. He hadn't left more than thirty minutes ago, so why was he back so soon? Taylor didn't think he would stop by until later. But who else could it be? She didn't know that many people on campus yet.

She moved to the window and pulled up the blinds, revealing Julian's broadly grinning, handsome face.

"Hey. Let me in! I can't float out here all night."

Brody's barking picked up again, relentless.

Taylor glanced at her dog. "What's gotten into you? It's Julian." She turned back to Julian. "What are you doing out there?"

"Open the window, and let me into your dorm. I'll explain everything," Julian said.

"Okay." Taylor unlocked the latch on the window and slid the glass up, stepping back so Julian could squeeze through it.

Brody followed Julian's every move, snarling as he entered the dorm and headed toward Taylor.

"Brody, stop it. You know him. You've never acted like this toward him before. It's just Julian . . ." Taylor stopped speaking as the person she thought was Julian transformed before her very eyes.

Julian's black, wavy, shoulder-length hair changed to chestnut, chin-length hair. Julian's warm, ocean-blue eyes changed to a darker, harsher shade of blue. The form filled out and aged, growing taller and more muscular. Facial hair grew on the jaw, completing the transformation.

"Seth?" Taylor gasped, taking several steps back. "What are you doing here? How did you—"

A smile curled up the corners of Seth's lips—a smile that suddenly felt familiar. Something tugged at the back of her mind, a memory of someone else with a smile like that.

"Taylor, you didn't even test me to see if I truly was your boyfriend, Julian. You can't be too careful nowadays. You really shouldn't trust anyone so easily. I thought you knew better than that." Seth stepped toward her, moving fluidly and almost gliding across the floor, not human-like.

"How did you sneak on to the campus? And why are you here?" Chills crept up her spine. This situation was bad. Very bad.

"Your little friend Kylie provided the perfect opportunity. It only took a slight nudge to convince her to follow you here earlier today. While everyone was distracted with the human breaking through the protection wards, I was able to sneak onto campus, unnoticed," Seth said.

Taylor reflected on everything she knew about Seth. The way he had inserted himself into Sarah's life and how their relationship had become serious so quickly. His irrational anger at the restaurant. The way he preferred to eat meat rare. Plus, he was a terrible cook. But Mel was too, so maybe that didn't matter.

Then Mrs. Fritz had died, her body a shriveled-up husk, as if the soul had been sucked right out of it.

Taylor had found the snake in the bathroom, then it disappeared, as if by magic.

Brody didn't like Seth and had sensed something off about him from the first time they met. He always barked or growled at him, and he had never acted like that toward anyone else. Except for Ammitt.

Brody was a smart dog, but she was beginning to wonder how intelligent her new pet truly was. After all, he had been the dog of Camille, a powerful supernatural being who served Ammitt, the demon lord. What if Brody wasn't an ordinary dog? But Taylor would worry about that later. For now, she needed to protect herself. And Brody.

"You're a demon," Taylor said, her breathing becoming erratic as she took a step back from him.

Seth chuckled.

Taylor gulped, fear slithering across her body. She wasn't sure she had fully recovered from her outburst of magic earlier. How would she defend herself? If she attempted to perform a spell, could she manage it on her own? Julian wouldn't be back for a while, and Grace still hadn't returned. She might be able to hold him off until one of them showed up. It was her best bet. Her best chance of survival. She wasn't going to back down. She had to fight.

Taylor clenched her hands into fists, running through the list of spells she had memorized. Which one was best to use in this situation? She was only a few weeks into her first semester at the academy, and she certainly hadn't learned enough to defeat a powerful demon by herself.

Seth brought his hands together in a pitifully slow, mocking gesture. "You know, I was beginning to doubt your intelligence. My brother warned me about you, but I see now that he was wrong. He was too weak, too single-mindedly focused on himself and his own goals and desires. He could have easily defeated you if he had only paid attention. Not that I'm surprised he screwed up. The youngest sibling usually does."

Taylor gasped. "Ammitt is your brother?"

"Yes, my younger brother. I'm the middle child."

Taylor swallowed hard, wishing she could swallow her fear and anxiety and get rid of it. "There are more of you?"

"We have an older sister named Ray too. She thinks she's the most powerful, but"—Seth scoffed—"I don't need her to accomplish this mission. I can handle this on my own. Then when I tell her of Ammitt's mistakes and my success, I'll be the one who receives the commendations. I'll be the one who saved the demons.

"Humans have been existing in this world for long enough. It's our turn to be in charge. We deserve more than being banished from the mortal realm and confined to our own world. What fun is that when we can live in the mortal realm and enjoy ourselves so much more?" He inched closer to her, his voice a near growl. "Especially with such cute little demon hunters to use as our playthings."

Taylor dug her fingernails into the palm of her hand and let out her breath. She could do this. She had to. It wasn't just herself, Brody, and her loved ones' lives at stake. If Seth was one of the demon lords, then everyone at Grimwood Magical Academy was in trouble.

The first spell that crossed her mind was *ignis*, the fire spell.

"*Ignis*!" she yelled, harnessing her power and hoping it worked.

A small, pitiful flame, about the size of a flame from a lighter, came out of her palm.

Seth laughed harshly, came over to her, and extinguished it with a wave of his hand. "You are the great Taylor Windsor? The demon hunter who banished my brother back to the underworld, a feat many demon hunters decades older than you couldn't accomplish on their own?" Seth asked incredulously.

"Yes," Taylor replied, gritting her teeth.

It hadn't been long enough for her to recharge. She needed more energy. Without rest and time to heal, she wouldn't be able to summon a spell powerful enough to kill Seth, and certainly not a banishment spell like the one she had used on Ammitt. What could she do?

"Is that the best you've got?" Seth asked, clasping his hands, palms together, in front of him, as if patiently waiting for her to try another spell.

This was all a joke to him. He wasn't taking her seriously. She was filled with an innate need to prove him wrong. To prove to everyone how powerful she was.

"No!" she screamed. This time, she attempted the water spell, holding out her right hand, palm out, facing Seth. She prayed to God that it worked this time, because if it didn't, she wasn't sure she would get another chance. "*Unda*."

A spray of water shot out of her hand, hitting Seth in the face, making him sputter and cough. But that was it. One pathetic burst of water.

Taylor hurriedly tried again, not wanting to lose her momentum, but also fearing that was all she had left in her. "*Unda*!"

A few tiny drops of water splashed onto the carpet.

Taylor stared at the water droplets, then looked at Seth, who smiled devilishly as he stalked toward her.

"Shit."

Taylor

A booming sound came from the hallway. The door splintered into dozens of pieces. In the hallway stood Julian, his chest heaving. His fingers shot out a mixture of pale blue and electric green bursts of magic. He glared at Seth, with fury in his eyes as he entered Taylor's dorm. Why were his magic bursts two different colors? Maybe the magic bursts changed colors when a demon hunter was emotional? Or because he was more experienced than her?

"Get away from her," Julian commanded in a booming, powerful voice so unlike his usual voice.

Seth sneered at Julian as he walked further into the room. "Ah, Julian Cromwell. How nice to meet you."

Julian glowered at the demon. "How do you know who I am?"

"The Cromwells are one of the five ancient demon hunter families. My siblings and I are well-acquainted with our adversaries, whether they're aware of us or not," Seth replied. He blocked Julian's path so he couldn't reach Taylor. "Have you come to rescue your little girlfriend? I think she needs your help. Despite my brother's warnings about her strength and power and everyone's assumptions that she's The Chosen One, she's weak and inexperienced. I'll allow you to help her." He paused as a smile curled up his lips. "Not that it will matter."

Taylor agreed with Seth. Even with Julian's help, she didn't see a way out of this. She was weakened to the point that she didn't think she could perform another spell. She needed to summon the remainder of her strength and focus on what she could do. Help defeat Seth, magic or no magic. No matter what, she couldn't let Julian get hurt protecting her. She couldn't stand to lose him. Not when they had just gotten close.

Taylor stood firm in her offensive stance, hands up in front of her chest, right foot slightly back, prepared for whatever was to come.

Seth glanced back and forth between Taylor and Julian and chuckled. "Do you two honestly think you stand a chance against me?" he asked in a lilting, teasing tone.

"Maybe not, so it's a good thing they have us to help too," a female voice said, entering the room behind Julian.

Grace came into the dorm at last, flanked by her younger sister, Molly, and someone who could only be her older brother, Oliver. Oliver's face was pale and sunken in, with dark circles under his eyes. His lips were bright red with fresh blood, and when he opened his mouth to smile, his razor-sharp vampire fangs stood out in plain sight.

Although Mel had told her Oliver was a vampire, Taylor had never seen one in person before. Oliver was the one who had fed off Mel for five days. Why was he here? A shudder passed through her body.

"Ah, a vampire? How very interesting the company you keep. I wouldn't have expected that from innocent young demon hunters. What trouble have you gotten yourselves into? Vampires can be tricky," Seth said in a purr as he stared with interest at Oliver.

"Grace, how did you know to come here? And why did you bring your siblings with you?" Taylor asked.

"Julian had a premonition that you were in danger. I was napping in the car on the way back to the academy, and he dreamwalked to tell me what was going on. My siblings were in the car with me. My mom was dropping Molly and me off at our dorms for the week. Oliver insisted on coming too. My mom had to speak with the headmistress, so she's in her office now, but she's supposed to come here after her meeting," Grace explained.

Taylor froze at Grace's words, taking a moment to gather her thoughts. "Wait, but how did Julian have a premonition? He's a dreamwalker. Premonitions aren't one of the Cromwell's gifts . . ."

Grace's face fell, as if she hadn't thought about it yet either.

Seth snickered, apparently connecting the dots before anyone else. "Uh oh. Looks like someone's mommy was unfaithful and slept with Alastair Price." His dark blue eyes flickered with delight as he surveyed Julian again. "So you have two gifts then. This is an interesting turn of events." He glanced at Taylor briefly, then back to Julian. "I think everyone has been wrong all along. Taylor is likely not The Chosen One." Seth paused, relishing in the anticipation that seemed to be building in the air, crackling like electricity. "Julian must be the real Chosen One. Cromwell, you might be one of the most powerful demon hunters alive. With the gift of premonitions and dreamwalking, if you hone your powers, you would be unstoppable. Picture it. You could join me and my siblings and help restore the world to its rightful order. Humans at the bottom as our food and playthings . . . Then the demon hunters and other supernatural beings. Then the demons at the top, where we belong."

Julian laughed harshly as green-and-blue sparks of magic continued to emanate from his fingers. "Trust me, I'm not The Chosen One. It must be Taylor. She's special."

Seth shook his head. "I don't think so. I was warned of how powerful she is, but it's been ages since a demon hunter has been born with two gifts. It's a rare power, one that should be treated with the utmost respect."

"What would you know of respect?" Julian practically spat. "*Magicae uptis*!" he yelled, as the mixture of electric-green and sky-blue magic bursts shot forth from his fingers, toward Seth.

Seth deflected the display with a wave of his hand. "Nice try." He raised an eyebrow. "Is that the best you can do?"

Grace and Molly both ran forward into the room. The sisters screamed, "*Magicae uptis*!" in unison. Their magic sparks were bright yellow.

Julian cast another spell. "*Ignis*!" Flames erupted from his hand, engulfing Seth and catching him off-guard as he deflected the attack from the Ellises.

Seth screeched. "You stupid brats." His skin was burning to a crisp, but he used the *unda* spell to extinguish the flames.

A gush of water washed over the room.

Julian cast the *ignis* spell again. This time, a steady barrage of flames crept across Seth's body, spreading quickly across the room. "Get out of here!" Julian warned the others.

"No, I'm not leaving you," Taylor protested.

"Leave. It isn't safe. Let me handle this," Julian insisted.

Meanwhile, Oliver crept closer to Seth, biting his flaming hand before slinking away.

Taylor wasn't sure how a vampire bite would affect a demon. Would it harm him?

Seth summoned the water spell again, engulfing the room with a flood. The demon hunters all choked and gasped for air as the water rose higher and higher in the dorm room. Taylor swam toward the door. She called for Grace and Molly to follow her.

"Julian, come on, let's go. We can get the headmistress and tell her what's going on," Taylor said.

Seth sputtered as he floated to the top of the water, swimming to stay afloat. "No," he uttered. "Julian will be coming with me to the demon realm."

Julian laughed and shook his head. "I will not!"

"If you want to keep your friends safe, then you'll come with me. Don't test me, child. I'll kill Taylor without a second thought," Seth warned.

Julian's eyes flashed with menace. "Don't you dare hurt her."

Seth flicked his wrist.

Taylor's body became heavy. Swimming grew increasingly difficult. Her oxygen supply was cut off. She struggled to keep her head above water. She continued moving her arms and legs, so she didn't drown. Julian swam toward her. Seth flicked his wrist again. A wave came out of nowhere, pulling Taylor underwater.

Taylor closed her mouth as she went under, deeper and deeper. She pushed toward the surface. Her lungs burned as she kicked her legs with every ounce of energy remaining. She was nearly at the surface when she heard Julian's next words.

Taylor's head breached the surface of the water, gasping for air.

"I have to finish this. I only care about keeping her safe, and if this is what I have to do, I'll die a thousand deaths to save Taylor." Julian stared Seth down, chewing on his lip as if he was mulling it over. He moved closer to Seth, standing beside him.

"Julian, no!" Taylor screamed, swimming toward him with every bit of strength she had left.

Seth swiped a hand toward her. Taylor slammed into the wall, crashing back into the water. She winced and raised herself up.

Oliver snuck over to Seth while he was distracted and sunk his fangs into Seth's exposed arm.

Seth screamed and raised his hand, throwing Oliver's body against the window. Oliver fell underwater.

Grace and Molly uttered a spell, and the water dissipated from the room. They both headed for their brother, who was lying unconscious by the wall.

Her chest heaving, Taylor leaned against the wall. She began to crawl, trying to reach Julian in time to stop him.

Seth smirked. "I don't take kindly to vampires trying to bite me. He must be punished if he can't play nice." Seth flicked his wrist toward Oliver, whose body burst into flames.

"*Unda*!" Grace screamed. Molly joined her, trying to put out the flames.

Taylor watched in horror as Oliver's body turned to ash. She continued crawling to Julian, unable to worry about Oliver at the moment.

Julian looked back at her and shook his head sadly, his blue eyes dulling as he accepted his fate. "Seth is right. I have more power than I know what to do with. I realized the truth months ago, but I wasn't sure what my next step should be. I've always felt out of place here, out of sync with the other demon hunters. Maybe this is why. I'm meant for another life. Another world. Something far greater than being a demon hunter."

"You can't seriously believe that crap he's spewing at you," Grace interjected. "He knows how powerful you are, and he doesn't want to fight you. Together, we can take him down! He wants to control you and take advantage of your powers."

Taylor's voice was raspy as she spoke. "Julian, please, don't do this. If not for me, then think of your family. Your sister and parents . . . Your friends . . . They all need you here. If you go with Seth, if you abandon the demon hunter way of life, they'll never let you come back. If you help the demon lords, they'll become unstoppable. We won't be safe anymore. All of humanity will cease to exist. Please don't leave," Taylor begged, tears dripping down her cheeks.

"I'm sorry, Taylor. I have to do this. It's my destiny," Julian said, turning to Seth with a nod.

Seth smiled, that same devilish smile Ammitt had once worn. He waved his hand in a circular motion. A swirling, multicolored vortex of light appeared. A portal. He waved his hand toward the portal, gesturing for Julian to go first. "After you, Cromwell."

Without turning to look at Taylor again, Julian stepped forward into the portal, vanishing from sight. Soon after, Seth did too. Taylor lunged forward, her fingertips reaching out to grasp Seth's cloak or hair, anything she could get her hands on. But her fingers went through the air. The portal was gone, and so was Julian.

Taylor fell to her knees on the carpet as sobs wrenched their way out of her throat. She jerked her eyes to where the portal had been and felt the complete and utter loss of Julian's presence.

Grace kneeled beside her, wrapping her arms around Taylor. "It will be okay, Taylor. We'll talk to Headmistress Lockwood and tell her what happened. We'll come up with a plan and—"

Taylor shook her head, sniffling as she stopped crying. "I'm going to find Julian and bring him back here. If he's really The Chosen One, then we need him on our side. We can't stop the demons without him. The fate of our world depends on bringing him back."

TO BE CONTINUED . . .

Deadly Portals Sneak Peek

NICHOLE HEYDENBURG

DEADLY PORTALS

BOOK 3: THE SHADOW BOUND CHRONICLES

Taylor

Julian was gone.

Oliver was dead.

Taylor sat on the floor with her head in her hands. Grace and Molly were on either side of her.

The events of the night had sunk in, but Taylor knew she had spent enough time moping. She needed to find a way to go to the demon world and bring back Julian safely.

With her hands on her knees, she pushed herself upright and leaned against the wall. Their dorm room was destroyed. The water spell Seth cast had done massive damage. Most of Taylor's belongings were soaked or ruined. She had already lost all of her earthly possessions once, so to lose so much again . . .

This time, though, she was filled with a righteous fury.

"Taylor, are you okay?" Grace asked softly, turning her tear-streaked face toward her. "We should go talk to the headmistress." She squeezed Taylor's shoulder gently. "We need to tell her what happened and . . ." She looked around their dorm room. "Maybe she knows a spell to help us fix our dorm."

Taylor turned to Grace, with tears shining in her eyes. "How can you be worried about me at a time like this? Oliver is . . ." she trailed off, unable to say the words out loud.

"I know, but the demon hunter's council was planning to kill him. He came out of hiding because he wanted to help you. He was trying to right his wrongs before he died." Grace sniffled and wiped her eyes. "They wouldn't have let him continue existing. It was only a matter of time. At least, this way, he died an honorable death. I can be proud of my brother." Her voice cracked at the end of the sentence.

Molly was bent over, sobbing uncontrollably still. "How can you say that, Grace? Ollie is dead!"

Taylor stood on shaky legs, attempting to comfort her new friends. "I'm so sorry. This is all my fault. If I hadn't let Seth into my dorm, none of this would have happened." Taylor shook her head in frustration. "I was naïve to think it was Julian and let him in without thinking it through. I should have questioned why Brody was barking at him."

Molly finally looked up from her crouched position. "It isn't your fault. I might be mad that Oliver is gone, but I wasn't blaming you, Taylor. I don't even want to know how Mom and Dad are going to react." She shot a concerned look at Grace.

Grace sighed loudly and rubbed her forehead. "We'll worry about that later. For now, let's go talk to the headmistress and see what she thinks the best plan of action is. She must have something in place for things like this happening."

Molly chuckled sarcastically. "For one of the demon lords infiltrating campus, killing a demon hunter turned vampire, and taking another training demon hunter captive?" She snorted. "Yeah, I'm sure things like this happen all the time."

Grace hit her sister on the shoulder.

"Ow!" Molly complained, raising her hand to hit her sister back.

Taylor grabbed Molly's hand. "Hey, stop it, both of you," Taylor interrupted the sisters' fighting. "I might not have any siblings, but I know this isn't the time to argue. I think Grace is right. Headmistress Lockwood will know how to get Julian back."

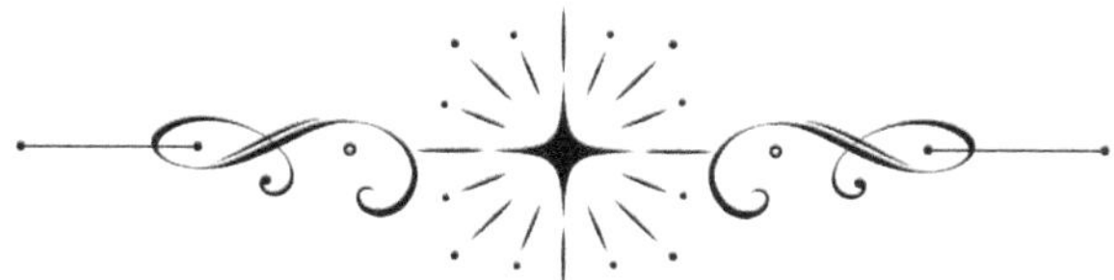

The three teenage girls sat in Headmistress Lockwood's office. She had still been working because of the chaos that had ensued on campus earlier. She was putting more safety protocols in place to ensure nothing like the day's earlier events ever happened again.

The headmistress looked up from her desk, surprised, when they barged in. She glanced at her phone. "Girls, it's after 10 p.m. Why are you here so late? You should be in your dorms." She eyed their disheveled clothes, soaked hair, and bruised and injured bodies, then abruptly stood from her chair. "What happened?"

Taylor looked at her friends and then at the headmistress. She should be the one to explain it because it was all her fault. She cleared her throat. "A demon lord was on campus. I let him into my dorm because he disguised himself as Julian. As soon as Brody started barking at him, I knew something was wrong. He transformed into my next-door neighbor, Sarah's boyfriend, Seth. Then I started to piece things together and realized he had been pretending to be a human male for months to get close to me and Mel. He tricked Sarah and made her fall for him, so he could infiltrate our lives. Thankfully, he never hurt Sarah or her daughter, Kylie, but tonight, he fooled me . . ."

"Oh my goodness! Where is the demon lord now? Did he leave? Are you all right?" Headmistress Lockwood asked, putting her hand to her mouth with concern as tears welled in her eyes. "Do you want me to get the school healer?"

"Actually, that isn't a bad idea," Taylor said. She took a deep breath. "I did my best to fight off Seth, but I was weakened from my earlier outburst. I could barely summon any magic, even the most basic spells were difficult. Grace, Molly, and Oliver showed up with Julian, and they helped me fight off the demon lord. I wouldn't have survived without them."

Headmistress Lockwood pursed her lips. "And where are Oliver and Julian now? Why aren't they with you?"

Molly's gaze dropped to the floor, and she threw her arms around her older sister.

Taylor exhaled before replying, "Oliver sacrificed himself to save us. Seth killed him. And Julian . . . Julian went with Seth to the demon realm."

Headmistress Lockwood nodded. "Alright. Well, we will have to make arrangements. I'll call your parents and tell them what happened. I imagine they'll want to come to campus and speak with me."

"What about Julian? How are we going to get him back?" Taylor asked.

"That isn't your concern, Ms. Windsor. Please leave that to me and the demon hunter council to figure out," Headmistress Lockwood said. Then, in an even sterner tone, she added, "And that goes for you too, Grace and Molly. I don't want to hear about the three of you getting into any trouble or getting into another situation over your head. I know you care for Julian, but it isn't safe for you to be involved. Don't go doing anything stupid."

Grace and Molly nodded in understanding. Taylor gave a brisk nod. But she had no intention of listening to the headmistresses' orders.

Hi Reader! The Shadow Bound Chronicles has been a labor of love, and I'm thrilled you decided to read this series. Thank you so much for reading my latest book. If you want to help me, I would appreciate it immensely if you wrote an honest review for *Deadly Betrayal*. Posting your review online is one of the best ways to support indie authors. Reviews help other readers decide which books they want to buy and allow indie authors to gain more exposure to new readers. Please consider posting a review on the book retailer website where you purchased the book and/or on Goodreads.

If this isn't your first Nichole Heydenburg book, you can probably guess who I want to thank first—my wonderful, wonderful husband, Zed. I'll forever be grateful that he agreed quitting my full-time job was the right move, so I could write full-time.

At this point, almost five years into my indie author career, there's no way I could ever go back to working a corporate job in an office, working for someone else. I'm living my lifelong dream, and it's all thanks to Zed. I also want to thank him for attending all of my book signings, always carrying the heavy stuff, being understanding when I have to work nights and weekends sometimes, and celebrating every milestone with me, big and small.

Miblart designed the cover for *Deadly Betrayal*. They have been great to work with for my new YA urban fantasy series. I'm excited to reveal the other covers in the series!

Sarah, owner of Three Owls Editing, has now edited five of my books. I'm happy I finally found an editor I can trust. She always catches my mistakes and cleans up my writing.

My amazing beta readers: Robert, Holly, and Carol. I couldn't be more thankful for their help. They always pinpoint exactly what is missing and help me strengthen my writing. I appreciate their willingness to read my crappy early drafts and for being honest with me about what needs to be changed, while being my biggest cheerleaders.

And finally, to you, my readers. Whether you've been reading my books since *The Long Shadow on the Stage* back in 2020 or you've just discovered my books, I appreciate your support. I hope you were able to escape reality for a few hours and that you enjoyed the twists and turns.

I want to extend a heartfelt thank you to every person who backed the Kickstarter for *Deadly Betrayal*. This campaign wouldn't have been a success without your support and your belief in the second book in The Shadow Bound Chronicles. I appreciate your support, and I hope you fall in love with the characters and the world I've created.

Thank you to my wonderful Kickstarter backers!

1. Jamie Davis

2. Jean-Maire Cole

3. Shannon J

4. Zilla

5. Valerie Anne Sizemore
6. Amanda Thompson
7. Katherine Webb
8. Rob Steinberger
9. Julie McAtee
10. Holly Shilts
11. Michelle and Steve LaBarge
12. Holly Hook
13. Amanda Siri Hill
14. Kate Postma
15. Alex Gould
16. Tiffany W
17. Zedekiah Heydenburg
18. Glen Campbell
19. Leslie Twitchell
20. Cate Dean
21. Victoria P
22. Jamie Lee Fry
23. Samantha Newberry
24. Alicia Banac-Aricayos

25. Alexandra Corrsin

26. Florentina

27. J.L. Hendricks

28. Johanna Miller

29. Kait Miczek

30. Anthea Sharp

31. Janine B

32. Antonietta L. Griesch

If you're interested in being a part of the first group of readers to learn about:

- Upcoming book releases, Kickstarter campaigns, and works in progress
- Cover reveals, beta reading opportunities, and ARCs
- Exclusive book content
- Book sales, giveaways, and freebies
- In-person book signings

Sign up for my newsletter on **www.nicholeheydenburg.com**!